ANG[illegible]N

by

JESSICA RAEL

CHIMERA

Angel Faces – Demon Minds first published in 2004 by
Chimera Publishing Ltd
22b Picton House
Hussar Court
Waterlooville
Hants
PO7 7SQ

Printed and bound in Great Britain by
Cox & Wyman Ltd, Reading.

The characters and situations in this book are entirely imaginary and bear no relation to any real person or actual happening.

ANGEL FACES – DEMON MINDS

Jessica Rael

This novel is fiction – in real life practice safe sex

'Give me something!' Amber shouted to the crowd of excited teenage girls gathering around the fight like a pack of hungry dogs. Someone threw a pink plastic belt and Amber caught it in midair. 'Hey, Jenny,' Amber said into the pained face of the blonde as she twisted her arms further up her back, 'this will look sooo cute on you, don't you think?' She laughed as she tied the blonde's wrists behind her back with the belt, and then dragged her by the hair into a toilet cubicle. The pack of girls crammed into the narrow doorway, jeering.

Jenny fought back tears; no way was she going to let this crowd see her cry, but it felt like the redhead had broken her arms. Jenny was a year older than her assailant, but the bitch was strong and fast. Not that Jenny was any slouch; you didn't survive long enough to make it into a shelter by being a wimp.

Part One – The Protégée

Prologue

The Inquisitor slid her fingers carefully round the base of the small yellow flower, then pinching the stem she plucked the desert bloom, dropping it in her palm so she could look at its fragile beauty. A Chiotilla bloom: the delicate, pretty daughter of a hardy desert plant. She smiled as a soft breeze rippled the petals, a vivid reminder of the flower's fragility, its newly discovered dependence on her.

Rebecca slid her thumb into the elastic waistband of her panties, catching the black silk, and pulled them away from her flat, toned stomach. Then she gently tipped the Chiotilla bloom into the sweet-smelling, moist darkness between her legs. The Chiotilla's petals tickled her labia and, as she let her waistband snap back, she could feel the little flower pressed firmly against the opening to her vagina.

Rebecca climbed back on her mount, and the animal reared slightly. The Chiotilla flower was crushed into her sex as she rode, grinding the bloom to a perfumed mush between her legs.

The flower had been taken, with care and precision, then when it surrendered and kissed her most private of places, it was crushed. Destroyed mercilessly as it struggled to retain its identity between her muscular thighs. Complex organizations survived only under rigid discipline. Symbolism and ritual served to reinforce that discipline, to give a sense of order, to underline power. A shame for the Chiotilla flowers, but the ritual she had just performed would be repeated by all those on the hunt. And the symbolism wouldn't be lost on them, either.

Naked in the Land of the Scorpion

A hot wind blew across the dry scrub desert east of San Diego. The breeze ruffled Rebecca's long dark hair, blowing it into her face. She let the horse's rains fall across the saddle and casually tied her hair back into a ponytail with a black band. Rebecca was thirty-six in a few months, but she could pass for ten years younger, a fact that was helped as much by her unlined face as her muscled body. Not the product of a high-priced executive gym (though she could certainly afford one) but from hours in the saddle, and her fearlessness at chasing down and tackling the constant stream of illegal immigrants that drifted across the Mexican border. Not that she was what you would call a model citizen, or even a patriotic American; it was all part of her work for the Cruza Cartel.

Citizen border patrols were nothing new in the San Diego area. The illegal immigrant problem was reaching epidemic proportions, and the local border police patrols were grateful of the help. The basic idea was that a watchful citizen, on volunteer duty, would locate and pinpoint illegal crossings and then radio in the position to the nearest police patrol – in theory at least.

The Cruza Cartel had infiltrated the operation years ago, seeing an obvious opportunity. The exclusively female organization was dedicated not to the prevention of illegal immigration, but to the pursuit of profit, and the satisfaction of the perverted sexual desires of their clients. Operatives would scan refugee groups, and if there were young, attractive female members they would be intercepted privately and with no police involvement, then given a stark choice: either hand over the female or females and be escorted safely into the city, or be rounded up and deported. Different cultures produced different priorities, and in order to save the family most would sacrifice a teenage daughter rather than face almost certain ruin and possibly worse. And so the Cruza would gain a prized piece of property.

Scanning the horizon from the shade of a low rocky ridge, Rebecca noticed movement. Nothing too important, she would see dozens of them every day, wandering half dead across the arid wastes. Some she would intercept for appearances sake, but most she would ignore, unless they had something of value to the Cruza, of course. The tall brunette took a pair of binoculars from a pouch at her side, it was military desert camouflage colors and matched the rest of her outfit. But style was everything, and Rebecca's work clothes had been expensively tailored so that she would resemble a goddess rising chameleon-like from the sands, rather than a scowling infantry soldier. The binoculars picked out two figures, a youngish Latino male and… something very interesting and definitely unexpected. She pulled the horse into action and began to ride towards the figures.

Rebecca's horse broke into a gallop and she lifted the radio from her jacket pocket. 'State Girl, this is Dark Horse, do you read? Over.'

The radio crackled for a few moments, then a woman's voice replied, 'Dark Horse, this is State Girl, do you have a flower in the sand?'

'Most certainly do.' Rebecca sounded breathless as she rode her horse hard over the desert terrain. 'A wild orchid,' she laughed, knowing Dakota would probably have never heard that code. You'd have to go deep into the Cruza manual to find it.

'A *wild orchid*?' Dakota sounded puzzled. 'What the

fuck's that?'

Rebecca laughed again. 'A birthday present for my niece, that's what. GPRS data coming your way, State Girl, and don't take all fucking day, I got young musk out here, could be trouble.'

The couple looked frantically around as they saw her coming, but they had few options against someone on horseback. They could have split, of course, and that would have been a pain in the ass. But luckily the girl wasn't that bright. She froze. The man looked to be about the same age as the girl; early twenties, Rebecca guessed. He turned and ran, west towards the city. Not that he would get far, but Rebecca was in no mood to fuck around, she wasn't losing this prize. Rebecca was an Inquisitor, one of only seven, all members of the Cruz Cartel's inner circle, and nobody ever fucked with an Inquisitor. She pulled a 9mm pistol from her belt and fired into the dirt at the young man's feet. He stopped in his tracks. *Smart*, thought Rebecca. The girl screamed, dropping to her knees in the dust.

'Stop!' she cried in panic. 'I'm an American citizen! I'm an American citizen! Please, my passport's in my backpack.' She began sobbing, and Rebecca gestured with the gun.

'Take it off and throw it over there.' The girl did as she was told, tears beginning to run down her cheeks. Rebecca could hear the jeep somewhere to her left, and without taking her eyes off the male and the girl cowering in the dirt, she pulled out the radio. 'State Girl, that you?'

'Yep,' came back the familiar voice, 'hundred yards to your left. So that's a wild orchid? Fuck.'

'Oh yeah, State Girl, that's a wild orchid alright. If the musk plays ball it's gonna be one hell of a birthday for Lauren.' Rebecca clicked off the radio and slipped it back in her pocket. 'Oh, and by the way…' she said to the girl still squatting in the dust, 'you try to run and I'll kill you before you get two paces.'

'Please,' the girl sobbed, 'don't hurt him. Don't send him back. I have money.'

'Don't worry, I'm sure he'll be just fine. He looks the sensible type. Your boyfriend?' The girl nodded and Rebecca laughed. 'One born every fucking minute.'

The jeep pulled to a halt in a cloud of dust and two women jumped out, both dressed in adapted military fatigues, as Rebecca was. Dakota whistled, staring at the kneeling girl. A shorter but equally stunning redhead climbed out beside Dakota, McKenna Jacobs, only twenty-six but rapidly gaining respect in the Cruza for her ruthless efficiency. Rebecca had hand picked the two women; she trusted them and the three worked well together. Minimum fuss when a take was in progress, and no fuck ups.

Dakota stayed with the girl while McKenna walked over to the male with Rebecca. 'You speak English?' the Inquisitor demanded, but the young man just stared at her. 'Don't fuck with me, dick-for-brains; you want in to town or not?'

He paused for a moment, puzzled, then nodded. 'Fuck, sure I want in to town. But you lovely ladies just gonna let me go? You go to all this trouble just to let me walk? No fucking think so.'

'Smart fucker, ain't he?' grinned McKenna.

'Okay,' said Rebecca, in an emphasized tone of bored impatience, 'let me tell you what I think and you tell me if I'm right. You met this stupid bitch in a bar while she was playing happy backpacker. You paid her compliments all night and after enough tequila you fucked her... bet you're good at it, too. Then just as she's cumming you tell her you love her, how you wish you could be together, but... now here's the sad part. You've already been deported from the States, so you can't ever go back even if she agrees to marry you. Which is about the only fucking true thing the bitch knows, right?' The man didn't answer, but she had his attention now. 'Now let me see…' Rebecca tapped the 9mm against her thigh, 'you're a smart shit, so you worked it so it seemed that *she* came up with the next part: she'd help smuggle you across the border. Brilliant. I mean, who would bother to stop a couple of backpackers, especially if one of them is a cute little blonde. Not your typical illegal dash, huh? Bet she thought she could just sweet-talk any border patrols if you ran into one; use that girly charm. But then you ran into us; tough break.'

The Latino male grinned, losing some of his nervousness. 'You wanna cut a deal, right? I been down that road before, miss-whatever-your-fucking-name-is. You want me to run a drugs pack? Well, I ain't that stupid, okay? So don't go thinking I am. I ain't swallowing condoms full of bad shit for no fucker, but if you got a car, and the shit's well hid, y'know, professional like, then yeah, let's talk.'

Rebecca smiled. A real lowlife, probably had a drug record to go with the deportation, and he didn't give a shit for the girl. Perfect. 'Well, looks like it's your lucky day, you sad fuck. Now listen, and listen good; we take the bitch and you never even think about her again. You got me? You never mention her; you don't even allow her in your fucking dreams. She ceases to exist for you from the minute you agree to this deal. Got it? And for you? You get a pretty new name, nice little fake green card, and plane ticket to New York. Hey, I'll even throw in a ride to the airport. Think it over, amigo, you got two minutes.'

'Fuck,' grinned McKenna, 'nice deal. More than that little shit deserves. All they usually get is a safe ride past the patrols and in to town.'

'Yep,' said the Inquisitor, 'but then they're not usually in possession of a wild orchid, now are they? Any idea what a pretty blonde barely out of high school is worth?'

McKenna just smiled. 'Exactly,' said Rebecca.

'Okay, shit, what's it gonna be?' she asked. 'Although I'll bet I can read your mind; an offer you can't possibly refuse, right? So there's gotta be a catch. Well, correct, and here it is: don't underestimate us, we'll be keeping tabs on your sorry ass, and if you ever speak about our deal or ever acknowledge you ever knew that bitch or have even seen her, then I'll ruin your party in ways you don't want to think about.'

His grin grew even wider, and then he whistled. 'Shit, lady, you think I ain't worked that out? If you deal in people then you're bad fucks, y'know. And I mean that with respect, right?' Rebecca nodded. 'You got yourself a deal, lady; my amnesia starts the minute I get on that plane.'

McKenna led the smiling man to the Jeep. 'You sure hit paydirt in that fucking bar, huh? You lucky shit.'

Rebecca walked over to Dakota and the kneeling girl. She seemed to have calmed a little, which was ironic. 'Did you call the car?' she asked her lieutenant.

'Yeah. ETA about ten minutes. Want me to wrap Lauren's birthday present?' Dakota laughed.

'Only until we get it back from the store, then you can do a proper job.'

Rebecca's lieutenant produced a handful of cable ties from her belt pouch and a role of duct tape. The girl looked on in horror and started to protest.

'I told you, I'm a US citizen, you can check in my backpack.'

Dakota moved with practiced ease, and her hands shot out like two startled snakes as she pressed the strip of tape firmly across the girl's mouth, the force pushing the captive onto her back in the dust. The girl's hand came up instinctively to her mouth, but Dakota instantly had hold of her wrists and in well-rehearsed motion she rolled the girl onto her front. The cable ties were on the girl's wrists before she hit the dirt, then before she could even think about kicking out her ankles were swiftly bound together. Then the Cruza lieutenant grabbed the girl by her shoulders and rolled her onto her back again.

Rebecca nodded her approval; swift, efficient and with zero damage to the goods. Very professional. By now the girl had realized something was very wrong. All thoughts of border patrols and the lies she had ready for any police interrogation evaporated in a growing panic. She began to writhe in the dust, tugging at her bonds. The two women ignored her.

The SUV pulled to a halt at the rear of the large house in the shade of a small bougainvillea tree. The equipment bag was designed to hold field expedition kit, but the Cruza had modified the design to incorporate a fine mesh so the occupant could breathe. The words *San Diego Botanical Research Center* were written clearly in white along the side – as they were on the SUV. The Cruza Foundation, as it was more commonly known, was a large donor and no official body kept track of what vehicles were operating in the desert.

Dakota opened the rear door of the SUV and unzipped the bag, and then with McKenna's help she reached in and dragged the young woman out of it. The captive wavered a little but managed to stand, blinking at the sunlight. Obviously terrified she shivered, even in the heat. Rebecca smiled; the bitch was quivering in front of the Inquisitor, every muscle in her tanned body trembling, tears welling in her eyes, and she was sobbing behind the gag.

Rebecca suddenly grabbed the girl by the hair and yanked her head back hard. The Inquisitor pulled a towel from the back of the SUV, loosened the girl's gag and wiped the tears from her face. The girl began to scream in alarm, but the older woman's mouth closed on hers like a lioness tearing at a gazelle's neck. Rebecca felt hot breath as the girl screamed into her open mouth, her hand tightened on the captive's hair, pulling their faces together; captor and captive, locked together by the Inquisitor's vice-like grip. The girl tried to close her mouth, but Rebecca's free hand moved swiftly and grabbed the blonde's nose and the mouth opened again. Rebecca probed with her tongue, pulling the girl even closer, then just as suddenly she let go, dropping the girl to the ground. The Inquisitor looked down at her property.

'Aw, didn't you like that, honey?' she taunted. 'Well don't worry; that was the last time you'll ever be kissed. I know someone who's got plenty of plans for that mouth of yours, and believe me, no one's ever going to want to kiss it again.' Dakota and McKenna laughed as they picked the terrified blonde up from the drive and began to drag her away.

The Shadow Stalker

Faith said the tip-off had come from a Lithuanian woman working in a fried chicken shop on the lower east side. Shalyn remembered laughing when Faith told her about 'the take' as the two women sipped margaritas on the balcony of Shalyn's expensive Manhattan apartment.

'Where the fuck's Lithuania?' the forty-four-year-old blonde had giggled.

Faith smiled. 'Nowhere we have any pull, sweetie.' Not that Shalyn had believed her; there was nowhere the Cruza didn't have pull. 'Anyway,' Faith continued, 'she tells us about this Indian cabdriver who comes in for a large bucket of wings every Tuesday and Thursday, and how he's illegal and how pretty his young Hindu wife is, hidden away in that dingy brownstone all alone, and how he just whines about how much easier it would be without her. Well, luck was on our side with that one. While we're planning our approach, Immigration picks him up. So we swoop.' Faith drained her glass then refilled it from the steel decanter. 'The immigration guy is on our payroll, so no problem. We just scared the stupid fuck cabbie for a while then went for the deal. A green card for a wife you don't want anyhow? He didn't even need thinking time.'

'Fuck, I just love those Indian bitches,' Shalyn shook her head.

'I know, sweetie; why do you think I'm telling you this? Jenna has a job for you and she told me to make you this offer. You take out the pimp that's treading on our toes and you get the Indian princess for keeps. Deal?'

'What condition's she in?' Shalyn placed her glass on

the table, careful to conceal her eagerness.

'Near perfect,' said Faith. 'Jenna kept her as a rent out, but she was always a plaything – no sado type stuff.'

Shalyn had been standing by the curbside for only about five minutes when the car pulled up. Timing was everything in her profession. She was dressed in boots and split leather skirt. A black guy jumped out of the car screaming and waving his arms.

'This is my turf, bitch! You ain't gonna get much work without a face, huh?'

Shalyn watched him with a vaguely bored expression, and then shot him in the dick. Blood exploded across the front of his jeans and he fell to his knees, strangely silent.

'No face,' Shalyn said to no one in particular, then after a moment she simply added, 'cool,' and fired five shots into the pimps face, obliterating it.

Her Indian princess arrived twelve hours later, as agreed.

Shalyn slipped off her bathrobe and stood naked, feeling the luxurious, thick red carpet beneath her bare feet. She wandered into the large bedroom suite. The bed, in keeping with the room, was vast and alluring, and beneath it was a large drawer. Shalyn pulled it open and gazed down at her naked Indian princess, locked by her ankle and wrist cuffs to the corners of the padded drawer.

'How ya doing, princess?' she asked, a little drunk from the wine and still heady from the kill. The half-empty bottle of Chianti hung loosely from her hand. 'What's the matter? There's probably more room in there than that fucking shit-hole you used to live in.' Shalyn unclipped the girl's hands and feet, turning her on her side while she locked her wrist cuffs behind her back. The assassin then attached the Indian girl's ankles to a spreader-bar, set on a modest two-feet span. She then grabbed the girl's leather collar, dragging her out of the drawer and throwing her onto the carpeted floor.

The assassin tugged the girl up to her knees by her thick black hair, then lay back on the huge bed and spread her legs so that the princess was staring directly at her owner's sex. 'Dance for me while you eat my cunt, bitch,' Shalyn laughed.

The Indian girl swayed her hips, jiggling the little bells Shalyn had attached to her waist-belt and cuffs. Her face was buried deep in the middle-aged blonde's pussy, her tongue working to some imagined rhythm. Shalyn lifted her legs, bringing her knees to her breasts, and the Indian girl pushed her tongue into her owner's ass, and then began to fuck the assassin's tight anus with deeply penetrating strokes, moving her whole face in and out in sequence.

'Wow…' murmured Shalyn. 'Jenna's people teach you that, or some fat bitch you were rented out to? It's some move, whichever.' Shalyn lowered her legs, locked the girl's head between her thighs, and squeezed hard. 'Climb up my cunt, slut, and fuck me with your head.' The blonde laughed drunkenly, amused as much by her own need to talk dirty off-duty as the slave's panicked attempts to drive her tongue deeper and deeper into her pussy. Shalyn reached to open the bedside cabinet and pulled out a length of black leather rope, the twisted fronds reminding her of the licorice strands she used to buy as a kid. She dropped it onto the bed, where it lay coiled like a dark viper.

The little princess could see nothing but her owner's pussy and the thighs clamped to her head silenced her world, but she felt the older woman twist as she reached for the drawer, knew what was kept there, and began to cry.

Without releasing her grip on the slave's head, Shalyn leaned forward, reached out and slipped the leather rope through the short chain that linked the slave's ankle cuffs together, tying it off. The assassin then lay back and pulled hard, raising the girl's feet up her back till her ankles passed her bound wrists, bending the little princess into a beautifully curved arc. The assassin grabbed the shapely ankles, clipping the short chain to the slave's collar, pulling the girl's face away from her pussy; and this was where the leather rope came in. Shalyn looped the free end of the whip-like rope through the sturdy brass rail at the head of the bed and pulled hard on the makeshift pulley. The princess rolled forward like a human wheel, until almost her entire weight was brought to bear on her face, again driving it deep into her owner's pussy.

Shalyn's body began to judder in ecstasy as the licking face squirmed in her wet slit. Orgasms pulsed through the older woman's body, one after the other as she pulled harder on the rope, driving the little princess' face deeper between her thighs.

Shalyn orgasmed countless times, then let go of the rope, allowing the exhausted Indian girl to flop back, her pretty princess face glistening with sexual juices. Shalyn got up and looked at the crumpled shape on the bed.

'Mmm... didn't really feel your heart was in it, slut,' she grumbled. 'If I didn't know better I'd say you weren't enjoying our little games.' Shalyn pulled the leather rope from the brass frame, and then stood on the bed and stretched up to the ceiling, feeding the rope through a metal ring bolted there. The princess began to whimper as the older woman threaded the rope through the pulley mechanism behind the ring, then with the casual press of a button on the wall beside the bed the electric winch lifted the sobbing slave into the air. The beautiful young Indian woman hung above the bed, swinging gently to and fro by her ankles.

Shalyn switched off the lights and slipped between the smooth silk sheets and lay there, listening to her slave quietly sobbing in the dark. 'Maybe by morning you'll have regained your enthusiasm, bitch,' the assassin slurred, swigging directly from the wine bottle. She then stretched out a shapely leg and gave the dangling princess a little shove with her foot, lounging back and watching the shadow of the intriguing puppet rocking gently on her string. 'Perhaps by morning you'll be in the mood to put a little effort into our games. Maybe then you can even find the enthusiasm to get that useless tongue of yours deep enough in my pussy and ass so I can have a decent orgasm.'

The phone bleeped gently in the darkness, and Shalyn reached sleepily out and picked up the receiver. 'Yes?'

'Good morning, sorry to disturb you so early,' said a deceptively polite female voice, oozing false sincerity.

Shalyn ignored the introduction. It was formulaic. The phone line was not scrambled, though it could have been easily enough, but if you scramble a line then it draws FBI agents to it like flies to shit. 'That's okay, just about to make a start on the day, anyhow.'

'This is Xansa Inc., San Diego, we have a virus problem,' the voice continued. 'Got into our machine here somehow, but we're worried it's infected our systems in New York. Do you have room in your schedule to help?'

'Shouldn't be a problem, just send me the details and I'll take care of it,' Shalyn said. 'Just for my records, who am I speaking to?' Now for the crucial part, Shalyn held the pen over the notepad.

'Ms S. Dickinson,' the woman said, then added, 'thanks for your help.' The phone went dead. It wasn't a real name but an email account, and Shalyn already had the password.

Las Flores

Amber moved too quickly for the other girl to realize what was happening. The shouting match was still in progress when the eighteen-year-old redhead suddenly lurched forward and shoved the startled blonde through the door and into the girl's bathroom. The bitch landed on her ass on the tiled floor, Amber kicked her in the face and she fell back moaning. The redhead was on the dazed girl so fast she had no time to think, and within seconds her arms were being painfully twisted behind her back.

'Give me something!' Amber shouted to the crowd of excited teenage girls gathering around the fight like a pack of hungry dogs. Someone threw a pink plastic belt and Amber caught it in midair. 'Hey, Jenny,' Amber said into the pained face of the blonde as she twisted her arms further up her back, 'this will look sooo cute on you, don't you think?' She laughed as she tied the blonde's wrists behind her back with the belt, and then dragged her by the hair into a toilet cubicle. The pack of girls crammed into the narrow doorway, jeering.

Jenny fought back tears; no way was she going to let this crowd see her cry, but it felt like the redhead had broken her arms. Jenny was a year older than her assailant, but the bitch was strong and fast. Not that Jenny was any slouch; you didn't survive long enough to make it into a shelter by being a wimp.

'Get the fuck off me, you bitch!' Jenny screamed, the pain increasing her fury.

Amber laughed at the girl's bravado; Jenny was no

match for her, and she knew it. Most of the girls in here had learned how to take a beating from a shit-drunk father, or one of their mother's perverted boyfriends, until someone moved them to the supposed safe haven. But Amber's dad, well, he used to be a policeman, so he knew a thing or two about not leaving marks. Most of them he'd used on Amber at one time or another, and that's why it took so long for anyone to figure out what was going on. No one figured it out when she was a kid, and things hadn't changed much since she'd grown up. He was still fast, even though he'd barely been sober for two days in the last five years, but Amber just got faster. She was a survivor. She'd see the fucker in his grave and she'd still be okay. She was always going to be okay.

Jenny struggled against the belt and the redhead's strong grip, the pain in her arms making her woozy. Amber had pushed her opponent down onto the filthy toilet seat and was pinning her there, but Jenny could see her attacker wriggling. She tried to push back, but her strength gave out and she collapsed heavily onto the dirty black seat. Looking down she could see her attacker's tennis shoes. A pair of off-white panties dropped to the redhead's ankles, laying limply on her grubby shoes. Amber began to slip the panties from her feet, and it even took Jenny's fairly sharp brain a few seconds to click in.

'Don't you fucking even—'

That was all Jenny got out before her assailant's underwear was stuffed into her mouth. The crowd of baying girls howled with laughter as Amber then pulled a bandana from her backpack and tied it round the blonde's head, covering her panty-stuffed mouth. The humiliated nineteen-year-old lay across the dirty toilet seat on her belly, hands tied painfully behind her back by the thrift-store plastic belt, her cheeks bulging as she sucked on the redhead's underwear.

Jenny could feel her saliva soaking into the panties. Her

mind reeled in disgust as she thought about the cotton rubbing against the little slut's unwashed cunt. The bitch probably hadn't changed them in a week. Jenny wanted to vomit as musky tastes filled her mouth, then something else, something salty, maybe piss. Jenny groaned and her stomach heaved, but she held it down.

A pair of hands slid around Jenny's waist with a strange tenderness that made her want to retch again. She twisted her head and saw the redhead grinning at her. The hands reached the waist button of her jeans and popped the stud, then eased down the zipper. Amber pulled the blonde's jeans and panties down to her ankles in one swift move. Then she placed the janitor's mop against the cubicle wall and aimed a kick to the middle of the wooden shaft. It broke in two, and Amber held out the rounded tip of one segment of the wooden shaft to the gang of onlookers.

'Don't just stare at the fucking thing,' she growled, 'spit on it. C'mon, losers.'

The girls obeyed until the end glistened with saliva. Jenny tried to get up, but Amber just placed her foot on her neck, holding her in place. Most of the girl's had been in and out of care homes when they were younger, not places that breed wimps, and now they were in a shelter, meaning someone had tried to do them serious harm. They'd seen a lot of stuff go down in their time, even though the eldest was only twenty-one, but now they were strangely silent as they watched Jenny Moyse getting ass-fucked in a toilet cubicle. Amber pressed the lubricated pole at the entrance to the girl's anus and laughed as the blonde went frantic, writhing and twisting and yelling into her gag. Then, with her typically casual indifference to the suffering of others, she pressed the thing deep into her opponent's ass. The nineteen-year-old went as stiff as the pole impaling her and stopped struggling, and didn't move again the whole time the psychotic redhead buggered her with the length of wood.

Amber worked the improvised dildo in and out of the tight anus, plunging it deeper with every stroke. The other girls gasped and mumbled in fascination as Amber worked on her victim, long, slow strokes, penetrating at least six inches. The redhead began to work the pole in the tight ass with rapid movements, making the sound of someone having an orgasm, laughing as she did so.

Then the misfit just stopped, seemingly bored with the humiliation of the older girl. Jenny Moyse remained as still as she had throughout the ordeal, but several girls noticed the tears meandering down her face as Amber left the pole sticking out of her ass.

'Show's over,' she said to the crowd, her tone menacing. 'That means fuck off, for those with a less than average brain cell count.' The girls drifted away, and the redhead pulled the cubicle door shut. 'Hey thanks, Jenny, I really enjoyed that,' she gloated. 'How about you?' She tore the duct tape from the blonde's mouth and pulled out her soaked panties. She dangled them in front of her debased opponent's face. 'Wow, cleanest I've ever seen 'em; better than that fucked-up washer in the basement, anyway. Be cool if you could suck all my dirty underwear clean, wouldn't it, huh?' Amber laughed, then hitched her denim skirt over her slender, tanned thighs and squatted over the blonde girl's shoulders. She relaxed her bladder with a relieved sigh and pissed on Jenny Moyse's head.

The older girl could feel the warm liquid soaking her hair. It ran down her cheeks, dripping off the end of her nose, forming a puddle on the floor.

Miss Parrish sat uncomfortably in her worn chair, grateful for the distance the desk put between her and the girl's cold stare.

'Jenny left last night,' the plump, middle-aged woman said. 'Some of the girls said you attacked her, that you did something very bad to her. Did you?' She tried to meet the girl's icy gaze, and failed, so she fiddled with her spectacles instead. 'Did you, Amber? Did you do something very bad to her? Something that would make her leave, even though she's supposed to be here for her own protection. Do you know what will happen if her boyfriend finds her, Amber?'

'Girls leave all the time, you stupid bitch,' the girl sneered. 'Facing down some macho prick with a knife is probably better than staying in this shit-hole. Be more fucking fun, anyways.' Her tone was one of bored indifference. 'You only stay cos they pay you.'

'Amber, I don't think you understand the seriousness of what has happened. If Jenny's boyfriend hurts her again, or she gets involved with drugs again, the police are going to want to know why she wasn't here. They'll be looking at you, Amber, asking what you did.'

'Fuck you.' Amber folded her arms. 'You just want something to write in that fucking book of yours, so you can go home and forget about it.'

'Now you know that's not—'

'Okay,' the hard-eyed girl interrupted, 'you don't have to worry about her getting hurt, or into trouble, because I killed the stupid slut. Cut her fucking throat and left her body in the dumpster by the kitchens. Oh, and it got emptied yesterday so she's probably in a landfill by now.'

Miss Parrish stared, and swallowed slowly. Then Amber burst out laughing. 'You think I'd waste that on her? If I ever kill someone it's gonna be someone more worthwhile than a fucked-up little trailer slut. Maybe someone important like you, Miss Parrish.' The redhead winked at the center's chief administrator.

'A-Amber, I think you'd b-better go now,' the woman stumbled, and without another word the girl got up and left the office. Miss Parrish could hear her popping gum as she closed the office door.

The chief administrator poured herself a glass of tequila

and sat it on the desk beside the phone – moral support of a very basic kind. She always knew she'd have to make this call someday. They had always paid her on time, and in cash. A small brown envelope with her name typed on the front lay on her desk the first Monday of every month. The locks had been changed a while back after a break in, but the envelope was there the following month, as usual. Miss Parrish had no idea how they got in, and she didn't want to know. But she always knew she'd have to earn that money one day. They hadn't asked much, but the woman sometimes felt like she was swimming in a tank of sharks, waiting for the day when the keeper forgot to feed them. She picked up the phone and dialed the number she'd been given.

'Hello?' said a calm voice.

'It… it's Miss Parish… from the Las Flores Young Women's Shelter,' she announced, falteringly.

'Yes, Miss Parish, I know. You're calling the number we gave you.'

'Oh… um, well…' The plump woman fiddled with the piece of card she had written the instructions upon. 'I… I think the package you've been waiting for has arrived.' There was a short pause, and then the voice spoke again, as emotionless as before.

'What color is the wrapping, Miss Parrish?'

'It's red. That's okay, isn't it?' The plump woman's hands had begun to shake. Something in that polite voice was making her very nervous.

'Yes, Miss Parrish, that's fine. We will send someone round shortly; please make sure you put the package somewhere safe till we get there.' The phone cut off and Miss Parrish sat listening to the hum of the dead line for several minutes.

Last Stop New Jersey

Shalyn lowered the exhausted princess onto the bed, and then carefully packed her away. She wrote a brief note, instructing her Philippine maid to shower the slave, then make sure she was fed and watered, and made to run the treadmill for at least an hour before being placed back in her drawer. The Shadow Stalker had memorized the contents of the email, and ran the details through her mind one more time as she headed for Newark airport. A thoughtful touch. Shalyn doubted the man would have argued much about not going to JFK, just like he was happy to sit economy, but Newark gave her the necessary degree of freedom to stop things getting overly complicated.

Miguel strolled off the plane smiling broadly. He'd always intended to dump the white bitch when he got to San Diego; she looked the type that could make a lot of unwanted fuss. But this, a lottery win, a green card and a free flight to New York, and the bitches gave it to him in return for a slut he was probably going to waste anyhow sooner or later. Miguel joined a line for a routine security check, and a black security guard moved down the line and stopped at him.

'Excuse me, sir, but the computer says you've connected from an overseas flight?' Miguel didn't detect anything particularly worrying in the security man's attitude, so he nodded. He'd no idea what they'd put on the computer. 'Could I ask you to step into the side office, sir? We have some concerns about a new Asian virus and you'll have to have an inoculation before you can go any further.'

'But I didn't come from Asia, man,' Miguel argued. 'Never been there.'

'Sorry, sir,' the man said curtly, but without much interest, 'it's procedure. Over there to your left, second door.'

'Fuck,' Miguel muttered under his breath.

The office was bare apart from a small table, a couple of chairs and some medical equipment. The doctor told him to sit down and relax, and to roll up his sleeve. Miguel did as he was told, and watched the doctor preparing the vaccine. She was attractive and blonde, and he liked that. A bit old for his tastes, but in good shape. She returned to the table and tied a rubber band around his upper arm.

Miguel winced. 'What you doing that for?' he asked. 'It's a vaccine, woman, not fucking heroin.'

The woman smiled pleasantly. 'We don't have time to allow the vaccine to work its way through your body, sir,' she told him. 'But I can administer it subcutaneous if you don't mind staying the night with security.'

Miguel stared at her for a minute. 'Nah, just fuckin' do it, I got things to do.'

She stuck the syringe into his vein and he felt the cold liquid mingle with his blood. 'Can I go now, woman?' he asked disrespectfully as she removed the band. She was smiling at him strangely, and packing her things into a black bag.

'Oh, I doubt you'd be able to stay even if you wanted to.' She held the hypodermic up for him to look at. 'Sodium pentothal and potassium chloride. It's what they give the bad boys on death row since they started taking the chairs out.'

'What?' Miguel blinked, unsure what he'd just heard. Then he felt his arm go cold... really cold. The icy chill spread across his chest and he sank slowly back into the chair. 'You fucking...' A dark, inky blackness smeared the edges of his vision, creeping in toward the center. It was like someone was drawing a heavy black curtain across his eyes. He thought about screaming, but couldn't remember how.

The city coroner unzipped the heavy vinyl bag and gave the body a cursory once over. 'Male, early twenties, Hispanic, heart attack, most likely drug misuse.' He scribbled hastily onto a yellow form.

'Autopsy?' his bored assistant enquired.

'Nope. No time. Can't go around cutting up every illegal immigrant that gets dragged in here. You seen my backlog? People with families first, Dave. How many times do I have to tell you? No family, no complaints. Simple.' He closed the bag.

The Protégée

Amber spread out on the smooth leather seats in the back of the limo. She was still wearing her denim skirt and the black leather felt cool against her legs. Miss Parrish had left Amber in her office, and then locked it. Then this woman came and told Amber to come with her, probably one of the Las Flores governors. If this was about Jenny then they could all go fuck themselves; the bitch had it coming.

The car paused at a set of huge wrought-iron gates, and a tall black woman in a dark suit walked slowly towards them from the other side. Amber watched her with mild interest. She looked tough – really tough, like she could even take her dad. Well, when he was drunk, anyhow. The black woman nodded at the car, then took something from her pocket, pressed it, and the gates swung slowly open. The car crunched up the long driveway to the huge white house, and Amber stared out of the tinted glass and let her mask of bored indifference slip.

'Fuck. You live here?'

The woman driving the car laughed. 'Yes, I live here, honey, but it's not my place. I live here because I work for the woman who owns it.'

'Shit. I guess I'm in real big trouble this time, huh? I thought Miss Parrish was fucking with me. Y'know, she usually does, she's a total loser.' Amber pressed a button and wound down the window, and leaned out. The teenager whistled as the full scope of the house, its outbuildings, ornate gardens and fountains came fully into view. The car pulled to a halt in front of white stone steps and Amber felt like she'd been driven straight into a movie, one of the good ones where people had money and got to do cool stuff.

The driver looked round at the teenager. 'Don't worry, kid, you're not in trouble,' she said. 'Miss Rebecca just wants to talk to you, that's all.'

'About Jenny?'

The woman laughed again. 'Maybe. But not for the reasons you're thinking. Just relax and enjoy your visit, okay?'

Amber nodded.

The inside of the house was as mind-blowing as the outside. The driver lady led the teenager to a grand room and sat her in a sumptuous, high-backed chair, picked up a phone on a table and ordered a coke. The woman then smiled pleasantly and left.

Amber sat for a few minutes, feeling like a turd in swimming pool. Any moment now someone was going to notice the mistake and throw her out that big gate.

A pretty oriental woman hurried into the room and handed the girl a coke on a silver tray. Amber took it silently and the woman left. Then she heard a door at the far end of the room open and a tall, dark-haired woman glided in. She was impossibly elegant, and she looked at the girl with a burning strength Amber had never seen before. Her dark eyes held the girl's gaze, and she smiled.

'Amber, isn't it?' she purred. 'I'm so glad you could come.' Amber stood up and the woman held out a slender, manicured hand. The teenager moved to shake it, but the woman took her hand and held it, squeezing gently but firmly. Their gaze locked and Amber felt overwhelmed. She had no idea what was going on. She had no idea what to do or say. Even the fight had left her. Amber had faced down her father's full two hundred and sixty pounds of drunken fury. She never backed down. Never. And here she was like a deer in a headlight. Frozen and waiting… for anything.

'Sit down,' the woman said, releasing the girl's hand, and Amber dropped back into the chair. 'My name is Miss Rebecca, and I have a few very simple questions for you, Amber. That's okay with you, I presume?' The woman sat in a chair opposite the stunned teenager, who nodded weakly. 'Good. Well, Amber, I need a simple yes or no at this stage. Nothing more, and certainly nothing less.' Amber nodded again. The woman smiled. 'Verbally, my dear… yes?'

'Yes,' Amber muttered weakly.

'Good, then I will begin.' The oriental woman appeared again with a tall glass containing lots of ice and a dark-red liquid – which Amber thought looked like blood – and handed it to Miss Rebecca. 'Would you like to return to live with your father in the trailer?' Rebecca asked, sipping the margarita.

'No,' Amber said, remembering the rules of the game.

Rebecca smiled; the girl caught on quickly. 'Would you like to return to the Las Flores Shelter?' The woman took another sip of the blood-red drink.

'No.'

'Would you like to live here?'

Amber paused. 'Yes.'

'Are you sure?'

'Yes.' Amber took a sip of the coke to wet her dry throat; she was smart enough to understand that this was becoming a very, very serious situation.

'If you were given the chance to live here, would you be able to leave everything you have ever known before behind? To have absolutely no contact with your previous life?'

'Yes.'

'Your friends?'

'Yes.'

'Your father?'

For the first time Amber smiled. 'Yes.'

'Amber, I make the rules that govern this house. My word is law here. Could you agree to obey those rules, even without knowing them yet?'

'Yes.'

'Would you accept my rule absolutely?'

'Yes.'

'Would you be loyal to me, Amber?' There was a subtle shift in the woman's tone.

Amber blushed. 'Yes.' The confirmation came out muted, but she wanted to shout it, scream it, and Miss Rebecca knew. The woman stared at the teenager with her unwavering gaze. Amber never learnt much at school, but she wasn't stupid. Her life had just switched lanes, suddenly and from nowhere, like a fast car on the freeway. Nothing would be the same again. This wasn't a game, it wasn't bullshit. People like this didn't bullshit. That's what people like her father and Miss Parrish did. 'Yes,' Amber said again, a little louder, and Rebecca smiled.

Amber stayed in the house. She didn't bother to collect any of her things and her personal assistant – which Amber thought a totally cool and wild idea – would get her anything she asked for, without question. And best of all, everyone treated her with respect. Amber looked around her large, beautifully decorated room, with its en-suite bathroom and huge tub, with disbelief. Something was going to turn up to ruin this dream, it always did. Then she'd wake up back in the stinking trailer, or the fucking care home, watching her back for the next scumbag to come at her. But it seemed real enough right now, so she dressed herself in the new jeans and tight baby-blue top she'd asked for, and slipped her new tennis shoes over her white socks and followed her personal assistant, Megan, downstairs.

Rebecca sat on the patio eating breakfast with her protégée. 'Did you ever see the film Caligula?' she asked the girl, who was steadily working her way through a large bowl of cereal. Amber shook her head. 'Perhaps you should sometime,' the Inquisitor continued. 'Then maybe you'll see some of the irony in my situation.' The Inquisitor peeled a piece of fresh passion fruit with a small silver knife. 'You see, I have my own Caligula. Or should I say, Caligulette? Lauren is the only heir to my empire, and at twenty-five she should already hold a senior position, but that's not the way it will ever be. Lauren has her own path and while she'll always be here with us, running the family business doesn't feature in her plans.' Rebecca smiled. 'Once it wouldn't have been allowed, but times change. Luckily for Lauren we have the resources to indulge her little hobbies, and it is also not outside my power to fill the vacant chair she left. So you, my dear, are my back up. A princess regent, if you like. If you make it, all the real power will rest with you one day; a more frightening responsibility than you realize.'

Amber said nothing as she sipped her orange juice, but she got the message. If she did okay, she could be as powerful as Rebecca. If she fucked up? Maybe someone would find her in a kitchen dumpster. But Amber had no intention of fucking up.

The Preparation of Stephanie

The curators managed the Cruza's property, and it was a rather archaic tradition that they did most of their work below ground. The idea that they skulked demon-like in basements amused most of them, though in truth their workplaces were usually well lit and rather sanitized. The decor was generally white, very practical for the job in hand, and in many ways the curator's workspace resembled a modern psychiatric hospital rather than a medieval dungeon.

Dakota and McKenna dragged Stephanie down a flight of steps into the subterranean levels of the house. They threw the bound blonde at a smiling black woman.

'Nice,' she said, drawing in a lungful of smoke from a cigarette she was holding. 'Makes a change from all the fucking Latinas.' The black woman threw the blonde roughly onto a black, padded table. The two Cruza officers left, chatting as they climbed the stairs, and the black woman produced a pair of large, pink-handled scissors. Stephanie began to sob and plead, but the black woman ignored her. There were no threats, no attempts to silence the frightened young woman, not even a gag. The curator hummed to herself in a workaday fashion while she snipped away the latest acquisition's clothing. Cutting along the seams of the girl's jeans, the curator tore them off and threw them aside, the same with her white cotton T-shirt. Stephanie stayed perfectly still and compliant during the process; the last thing to do when someone had a sharp metal object brushing the surface of your skin was struggle.

The black woman snipped the waistband on either side of the girl's panties and pulled them off, dropping them onto the pile of clothing on the floor. Stephanie hadn't been wearing a bra under the T-shirt.

The curator then put on a plastic apron, pulled down a hose from above the table and began to wash the acquisition, soaping her with a yellow sponge and then rinsing the suds away. Stephanie was in the human equivalent of a carwash, and the curator treated the experience as if she were hosing down trucks for five bucks an hour. The only part of the girl the curator bothered to dry were her wrists and ankles, rubbing them briskly with a white towel, then she turned the blonde onto her front. Practiced hands worked their magic, and Stephanie felt the cuffs being placed around her wrists and ankles, and the little click as they were locked into place. The same pair of pink-handled scissors sliced through the cable ties. Stephanie's hands pulled apart in reflex, but each cuff was clipped securely to its twin, then the same procedure was applied to her ankles. Stephanie's situation was unchanged, if perhaps a little more comfortable.

The curator reached up and pulled another hose from above the table. This one had a long plastic nozzle attached to its end, which the black woman inserted roughly into the girl's vagina, twisting to work it inside the girl's body. Stephanie jerked in surprise then started moaning pitifully, rising to full blown sobbing as the curator turned on the jet of soapy water and flushed the girl out like some cheap rubber sex doll.

After a few minutes the procedure was repeated in the girl's anus. Then she was rolled over onto her front again. The curator grabbed a silver container sitting on a heating plate on a side table, swirled the thick liquid wax around the pitcher, then emptied the contents onto the young blonde's sparse pubic hair.

'You lucky, bitch,' the curator said to the object of her

attention. 'Them Latina girls is hairy as fuck, have to do right round to their asses, and legs an arms, too. This little muff ain't nothing.' The woman waited for a few minutes, leaning back against the table and smoking another cigarette, then she glanced at her watch and hummed to herself while she ripped off the cooled wax leaving the girl's pussy as bald as a Thanksgiving turkey.

Stephanie yelped, but held back any further tears. The bitches just wanted to humiliate her before handing her over to the police, and she could put up with a bikini wax and enema. They'd pay when she got her hands on a lawyer, though.

But what happened next was a surprise, subtly undermining her theories about the women's intentions. The curator clipped nylon straps to one side of the table, then lay them across the girl's naked body, securing them to the other edge, and with a strong tug on each strap buckle she was held tight, unable to move at all. The black woman then slid a cold, metallic dental brace into the her mouth, then turned the knob at the side like she was winding an old wristwatch, and Stephanie felt her jaws being forced apart. She began to make gurgling sounds, feeling the saliva build at the back of her throat and had to swallow frequently to clear it.

The black woman pulled over a wheeled trolley packed with frightening metal implements, and Stephanie could feel the panic begin to rise in her stomach. The curator picked up a long thin implement with a curved spike at the end, leaned over the girl, and began to work on her teeth. Stephanie lay supine and helpless on the bench for nearly an hour while the curator performed an expert dental hygiene workout on her already neat white teeth. She lay there, swallowing her saliva while her mind hopelessly searched for meaning, and all she came up with were more questions.

The Birthday Girl

Amber hadn't been given any chores or other stuff to do, so she lay in bed longer than usual. Megan, her personal assistant, came in to wake her at about nine o'clock. The woman was of medium height and build, attractive but not pretty. She always wore her dark hair tied back, and had a neat, fastidious appearance.

Amber also suspected her duties included acting as her bodyguard. She had noticed the woman carried a gun, neatly tucked into a shoulder holster on her left side, and she rarely took her attention off her teenage charge, even if she was very clever at hiding it. But mostly Megan seemed interested that Amber learn some of the more basic Cruza ways, so it seemed she also doubled as a sort of teacher.

Deportment was a word the girl heard often. Basically it meant acting totally cool, and like she didn't give a shit. Everyone did it around here, and it was going to be really crucial when Amber met important people, and it was another reason why Lauren would never make the grade. In a way Lauren didn't give a shit, she did her little girl thing all the time, and Amber could see what Rebecca meant. Lauren wasn't going to change that for anyone. But that was cool. Amber had met Lauren at dinner yesterday, and she liked her. Sort of a big little sister, and one who had live dolls to play with instead of the plastic kind. Funny if you thought about it; a grown woman playing with live dolls. But Amber was a teenager, and weird was always cool as long as it wasn't geeky-weird.

Despite the act Lauren was definitely a woman. She

had a voluptuous figure, bordering on plump, Amber thought, and when she pretended Amber was her *big* sister, well, that was just funny. The games Lauren played weren't what you'd normally expect your little sister to be getting up to with her Barbie collection either, but that just made Amber laugh, and sometimes she even wondered what it would be like, pretending to be a kid again and making other women be dolls and stuff. Perhaps she'd take her *little* sister on the offer of a sleepover one night; after all, the woman had given Amber the biggest break in her whole life, and she knew when to be grateful.

Rebecca knocked on Lauren's door while the small birthday welcome group loitered in the hallway. A few seconds later the woman opened it, grasping her aunt around the shoulders and giving her a big hug, and Rebecca smiled in a genuinely fond way. Family was important to the Cruza. Everyone knew Lauren had sidestepped her responsibilities, and that wasn't the Cruza way, but most admired her for not bending to the pressure to conform, even if they did think she was a little flaky. The Inquisitor took a pragmatic approach; if her niece didn't have what it took she didn't have what it took, it was as simple as that. So steps had been taken to ensure a successor, problem solved.

'Happy birthday, honey,' Rebecca said. 'A big twenty-six today, huh?' The plump brunette nodded, ushering her aunty and Amber into her bedroom. The chef had already been informed to politely drop the twenty, leaving just six candles on the cake.

Amber smiled and wished Lauren a happy birthday, then hugged her and kissed her on the cheek. The two had become genuinely fond of each other, and though Amber wasn't very good at playing down her precocious nature she was still a teenager, and Lauren liked that. She also liked the way Amber talked. She like the slang and made

Amber promise to teach her. The twenty-six-year-old had a strange ability to draw people into her weird world. There were plenty of her family's genes operating behind that childlike grin, and now Amber really was the big sister because that's the way Lauren wanted it, and if Lauren wanted things a certain way then that's how they usually turned out. And Amber could fit the bill, all grown up and working with serious hard cases like Dakota, but young enough to be cool, too.

'You know I have to go out for a while today, don't you, honey?' Rebecca said, and Lauren just smiled and nodded. 'But I'll be back later so we can do something fun for your birthday, okay?'

'Is Amber staying?' Lauren asked.

'Of course, sweetie, Amber lives with us now, remember? She's family.' Rebecca motioned to Megan, standing dutifully in the hallway, who turned to her left and clicked her fingers.

'I got you a very special present, Lauren,' Rebecca added, moving aside as two women carried in a huge box wrapped in pink paper and decorated with pink ribbons and bows. 'Something you're always telling me you want.'

'No *way*!' squealed the birthday girl. 'Not a *real* doll! You're kidding me, right?'

'Open it and see.'

Lauren tore away the ribbons in an excited frenzy, and then ripped off the paper. She pulled the lid from the large box. Amber leaned over so she could get a look; she'd never actually owned a doll.

Inside the box lay a pretty young woman in her early twenties, her blonde hair pulled back into a ponytail and held in place with a red ribbon. She was quite naked and wearing pink ankle and wrist restraints decorated with little sparkly red hearts. In her pretty mouth was a pink rubber gag. Her finger and toenails were painted a delicate shade of rose, and she wore a pink collar with the words *I Belong to Lauren* in shiny silver lettering.

Amber smiled as she watched the surreal scene, beginning to like her new life. She looked at the new toy. Only the terrified look in the girl's stunning blue eyes broke the illusion, but Lauren didn't appear to notice, or maybe she just didn't care. Either way it was a cool present, and it looked way more fun than a six-inch piece of androgynous plastic. At least this one had a real cunt.

Fun and Games

Lauren ground her large ass down onto the sobbing girl's face, whipping the helpless toy. It looked a little more disheveled than when she'd gotten it that morning, but it was still cute. Lauren loved her Aunt Becky, she always got her such neat stuff, but this was definitely the coolest. She'd wanted a real live doll for so long she'd had plenty of time to think what she was going to do with it.

'Don't know what plans you had for your life fun-toy, but you can forget them,' she beamed. 'You're my property now, and you know what that means, don't you?' She smiled wickedly. She delighted in telling her slaves how they would spend the rest of their miserable lives. She loved to see the fear in their eyes and hear their pathetic sobbing; it made her feel like a goddess. A real one though, not some glamorous movie star. A real goddess, with the power of life and death, pain and relief, all in her little hands.

As if to check, Laura gazed admiringly at the pink glitter-polish on her perfectly manicured nails. 'You're the cutest toy I ever had, and you're gonna be licking some part of my body practically every minute and every day.' She paused for a moment, knowing there was something she'd forgotten. 'Well… unless I hurt you bad, then you'll be in the medical bay till you get better, I guess. Anyway, you're my best toy now, and I'll never stop playing with you. And toys don't get rest or anything. You'll even be doing *gross* stuff all night.' She giggled, her large breasts jiggling.

She let loose a well-aimed blow with the crop that hit the slave directly between the legs. She squealed with delight as she felt her plaything jerk in pain and then frantically wriggle and squirm its tongue deep into her ass. Lauren had masturbated about making a real live doll do this since she had first told Aunt Becky that she wanted one, and now she actually had it, and it was helpless and couldn't say no to anything she wanted... and she wanted lots and lots of things.

Stephanie tried to concentrate as she squirmed under the woman's suffocating ass cheeks, desperately trying to force her tongue deeper into her tormentor's anus, just to avoid the evil sting of the crop as it lashed at her exposed breasts and sex. The slave's pitiful screams and begging moans were muffled by Lauren's ample buttocks as the sadistic, childlike woman bounced happily on her face. Every now and again Lauren would lift her sweaty ass off the pathetic creature's mouth just long enough to listen to the funny toy beg for mercy, pleading for her sanity and some release from the degradation and pain. Lauren would laugh hysterically; she loved it when the toy begged her like that, it was totally cool. She would then drop her ass back onto the sobbing face and resume whipping the slave's exposed vagina, feeling the tickly feeling in her tummy as the tongue probed deep into her ass once more.

That night Lauren attached the special butt harness to her plaything's head, carefully explaining what it was for. She reveled in the despairing look in the girl's eyes as the young blonde thought about the degradation to come. Lauren giggled as she tightened the straps around the toy's head, then while her victim kneeled, bound and naked before her, she slipped on the goddess harness that was designed to attach to its counterpart. It fitted snugly around her waist and thighs. Then she grabbed the whimpering slut by the hair and dragged her onto the bed, with it's pretty pink quilt and sheets. She then threw the covers over the toy's quivering, naked, bound body, and climbed in herself, smirking at the delights that awaited her and the torment that awaited her property.

Once under the covers Lauren slid her stout thighs either side of the wretched slave's head and positioned her ass in front of her whimpering face. Then with cruel, deliberate slowness the twenty-six-year-old clipped the toy's face harness to the one she wore round her own waist and thighs. She grabbed the side straps and gave them a strong tug. The toy's face was pulled deep into her ass crack, so deep that her mouth was pressed firmly against her owner's anus. Lauren gave one last pull on the straps until it felt like the slave's head would disappear into her ass completely, and how she wished she could do that. She giggled, and then orgasmed just thinking about how totally cool *that* would be.

Stephanie could barely breathe, the woman's fleshy buttocks smothering her face. The private world that existed in the deep valley between the woman's cheeks was now her whole world, everything she could smell, and hear, and taste. The petrified girl obediently began to worm her tongue deep inside the anal passage pressed hard against her lips, and she could hear the sadistic voice, muffled by the strong thighs that gripped her head.

'Listen toy,' the psychotic woman said, 'if I wake up, even for one second, and find you're not licking my beautiful ass you'll be sorry. Got it, loser?'

As Stephanie continued probing the maniac's anus she thought how few people would ever understand just what *total* servitude was, spending nine hours licking a sleeping woman's ass just because it pleased her to have you do it, even though she would be unaware of almost all the degrading attention being lavished on her. It was unbelievable decadence at the expense of the unfortunate victim, but then the slave had now seen enough to know that the Cruza didn't consider their property human, or even animal. They were just expensive sex toys, nothing more.

The Black Glass Bar

To Sabrina the whole thing was becoming a massive headache. The club offered her prestige, sure. And there was no doubting she enjoyed the functions; who wouldn't? But now the pressure was on. How did you go about finding new ways to amuse a group of pampered, wealthy lesbians with a taste for the sadistic every month? The girl would do fine for a few days, of course. Sabrina watched with mild interest as the young woman began to stir, but the risks were getting too high. Perhaps it was time to make a strategic alliance, she idly thought.

Shelly awoke from the drug-induced slumber to find she could not move. Full consciousness returned slowly and in fragments. The twenty-two-year-old sociology student found herself naked and arched backwards, when what seemed like only moments ago she was enjoying a quiet drink in a lively bar. The girl opened her eyes but found she couldn't quite focus yet. She was on a bench of some kind, and it was lower at the head end, rising towards the end where her feet were. Then she realized her legs were raised in the air, and tied. She struggled for a few seconds, tugging at the restraints. Her hands were also tied, but down, folded under the bench and somehow attached to the underside.

Panic rose in her drug-slurred brain and she began to pull again at her bonds, but she was held tight. As the fog in her head began to clear she realized she was totally naked and spread out, like an insect in biology class. She was naked and she couldn't close her legs. She could never remember feeling so vulnerable.

Then her vision cleared a little. There were women in the room with her. Quite a few women. And there… there was the woman who had bought her a drink in the bar, the attractive dark-haired woman who had shown such an interest in her family – or lack of one. The terrified girl tried to call out, but her voice was just slurred nonsense. She heard the women laugh.

'Shout all you want, slut,' said a woman to Shelly's right. 'The only ones who'll hear you down here will be us, and we want you to make all the noise you can. Don't we, girls?' There was the sound of more female laughter from all around the frightened student, and a hand tousled her hair like she was a child.

Breakfast in Chains

Rebecca sliced a fresh bagel in two, carefully spreading cream cheese on one half with an engraved silver knife. She bit into it delicately while flipping through a leather-bound report that sat on the table in front of her. The Inquisitor glanced up at the attendees of the twice-weekly breakfast meeting. Dakota was dressed in gray sweat pants and a white T-shirt. She sipped chilled orange juice and waited for Rebecca to speak. McKenna was still in her dark-blue toweling robe, and she didn't appear to be wearing anything underneath. To McKenna's left sat Amber, in a baby-blue crop top, denim shorts and pink flip-flops with plastic daisies on the straps. Different worlds, the Inquisitor thought, observing the young woman, but that was why she had chosen her in the first place; tried and tested survival skills, verifiable aptitude for cruelty, and a sharp, streetwise intelligence.

'Okay,' she said, dabbing crumbs from her lips, 'McKenna,' the woman sat a little more stiffly despite the supposed informality of the meeting, 'catch up with me in my office after lunch and we'll run through these renovation costs. Either we get our clients to return our property in a little better state of repair, or we start charging for the clean up. Profit lines are going to slip if we don't keep an eye on this.'

'I'll talk to the head curator and see if we're running as lean as we can, but short of getting the bitches to hose the cum and lubricants off themselves when we get them back I don't think we can trim back anymore.' McKenna drained the last drop of orange juice from her glass, then picked up the empty jug from the table and waved it in the air, attracting the attention of a middle-aged woman watching from a respectful distance.

Juana stood perfectly erect in front of the middle-aged woman in the blue suit and white apron, just as she'd been taught to do. Her wrists and ankles were locked into leather cuffs, and she wore a broad leather belt around her trim waist. A chain linked her wrist cuffs together, and ran through a loop at the front of the belt. She had seen prisoners wear such things on work gangs. The young Latina girl had enough movement to carry a tray and clear away plates, but little else. Her ankle cuffs were also joined with a chain, which allowed her to walk carefully and slowly, but not to run, so she moved in a humiliating shuffle.

The twenty-year-old Mexican was a beautiful example of Latin perfection. Flawless coffee-colored skin, pert breasts, a well proportioned ass, slender legs and shapely ankles. The woman had fitted the girl with a leather collar, which also had a ring at the front, and she'd clipped one end of a gold chain to it and attached the other end to the girl's clitoris ring, so that it pulled painfully if she stood upright. The woman then forbade Juana from slouching; the girl had to carry herself properly at all times. Which meant walking elegantly with a straight back and head held high. So Juana did so, always aware of the constant pain in her clitoris. Every other day the woman would remove another link from the gold chain, and Juana's torment would begin afresh.

Juana had been a good student. It wasn't her fault her school closed in her sixteenth year when it ran out of money. The same way it wasn't her father's fault when the factory in the town where he'd worked for fifteen years closed because the American's found somewhere cheaper to produce their precious *things*. She had been struggling to keep up, working nights cleaning so she could carry on her education by correspondence. So in a way she was a little excited – as well as more than a little scared – when her father told the family they were going to America.

Even the small children knew the risks; they'd all heard of someone who had tried. Many got sent back but also, and very importantly to the people of her small village, some didn't.

But desperation breeds courage of a sort, so they packed up as much of their meager belongings as they could carry and took a bus to the border.

After several days in the desert they were already in trouble. They had tried to stay on one of the roads, where walking was easier, but there were police patrols and once a man in a car slowed down and shouted at them, telling them to, 'Get the fuck back to Mexico!'

That wasn't so bad, they never exactly expected to be welcomed, but the next day a truck slowed down and the three men in it started shooting guns at her family. Firing into the air and laughing, they then began to shoot at the ground around her father. They all ran, back into the desert and away from the road.

Later that day they met another Mexican family making the crossing. They had already lost a child to thirst and heat exhaustion. Things were bad. Then the jeeps came riding down on them like they were wild animals. Her father was sure it was the border patrols.

The women took her father and the man of the other family to one side at gunpoint. At first her father shouted, but then he went quiet. Very quiet.

A little while later a white bus bounced down towards them from the nearby road and her family filed silently inside. They did not look back at her, but some of the little ones were now smiling and happy. Even her father had straightened his shoulders a little, and he no longer stared at the ground in despair. Juana had no idea what was happening, and stood under the blazing sun with a girl from the other family, who looked a couple of years older than her. She felt very numb as the bus drove away, and as soon as it disappeared out of sight the women with the jeeps changed. They grabbed the older girl and tied her hands, laughing that she was the bad catch and not as pretty as Juana. Then they threw her in the jeep. Juana became scared as the women roughly tied her own hands behind her back, but then one of the women slipped a hand inside Juana's dust-stained blouse and mauled one of her breasts. Juana shouted at the woman and began to swear in Spanish, but the woman just grinned so Juana spat in her face.

While the other girl lay in the back of the jeep, the women had some fun with Juana in the dust, under the glare of the mid-afternoon sun. There were four of them, though one just watched. They stripped her naked, ripping her blouse and tearing her skirt like a pack of wild animals. When she was naked they began molesting her breasts and she felt a hand at her crotch. One of the women shoved two fingers into Juana's vagina and began to work them in and out, while another kissed her roughly, forcing her tongue into the virgin's mouth. The third woman forced her finger into Juana's anus, making her lift her buttocks off the dirt in shock. They laughed even louder and one began to suck her nipples. The onslaught lasted for about twenty minutes perhaps, it was difficult for Juana to tell, and then she was also thrown into the back of the jeep, lying next to the older girl. Juana felt strangely ashamed of her nakedness.

On her second day of capture the three women who'd taken advantage came to the place where she'd been washed and depilated and took her to another room further up in the house. There they tied her to a bed and used a thick needle to pierce both her nipples and her clitoris. They did not use any anesthetic, and seemed to enjoy the girl's cries of pain and pathetic pleading. They fitted her with gold rings in her nipples and clit, soldering the loops closed so they could never be removed, laughing at the girl's anguish as the rings heated up under the hot solder.

McKenna watched the naked Latina girl walking with practiced care from the house to the patio table. She could hear the ice chink in the fresh jug of orange juice she carried, and saw how she winced with each step as the gold chain tugged on her clitoris. McKenna looked at the painfully stretched little bud, guessing it had a long way to go yet before the girl was ready for the Cruza client with a fetish for that particular deformity. The girl bent awkwardly, and placed the jug on the table.

Rebecca was engrossed in conversation with Dakota, so McKenna decided a little impromptu practice for the bitch wouldn't go amiss. She grabbed the girl by the belt and told her to stay put, and then dug into the cream cheese pot with the knife, opened the front of her robe, and smeared the creamy white substance over her vagina, making sure it covered her labia and clit. Then she gathered some more, carefully slid the blunt knife into her pussy, smearing the inner walls with it. The Inquisitor and her lieutenant ignored what was going on, but Amber stared in fascination. McKenna smiled at the young protégée, then grabbed the Mexican beauty by the collar and pulled her face between her thighs.

'Don't see why you should miss out on breakfast, bitch,' she said. 'That wouldn't be fair at all, would it?' The girl shook her head while she buried her face against the woman's pussy and lapped like a hungry puppy.

Amber pulled her chair closer so she could get a better look, and the Cruza officer smiled at her again. 'Perks of the job, sweetie,' she purred, then squeezed the girl's head tighter against her crotch and casually drew the folds of her robe over her head.

Rebecca ran her finger down one of the sheets of paper in the file, speed-reading the details. 'What do we know about this *Black Glass Bar*?' she asked her lieutenant.

'Pretty much everything. A Sabrina Townsend bought out a dive club about eighteen months ago on what she managed to wrestle from her ex-husband in the divorce, which from what we could ascertain was a lot less than she should have got. He's mid-level money, a broker, on the take, but not a big game player.'

'So he's not hanging around waiting to start trouble?'

'Doesn't have what it takes, plus he got off light and I bet he knows it. It would only be a lose-lose for him.'

'Okay, so what about her?'

'On the level. Standard rich bitch into S&M games, no heavyweight contacts. Managed to get herself some clientele at the club into hard sado games, and it looks like she went with it for the money. Refitted the basement. Tacky and very seventies, so Carrie says. I sent her down to check it out anonymously last week. About three months ago one of the paid for masochists got hurt pretty bad and made a fuss. Cost Ms Townsend a lot of cash to stop that one in its tracks.'

'So how'd she come to be talking to us?'

'An opportunistic *take* basically. Grabbed a young woman from her own bar and used her for that night's party. That left her with three problems: one, what to do with the girl now she had her; two, how to get more because the party went so well; and three, Carrie's little chat after the party, explaining what happens to people who try to franchise Cruza operations without permission. Personally I think it was number three that got her attention.'

'Think we should legitimize her operation, or peg her

out for the crows in the desert?'

'It could be made to work, and she's compliant. We could always give it a couple of months before deciding if the little birdies need feeding or not.'

Rebecca smiled. 'Okay, you get on it.' The Inquisitor scanned the rest of the report. 'Only other thing here is the possible Los Angeles account.'

'Hannah Levis. Former porn actress with a hedonistic philosophy and a billion dollars from the sad death of her ex-husband. He was seventy-nine, so I think we've seen this movie before. Likes pretty girls, but we don't have a handle on what her taste in games are yet. Just needs checking out. Basic sales call.'

'Okay, but I want you on it. A billionaire could be a big account, so let's bring it in.'

'I'll take a look at the club this morning, then fly up and talk to our lady in LA.'

'Sounds good. Oh…' Rebecca reached for the orange juice and smiled at her protégée. Amber was watching the Latina girl with undisguised enthusiasm as she wriggled around under McKenna's robe, making all manner of sucking sounds. 'And take Amber with you; she needs to see the business side of the operation. Just tell her to stay quiet and follow your lead. And take Megan, she can ride shotgun on the trip.'

Dakota nodded, and reached for another bagel.

The Rainbow Girl

Amber sat in the back seat of the metallic-blue BMW, next to Megan, while Dakota drove. Megan was wearing black sunglasses that cupped her eyes so no light could get in. Amber had a similar pair back in her room. Everyone in the Cruza wore them when they went into the desert, but the girl wondered why her personal assistant needed them in the air-conditioned, tinted window comfort of the expensive car.

After driving for around an hour and a half, passing around San Diego proper to the coastal part of town, Dakota pulled up outside a building in a deserted street full of small industrial units.

It was dingy and cool inside the *Black Glass Bar*. Sunlight streamed in through the main door, dimly lighting the faded décor, but only when the main door was fully shut did Megan remove the sunglasses. Amber smiled with understanding; her personal assistant now had perfect night vision, unaffected like everyone else by moving from the outside glare into the cool gloom.

Sabrina Townsend was a mildly attractive, average brunette in her early forties who was probably used to having her own way, and feeling decidedly nervous in the company of the notorious Cruza members. Two large men leaned on the bar at the back of the club trying to look menacing, and failing.

'Those two,' said Dakota, pointing at the men. 'I want them out of here now.'

Sabrina Townsend swallowed visibly, and tried to hold

her ground. 'No, I'm afraid they stay until…'

The club owner never got to finish. Megan moved with impressive speed, pulling two electro-stun pistols from her jacket and firing at the men without warning. The two heavies jerked and twitched, falling heavily to the floor, unconscious. Megan sauntered over and began binding their hands with cable ties. Dakota stepped closer to the now scared looking Ms Townsend.

'If you ever disobey a direct order again, you die.' The lieutenant spoke calmly, which just increased her menace. 'Clear?'

Sabrina Townsend nodded weakly, and then led her visitors to a far corner of the room. Behind a concealed door lay a flight of steps that led to a second, heavier locked door. Sabrina handed over the key.

'Wait here,' Dakota told the woman. Then the lieutenant motioned for Amber to come with her. Megan remained with the club owner.

Amber looked around the gloomy basement. 'Yuk,' she said.

Dakota laughed. 'Couldn't have put it better myself. Looks like a set from one of those old horror movies. I keep expecting Dracula to come leaping out from behind those drapes. Fuck, you just can't buy class.'

They found a small side room containing a single iron-framed bed, with a stained mattress. Lying on it was Ms Townsend's un-hired victim. The girl was tightly hog-tied, her breath rapid as she sucked in air through a cute, slightly upturned nose. A wide strip of duct tape stretched from cheek to cheek, sealing her mouth. Two terrified eyes stared at the newcomers.

'Interesting,' said Dakota, pulling the girls matted fair hair away from her face. She looked the girl over for a few moments, and then led Amber back to the door. 'That…' Dakota jerked her head back in the direction of the terrified bundle, '…is what we call a rainbow girl.'

Amber looked at the lieutenant, puzzled. 'On account of the pretty colors,' the woman explained. 'This'll be good training for you. I want you to have a close look at her while I go talk to Townsend. She's probably shitting her panties standing out there with Megan.'

Amber sat on the bed next to the captive, running her fingers over the girl's body, feeling the raised lines where the cane had struck her. The teenager thought the rainbow girl looked beautiful. She gently peeled the duct tape from her lips, and the captive just lay there whimpering. Amber slipped a finger between the slightly swollen lips, and the abused girl began to suck on it, the feeling reminding Amber of a baby goat she'd once handled at the zoo. She guessed the frightened girl thought that's what she wanted her to do, and while she sucked Amber fondled one of her exposed breasts. The rainbow girl winced as Amber roughly handled her tender flesh, but she didn't stop sucking the finger in her mouth.

After a few minutes Amber slid her wet finger out and wiped it dry on the captive's hair. Then she carefully replaced the duct tape, and stroked the girl's breasts with both hands, giggling. She spent long minutes exploring the girl's body, noting where her abusers had hurt her most. Tracing the lines of the cane on the girl's inner thighs, even noting the red welts on her pussy lips. Strangely there were no stripes on her buttocks, but Amber noticed there were whip marks *between* her buttocks, striking directly across her anus. That was clever, noted the protégée. Someone with a lot of experience had worked on the girl, and she doubted it was Sabrina Townsend. Amber thought the club owner was actually pretty lame, looking like a total jerk when she'd tangled with Dakota and Megan.

A deal of sorts was agreed, though Ms Townsend had virtually no input but to signify that she would comply. The Cruza would supervise some refurbishment – at Ms

Townsend's expense – and would supply 'toys' for the regular customers. But there would also be house rules, and better security.

Amber mentioned to Dakota about the unusual way the captive girl had been whipped and the lieutenant was unusually pleased, then insisted Townsend divulge her client list. Sabrina confessed that this particular abuser had been a wealthy local lawyer. Dakota arranged a private visit; the woman was getting girls from somewhere, and it wasn't from the Cruza.

The three then climbed back into the BMW and drove towards the small airfield that housed one of the Cruza's private jets. They were being flown to Los Angeles for the second call of the day: to Mrs Hannah Levis, the recently widowed billionaire with a taste for female sex slaves.

'You did well back there,' Dakota said to the young protégée. 'Tell you what; I'll get you something nice for helping out. So what would you like? Some new clothes? Something pretty?'

Amber thought for a moment. 'Dakota…'

'Yes?'

'I'd like the rainbow girl, please.'

Dakota laughed. 'Sure babe, if that's what you want.'

The Silver Bullet

Two Cruza women had delivered her first purchase a couple of days ago. The Mexican girl was drugged and completely untouched, just as agreed. She lay peacefully sleeping on Hannah's large bed as her temporary owner slowly cut away sleeping beauty's clothes with a pair of surgical scissors. Then she rolled the girl onto her front, removed the cord she was bound with and attached the necessary leather restraints.

Hannah waited until the girl was coming round before inserting the rubber gag – just as the Cruza women had instructed, so as to not risk choking her. Then just before the girl became fully awake Hannah attached the blindfold as a final touch. Then she sat, watching with growing excitement as the girl's awareness slowly returned. The woman could barely resist fingering herself as she watched a state of panic consume the girl. It was delicious.

Training began early the next day. Hannah stretched the girl's legs wide, and then unpacked the bag the Cruza women had given her. She inserted a cold steel gynecological instrument into the girl's anus, following the enclosed instructions carefully. The blindfolded girl went wild with panic, thrashing around, but to no avail. The Cruza never scrimped on their play equipment, and the restraints were the best money could buy. But then, it wasn't as if Hannah had to count the dollars. The gynecological tool was an expandable hollow tube that slid deep into the girl's rectum.

Then Hannah took an inch long metal capsule from the bag, and raising the girl's pelvis with one hand, slid the capsule down the tube so it was lost deep inside the unfortunate captive. Then she set about showing the girl the exact purpose of the very expensive suppository.

Hannah removed the girl's blindfold and locked her ankle restraints together. 'Okay,' said the woman, smiling at the pair of beautiful but bewildered green eyes regarding her, 'I want this to be a quick lesson, so forget all the crap running round inside your head and pay attention. You belong to me until I'm done with you. I'll keep you for as long as you please me, and when I get bored I get to hand you back. But… and it's a very important but… you will never be free again. Got that?' Hannah watched the green eyes widen even more. 'All you will ever have to think about for the rest of your worthless life is how to please whichever woman is currently renting you. But I get to be the first, and as you're not trained yet they gave me that neat little thing in your butt.'

Hannah pressed a red button on a small remote she was holding, causing the metal capsule buried in the girl to emit a high voltage shock. She watched with amusement as the girl convulsed, arching her back in acute agony. Waves of pain rippled through the captive's insides, then just as she was about to pass out the pain stopped.

'Nifty little device, huh?' Hannah gloated, looking at the little control with obvious admiration. 'And the best thing is I don't have to take it out to charge it. I just have to strap a box thing around your waist. Apparently it works a little like an electric toothbrush, or so they told me. Can't remember the jargon, but it can charge the capsule without direct contact. Very, very neat.' She chuckled and placed the remote on the bedside table. 'So,' she continued in a menacing tone, 'let's see how far I can make you go before I have to use it again.'

Hannah lay back on the cool black silk sheets that covered her large bed, her naked flesh reveling in the sensation.

She arched her pelvis, forcing the silver strap-on dildo deeper into the young woman who straddled her. She smiled to herself as the girl gasped, the full eight-inches of the aluminum column driving deep into her vagina. The olive-skinned, dark-haired cutie was evidently not enjoying the experience as much as the woman beneath her. Hannah gazed lustfully at the girl's tight stomach, and watched her small breasts jiggle as she desperately bounced up and down on the stout strap-on. The girl's hands were bound behind her back, and Hannah could see the tension in those slim thighs as the exhausted girl lifted her body, sliding the thick dildo in and out of her cunt.

'Work it, bitch,' Hannah growled. 'You're getting lazy.' She pulled roughly on the thin silver chains attached to the girl's nipple rings, then lay back, smiling as she recalled putting the rings in the week before. That Cruza woman hadn't objected. Shit, she could pay for anything she wanted. They'd even offered to do it for her, but where was the fun in that?

The piercing was a real homemade job. Hannah had tied the girl to the kitchen table and then pierced each of her nipples with a needle, before feeding the silver rings into place.

'That's enough, slut,' Hannah said, in a bored tone. She turned sideways, throwing the girl onto the bed, and then she pulled her hips back, extracting the dildo from deep within the girl's cunt. There was a squelching sound and then a faint plop as the silver torpedo pulled free. 'Maybe I should get a bigger one; that felt a little loose, didn't you think?' The woman laughed as she saw the worried look on the girl's face, but her captive lay quietly while Hannah undid the straps that held the metal monster and slid the harness down her legs. She dropped the beast onto the floor, and heard it hit the carpet with a satisfyingly heavy clunk.

Hannah then grabbed the girl by her ponytail and dragged the exhausted wretch between her thighs. She unclipped the rubber gag and pulled her flushed face to her pussy and held it there. She then dug her heels into the small of the poor bitch's back and began to undulate her pelvis, masturbating herself on her unwilling playmate's face. The billionaire picked up a riding crop from the mattress and cracked it sharply across the girl's exposed buttocks. 'Let's see if you can work that tongue better than you worked Metal Mary, shall we?' She sighed blissfully; the girl could barely nod her head, let alone speak with a mouth full of sopping wet pussy.

A week later and Hannah was genuinely surprised at how enthusiastically the slave had worked to avoid the device. She looked like a typical dumb slut with more curves than brain cells, but she was obviously smart enough to know that being in a load of pain was worse than submitting to the perverse demands of the woman who held her captive.

Hannah made her way upstairs clutching a black leather briefcase under one arm. She burst excitedly into the bedroom. The slave was lying on her back on the bed just as Hannah had left her two hours ago. It was warm out in the July sun, and Hannah had deliberately left the Mercedes' air-conditioning off. She struggled a little as she removed her damp, sweaty panties, sliding them down to her ankles and kicking them off. Then she pulled out the girl's gag and sat heavily on her upturned face. As she was now trained to do, the girl immediately began licking her owner's sweaty pussy, driving her tongue deep into the musky interior of the woman's vagina, lapping like her life depended on it.

Hannah entered the code into the briefcase lock and flipped the catches. She opened the case and pulled out the gleaming silver dildo. It was huge, at least ten inches long, and so thick she could hardly get her hand round it. She lifted her skirt so she could see the girl's eyes peering up from behind the thick fuzz of her pubic hair, gave the defeated green eyes a little wave, and chuckled. 'Hey,' she said to the slave, 'guess what. Tonight you get to meet Metal Mary's big sister. And there's an added surprise, just to make things even more fun.'

That night Hannah positioned the girl over the back of a large chair in the house's vast and opulent lounge. The slave's ankles were tied to rings on the lower chair legs, but she was still standing barefoot on the thick pile carpet. Her arms were twisted uncomfortably behind her back and her wrist cuffs were securely attached to her neck collar. Hannah had attached a strong clip to the girl's ponytail, and it was pulled forward and tied to the front of the chair so she couldn't straighten up.

Hanna slipped on her strap-on harness and inserted the new metal dildo into the ring, then spoke softly into her plaything's ear. 'Remember the surprise I told you about? Well, actually there are two. My, aren't you a lucky girl?' She giggled and laid a hand on the girl's bare back, feeling the muscles tense.

'First, this isn't going in your cunt,' she went on. 'Nope, I'm going to stick this big beauty in your ass.'

For the first time in many days the hapless girl resisted. She began to struggle against her bonds, but to no avail. She was held tight, and Hannah could hear her whimpering into the gag.

'And second…' the woman continued, '…is that this beauty is long enough to reach that magical little capsule in your ass. And as they're both made of metal and one is electrically charged… well, I'll leave you to figure it out. Oh, and don't worry about me, it's rubber at this end.'

The girl thrashed and writhed, wailing into the gag as Hannah pressed the huge metal dildo deeper into her tight rectum, and when it had penetrated to nearly its full length Hannah began to fuck the girl with long, slow strokes. Then as the lubricant she'd been kind enough to use made the thick shaft slick enough, the woman plunged harder and further, sinking the dildo deep into the girl. As Hannah's groin slapped against the girl's buttocks the dildo penetrated far enough to touch the capsule, and a burst of low voltage flooded the girl's insides with each stroke. Hannah thrust away, climaxing every few minutes as she felt the girl writhing involuntarily with the pulsing shockwaves.

As the dawn light made the heavy curtains glow faintly, Hannah, soaked in a sheen of sweat, was still pumping away in a sexual frenzy while the girl's exhausted body lay limp over the chair. But eventually Hannah withdrew, then wearily plucked a handful of delicate pink flowers from the ornate container on the oriental glass coffee table in the center of the room and inserted them, stalks first, into the girl's anus. 'Maybe I'll just keep you as a novelty vase,' she sighed.

Hannah picked up the phone and dialed the special number she'd been given. 'Hi, State Girl, anything new for me?' she asked. 'Really? Great. So can I expect delivery in the next few days? Fantastic. Oh, and can you send someone to collect poor little green eyes here. She's pretty used up, but maybe you can still get someone to take her on the low end of the market.' Hannah glanced over at the girl. She looked like a rag-doll that had been left in the yard during a rainstorm. 'Doubt you'll get more than twenty bucks for her now, but don't worry; I'll pay what you wanna bill me. After all, I had *so* much fun.'

According to Taste

Several links in Juana's chain had now been removed, and though the girl had become used to the constant pain in her clitoris, the sight of what should be a little pink nub, protruding like a tiny penis, shocked her. Juana's life seemed all about lessons, and her captors were teaching her more through the total and complete way in which she was now owned. Juana, the pretty, clever girl who would do well one day had become… well, it appeared she no longer had a name, but she was something to be played with, to be enjoyed by others, something to be bought and sold and tailored for the perverse pleasure of a woman she had never met.

Juana, like all the other pathetic slave girls here, was forced to carry objects of her own humiliation wherever she went. A rubber gag was clipped to her belt at all times in case it was needed. Anyone wishing to abuse her would remove it and stuff it in her mouth, silencing any annoying sounds she might make during the ordeal. Carrying the gag was an exercise in humiliation, though Juana could not understand why she needed one. Pain, humiliation and degradation were now the only words she would use to describe her life, but how could she describe anything when she wasn't even allowed to speak without permission.

In addition to the gag, slaves were also required to carry a flexible cane also attached to the belt. Should any of the many mistresses in the household get the need – or the whim – to discipline their property, a tool was always to hand. It was not considered polite for a girl to make her owner search for something to strike her with should the need arise.

While Juana had been on house servant duties, she would often be wandering the long hallways of the house, fetching and carrying for the *paid* servants. Once she passed a tall blonde who looked her over as she approached carrying an empty tray in her manacled hands. As Juana passed the blonde suddenly reached out, grabbing her collar, and she immediately stopped on the spot. The blonde then pushed open a door, and finding a cupboard filled with shelves of cleaning equipment and bundles of dirty laundry on the floor, pushed the slave inside. Juana cringed as she heard the door shut behind them, and felt claustrophobic with wild thoughts racing through her mind. She could die in here. The woman could kill her just for fun and no one would care. They would just make her pay what they thought Juana was worth – which probably wasn't very much.

The blonde unclipped the gag from the belt, feeding it gently into the naked Latina's mouth, and Juana's head jerked as the woman tightened it. Then, with equal assuredness, the blonde also unclipped the cane. Juana was always aware of the cane; she could feel it brushing against her leg constantly, it would tap against her naked thigh as she walked. So far no one had ever used it on her, but now a blonde she'd never seen before had her trapped in a storage closet and she was holding the cane, rubbing it on her palm and smiling at her.

They seemed to stand like that for an eternity. Juana felt like a tiny rabbit in the presence of a hungry coyote, hoping, in that state of desperation only the truly helpless ever know, that if she didn't move, didn't twitch a muscle, the woman would leave her alone. But those malicious blue eyes told a different story. Without warning the woman grabbed Juana by the hair, forcing her head down to her knees. The cane cracked across the Latina's buttocks and she yelped hopelessly into the taught rubber gag. The blonde began to thrash the slave, caning the backs of her thighs and her calves, the blows falling in rapid succession.

Then with as little warning as she'd begun the attack, the woman stopped. Juana had been sobbing into the gag but now she fell silent, again hoping she would become invisible to her cruel and powerful enemy if she could just stay quiet enough. But a foot locked around her ankle and with a quick move the blonde tripped the slave, twisting her so she landed on her back in a heap of old linen. The blonde stood over her prey, looking impossibly tall. A sheen of sweat covered her taught, muscled body, accentuating her tanned skin. The piercing blue eyes gazed down upon the doomed creature at her feet, impossibly bright blue eyes full of hunger. Not a coyote, the slave thought, a wolf.

The blonde swept the cane down on the slave's belly, causing the girl to double up in a protective reflex. As Juana's knees moved instinctively to her breasts the woman snatched the ankle cuffs and clipped them together in a swift movement. Then she pulled a length of flex from a cable drum on a shelf, looped one end around the upright beam on the storage rack, and the other she threaded through the ankle restraints, raising the olive-skinned girl's legs with amazing ease that let her helpless victim glimpse a hidden and dangerous strength. Juana now hung from the shelving, suspended by her ankles so that only her shoulders were touching the floor.

'Before I leave this closet,' said the blonde with chilling calmness, 'you will beg me to allow you to…' without warning she sliced the cane across the soles of the bound slave's feet and Juana howled through the gag, '…to use that filthy tongue of yours…' she struck again, '…to make me orgasm.' Another blow slashed across the reddened soles of the sobbing slave's feet.

The woman released the knot in the flex and the slave

dropped to the floor, lying amongst the dirty linen like a broken doll. The blonde then grabbed the slave's ponytail, and Juana was hauled to her knees. All slaves wore ponytails; the mistresses used them like handles on a sex toy, to position the girl's head just so for maximum pleasure when receiving tongue worship. The woman loosened the straps on Juana's gag and pulled it free. It fell onto the sheets, saliva and tears soaking into the soiled cloth.

'Beg,' the woman commanded as she stared down at the naked girl.

'Please, mistress...' Juana fought to keep the pain in the tortured soles of her feet from overwhelming her. 'Please allow my filthy tongue into your glorious sex. Please, allow me to lick your divine sex until you orgasm in my mouth.'

The blonde laughed delightedly. 'Do you even have the faintest idea what you're asking?' she asked, and Juana shook her head. 'I am everything you will never be, slut.' The woman spat the words venomously. 'I am wealthy, while you don't even own your own body. I am free, while you can't even take a piss without permission. I am in control, while you are controlled. I am respected and valued, while you are passed around and used like a cheap plastic dildo at a high school slumber party.

'And the best part is, I will grow more beautiful with every birthday and slip gracefully into elegance as I grow older, while you...' the wolf smiled down at the trapped rabbit waiting to have its throat torn out, '...will be used, fucked and beaten, and passed around to any bitch with enough dollars to pay. While I am a classic first edition on a collector's bookshelf, taken down lovingly and handled like the rarest, most precious thing in the world, you are like a cheap paperback in a public library, taken out every day and retuned dog-eared and grimy. And the best thing is, as you wear out the price goes down, and as the price goes down the owners of the cunts you get to stick your disgusting tongue in move further along the food chain, till you find yourself strapped on your back in one of our five-bucks-a-cum booths, while some druggie sits on your face grinding her unwashed cunt into your mouth.'

The blonde lashed out with the cane, catching the slave on her left breast. Juana yelped, earning another stinging swipe to her right breast.

'So, perhaps now you understand the honor I am bestowing upon you. You are going to taste *my* pussy juice. You are going to put your tongue in *my* perfect cunt. You are going to get to lick *my* heavenly ass. And while you do it, you're going to hear every word I've said echoing in that empty head of yours. Oh, and if you want to leave this delightful little room with any flesh on that scrawny body of yours, you'll make sure I enjoy plentiful orgasms.'

The blonde laughed gaily, then she slipped off her expensive red silk knickers, grabbed the Latina girl's ponytail and pulled the slave's tearstained face between her toned thighs.

The blonde used Juana in the utility closet for a few hours, grinding her pussy onto the slave's mouth as the Latina pushed her face against her abuser's vagina with all her strength, driving her tongue deep into the woman. The cane spurred the slave on, lashing her across the back and buttocks. Juices flooded the slave's mouth. She swallowed, drinking the blonde's flood. Her tongue wormed deeper into the clinging wetness. The woman held the back of Juana's head and pressed the slave's face tight between her legs, sniggering at the spluttering sounds the Latina made. The blonde shuffled her sandaled feet further apart and using the leverage rubbed her pussy up and down the slave's face, masturbating on the pathetic wretch like a horny pubescent teenager with a pillow jammed between her thighs. Hands pressed down on the slave's head, sliding the poor girl's face against sopping sex lips, locating the Latina's mouth directly over her abuser's anus. Juana's smeared face slid into place between the blonde's buttocks, lubricating the woman's anus with her own juices. The slave's tongue burrowed into the blonde's anus. She obediently pushed hard and her tongue slid into the waiting passage. The blonde grunted with delight, and moaning with pleasure she squatted lower on the slave's head. She grabbed the young Latino's ears and held her tight while a powerful orgasm rippled through her slender body. Juana summoned all her remaining strength, and drove her tongue deep into the woman's ass, wriggling it desperately. The blonde shuddered and let out a long groan as another orgasm pushed up from the pit of her stomach to surge through her body in waves of raw pleasure. The blonde held the Latino between her legs while her quivering body shivered and the last few spasms of ecstasy subsided.

Without a word the blonde straightened up, allowing the body of her victim to flop to the floor. The woman smiled dreamily. 'Not bad, slut,' she said dismissively, then picked up the red silk knickers and pushed them into the exhausted Latina's mouth. 'Something to remember me by,' she laughed, as she walked calmly out of the closet, straightening her tight dress.

Juana heard the click of the door as it shut behind her tormentor, and lay sobbing on the dirty sheets.

The Golden Girl

'Mrs Levis,' Rebecca smiled as she spoke into the phone, even though the woman couldn't see her. The billionaire had turned out to be the perfect client – appreciative, loyal, very discreet and punctual at paying her bills. Also, the woman never quibbled about paying for breakages or for any unexpected cleaning bills the organization incurred. In fact she was very unusual; Rebecca was used to dealing with the super wealthy, and they were usually a total pain in the ass. But Mrs Levis was different. The Cruza even supplied Mrs Levis' fulltime security needs, allocating her round the clock bodyguards. Of course, it also suited Rebecca to have one of her people around to protect her assets. It wouldn't do anyone much good if the woman got careless and attracted attention, but then Mrs Levis was not stupid and she genuinely seemed to appreciate Rebecca's people keeping an eye on her. Perhaps she could relax a little more and enjoy her games without worrying. Either way, the woman never quibbled about paying for security provisions.

'Please, Rebecca, call me Hannah. No need for formalities, we both know I have no family, and I'll be damned if I'm going to leave my money to anyone after what I had to go through to get it. So I'm going to spend every cent, and from what I've seen so far you're going to be the main recipient.'

Rebecca smiled; whether it was new or old money, she liked the woman's style.

'So what can we do for you today, Hannah?'

'Well, firstly I would like three entertainment packages for tonight.'

'Aha.' Rebecca scribbled the order onto a yellow notepad on her desk. 'Anything particular?'

'Surprise me,' replied the woman.

'We'll try our best, Hannah. Anything else I can do for you?'

'Well, I'm going to Aspen for the weekend and I'd like something to take along with me so I don't get bored.'

'Just send us the details of where you're staying and I'll have it waiting for you when you arrive.'

'Oh yes, and I'd like something for the journey up. I hate to fly but I get so bored in the car.'

'I see,' Rebecca said. 'How about I send over one of our limos to take you? Ours are, well, specially equipped, and there will be something to keep you entertained on the long drive.'

'That sounds fantastic, sweetie,' gushed the woman. 'Lets do it.'

Rebecca replaced the handset and smiled to herself. What a good way to end a day.

The Inquisitor made her way to the private gym and bathroom that led off from her large, light-oak paneled office, with its huge tropical fish tank, plants and ornamental fountain. She closed the door behind her and began to strip off her clothes, slipping off her sandals then wriggling out of her tight electric-blue dress like a gilded snake shedding its skin. She slipped off her bra, and then rolled her panties down her thighs, kicking them off her bare feet. The white tiles of the air-conditioned gym felt cool on the soles of her feet as she padded into the equipment area. She sat on a low bench that ran along one wall, and slipped on her white socks and tennis shoes. The Inquisitor stood for a moment, looking at herself in the wall-to-wall mirrors; she had the breasts of a teenager, small and pert, a trim waste and long tanned legs.

Rebecca's personal plaything was already in the room, prepared and awaiting her owner's arrival. The girl was a beautiful blonde Brazilian of mixed race. Rebecca had always loved the way her blonde hair contrasted with her coffee-colored skin. From that perfect face, with its flawless complexion and golden halo of hair, shone bright green eyes that were quite breathtaking in their beauty. She was an exceptional catch, even by Cruza standards. Rebecca acquired the girl about five years ago, in an opportunistic deal with a Peruvian drug dealer. She was a beautiful virgin and he was going to marry her, but the minute Rebecca set eyes on her she had to possess her. The price was understandably high, with Cruza operatives giving safe passage to a cocaine shipment with a street value of around seven million dollars.

Rebecca was the only person the girl had ever known sexually; the dealer was as good as his word, the girl was indeed a virgin. She even had an intact hymen, rare even in true virgins. The Inquisitor had taken that from her the first night, with a twenty-four carat gold dildo, fucking the girl as soon as she arrived back with her prize. In celebration the girl had been forced to drink champagne from Rebecca's pussy while the woman held up the dildo like a hunting trophy.

Rebecca still found the girl irresistible, and in five years she had lost none of her beauty. The girl was currently strapped to a curved bench, bending her bronzed, slim body back in an arch. The top of the bench was bolted to the back of Rebecca's exercise bike so the girl's head rested where the bike's saddle should be. A little clichéd, the Inquisitor thought, smiling to herself, but lots of fun anyway.

She climbed elegantly onto the bike, swinging a shapely leg over that perfect face till she stood upright on the pedals, her shaved vagina gently touching the tip of the girl's nose. She smiled down into those jade eyes and they looked back up with resignation. Rebecca had watched the girl's stare change slowly over the years, from horror moving through disgust at what she was being made to do, to shame and humiliation and finally… resignation. She had come to accept what her life was about. No husband, or children, or cars, or dresses, or friends, or career; just a sexual plaything. Nothing more than that – ever. A stranger life than she could ever have imagined. When she was not entertaining her owner she was being pampered, as a host of Rebecca's servants worked to keep the toy beautiful.

Rebecca worked out for an hour every day, building up a sweat on the bike, with the girl between her thighs. Instructions were unnecessary; the green-eyed girl knew the routine. She turned her head and began to lick the insides of her owner's thighs, moistening them initially so the woman's skin wouldn't chaff as it rubbed against her face. It was only necessary for the first few minutes, for the girl knew only too well that things would get very wet as her owner began to sweat and juices leaked from her pussy.

Rebecca lowered herself onto the girl's face and began to pedal. Her muscular thighs slid against the girl's cheeks as the girl worked her tongue into her owner's pussy. She nuzzled the woman's soft wet cunt as it bounced and ground on her face. She licked the wet entrance and pulled on Rebecca's clit with her lips as it slid across her mouth. After twenty minutes or so the girl's face was coated with Rebecca's sweat, juice, and her own saliva. Rebecca drove harder into her workout. The girl closed her mouth on her owner's labia and sucked the silky flesh. Rebecca came instantly, but then the girl had been learning what made her happy for five years. The woman pounded on the machine's pedals, driving herself harder as the girl struggled to drink all that leaked from her panting owner's vagina.

There was a short bleep as the timer told Rebecca she had completed her workout. She wiped the sweat from her brow and relaxed on the girl's face. The slave's golden hair was damp with Rebecca's sex juices, and rivulets ran down her throat, dripping to the tiled floor. The girl knew by now that she would have to get down on her knees and lick up anything that spilled after the session, just as the maids who cleaned her would wipe her face with a white silk cloth, which they would then make her suck until every drop of her owner's fluids were gone, just as Rebecca had instructed.

The Inquisitor sat unmoving on the girl's face, catching her breath. The golden slave continued to work her tongue on her mistress's pussy, bringing her owner to another shuddering orgasm before she climbed off.

Rebecca released the girl from the bench, though she still wore her padded cuffs. The girl stood up, hands bound tightly to her sides, and then began to lick the sweat from her owner's body. Starting with her shoulders and arms, sucking each finger, then Rebecca's neck, moving down to her breasts, then her flat stomach. The girl licked the woman's back and buttocks, and then worked her way down her thighs to her calves, stopping at her ankles. Rebecca pulled up a small stool and sat down, the girl kneeling before her, and then she slid off her tennis shoes and socks and sat quietly while the girl sucked on her toes. After the elaborate ritual was concluded the Inquisitor chained the girl to a metal ring on the wall where the maids would collect her, and headed for the shower.

Pink Lip-gloss and a Length of Rope

Amber sat on her bed looking at Rainbow Girl as she knelt on the floor. The young woman had spent some time in the medical center, and now her skin was fairly well healed. Amber had also had the curators subject the girl to a thorough cleaning after her removal from the *Black Glass Bar*. Now the young blonde sat on her haunches, freshly scrubbed and perfumed. She was still naked and bound, but then that's how she would always be. The woman belonged to the Cruza now, but even though the organization was her ultimate owner, everyone knew she was Amber's pet. Everyone had one – sometimes two or three – and it was customary not to use another member's pet without asking first.

Amber reached across to the dresser by her bed and picked up the thin cane. She watched Rainbow Girl's eyes closely, and could see the memories there, everything that had happened to her that night in the grimy dungeon still vivid. She backed away slightly from the cane, but she couldn't go far. Amber was curious; the way the captive's ass had been punished impressed her – and excited her as she imagined being able to inflict pain with such professionalism. It made the girl even more determined to cast off her past. Sure, she had always liked hurting girls, and the more her father had hurt her the more she enjoyed inflicting worse on others, but in her own way she'd been fumbling in the dark, learning as she went.

There was nothing particularly special about the white trash trailer park where Amber had grown up, a ramshackle collection of paint-flaking aluminum boxes and rusting trucks. The population of washed out women and feral kids presided over by a patriarchal collection of men: misfits, drunks, and criminals, in no particular order. About the only thing that held them together was their mutual love of bullying violence, alcohol, drugs and guns. The average white trash male ruled over his little slice of the kingdom using a simple rule; women were easy targets, and little girls the easiest of all. Under the stewardship of the unwashed, gun toting, truck driving bullies the trailer park became a violent zoo, seething with abuse, cruelty and loose sexuality. A place where teenagers roamed in hunting packs, preying on the weak and idolizing the strong, while little kids with poor hygiene and crappy diets lurked in the shadows of their older siblings, learning so they could recreate the same shitty world for themselves in a few years.

Mostly things were predictable; girls got pregnant at fourteen, marrying some loser who knew how to beat them just like their daddies did. The guys usually served their first jail term at about the same age. Amber had always known her pathetic bunch of so called friends just couldn't wait to walk the path, a can of beer in one hand, a baby in the belly, and a broken nose on a Saturday night. They just couldn't wait.

So Amber wasn't very old when she figured out that some people simply resigned themselves to abuse. It was as if they were raised to expect little else. But she had to wait till she was eighteen before she discovered another variety, a type born in the passion of sex, and it was about the same time she also discovered that some people might actually need it, might actually crave this kind of abuse. They sought it out. They thrived on it.

The last trailer on the park was tucked away by the service road. There were no kids, so she'd never had any cause to get to know the residents. Just some useless drunken old hag – Amber had never bothered to learn her name – and her quiet, withdrawn daughter, a woman in her late twenties called Jackie. It was Jackie who taught Amber who and what she really was, and it was an interesting lesson for the teenager, a girl who had fought back against abuse her whole life, who wouldn't back down, who would never accept what was being offered by the world. The hard-fighting, sharp-witted, and by a lucky dip of the gene pool, very pretty redheaded girl was suddenly confronted by someone excitingly different, someone who could only truly exist when she was being used, and the more she was, the more she thrived. A woman who, in a paradoxical way, was a little like Amber herself, sort of the flipside; the more you hurt her, the more alive she became.

It began one warm July evening when Jackie was sat out by the road watching the cars pass by. The teenager bumped the woman then shouted, 'Get out of my way, bitch!' Or something like that. Amber couldn't remember exactly. Her father had just hit her again and she wasn't in the best of moods. Usually you got into a fight pretty quickly if you talked to trailer trash that way, even if they knew you, but Jackie just stared at the ground and moved out of the way. So like a true pack animal Amber moved in for the kill, determined to press the advantage. But while she cursed at the strange, quiet woman the teenager noticed something in her eyes, or rather the lack of it. Despite timidly accepting the tirade of verbal abuse from the younger girl, her eyes lacked fear. The woman was allowing this to happen, encouraging it even, by her very silence. On impulse Amber slapped Jackie's cheek, a stinging blow, but the woman just stared at the ground. She didn't fight back, nor did she run away. It was something the teenager had never encountered before.

From that point on Amber became a little obsessed with the woman. She was someone the girl could control completely, someone *she* could hurt, someone who would never resist, never tell. The redhead knew it was a sexual thing, and while most of the white trash girls were fucking guys on a regular basis, Amber knew she wanted something different. Every night, after she'd found some excuse to hurt Jackie, watching as she took it all, puzzled by how her eyes seemed more alive than at any time she'd known her, the teenager would lie in bed and masturbate over what had happened, thinking about what she was going to do to the withdrawn woman tomorrow.

Amber even got a key to Jackie's trailer. She just demanded one and it was handed over. Even the smallest act of compliance would make the teenager wet, simply telling Jackie to get her a soda would dampen the domineering girl's panties. Amber would head for Jackie's trailer most evenings; the woman's drunken mother was hardly ever around, and the teen's father couldn't give a shit where she was, so things worked out pretty well. Amber was never very sophisticated with her new hobby, nothing like she'd seen at the *Black Glass Bar*, and certainly nothing like the Cruza. Back then, well, she'd been pretty crude at applying her natural talents, but everyone had to start somewhere. Certainly not bad for a white trash teenager making it up as she went along. The teenager was still experimenting, still not quite grasping what she was, so she would just beat Jackie with her hands, slapping her while she cowered by her bed, not fighting back, not even trying to protect herself from the blows the crazy teenager rained down on her. She just absorbed the abuse and never told, never changed the locks, never avoided the pretty redhead, and every day her eyes were more alive, taking more care over her hair, make-up and clothes.

One night when Amber was particularly fucked off with life, she tied Jackie to the bed. Just like that, she had no idea why, a crazy girl acting on impulse. Jackie lay there; her wrists bound to the bed frame with a piece of old laundry line. The woman lay still for a few minutes then she began to thrash around, pulling at the rope. That just excited Amber, watching her struggle like that, powerless, and if it occurred to Amber that Jackie should have struggled *before* the rope was put on her, she never thought about it. So the teenager just stood watching the woman struggling, moaning, thrashing around, and the damp patch in the girl's panties grew larger until she found herself looking around for something to hit Jackie with.

She rummaged through all the crap in the closet, and it took her a moment to realize she'd found what she was looking for. She stood looking at the leather belt in her hand for a moment, and then she stripped off her jeans, throwing them over the bedrail, and stood there in her crop top T-shirt and white socks. She twirled the leather belt around her head, glowering down at her struggling victim like a demonic cheerleader. Jackie started whimpering but she didn't pull back or curl up, in fact it almost seemed as if she almost imperceptibly raised her buttocks, taunting the teenager, so Amber brought the belt slicing through the air, landing with a satisfying *thwack* on the woman's ass cheeks. It couldn't have hurt much for the struggling bitch was still wearing her denim shorts, but she yelped anyway.

'Shut the fuck up, whore,' Amber shouted, lashing her again. But Jackie didn't shut up. Instead she started to moan, wriggling and struggling against the cord wrapped around her wrists, so again on impulse Amber pulled off her white socks and shoved them in Jackie's mouth, muffling the annoying sounds. It was a gross thing to do, and the idea of her socks filling the woman's mouth excited her, and then she went on another search.

It didn't take her long to find what she was looking for. In the bottom drawer of the kitchen cabinet, just next to the refrigerator, lay a roll of silver duct tape. She knew all the trailers kept some, especially the really crappy ones like Jackie's, because when it rained they leaked like sieves. She also found an unexpected prize; a six-pack of beer at the back of the refrigerator. She took them out and popped a tab on one of the chilled tins, rubbing it against her forehead. It was a hot, sultry night and the condensation mixed with the sweat on her brow, ran in rivulets down her cheeks and throat to disappear into her cleavage. A small damp patch appeared at the front of her white T-shirt as she held the can to her lips and let the chilled liquid trickle into her mouth, held the fizzing liquid there for a moment, enjoying the sensation, then swallowed, smacking her lips in satisfaction.

The yellowed lamp in the grimy bedroom illuminated the scene on the single bed. The teenager knelt on the woman's chest while she peeled off a length of tape, then she pushed the socks deeper into her mouth, squeezing her jaws shut tight, then pressed the tape firmly over her lips. Much better.

Jackie went strangely quiet, and instead of struggling against the new degradation Amber could hear her gently sucking on the cotton socks. The teenager stood by the bed, looking down at her victim while she swigged cheap beer from the can, then she raised the belt and lashed the woman's buttocks again, giggling at the muted yelps punctuated by sucking sounds. The alcohol seeped into her excited mind, unlocking buried desires like a magic key. She grabbed the waistband of the woman's denim shorts with strong hands and tugged them off. Jackie's panties came with them, leaving her naked from the waist down, and now she went wild, thrashing around like a freshly caught fish on a riverbank. The redhead thought the scene was electrifying, and stood watching until one of the woman's flailing feet kicked her in the leg. Jackie hadn't done it on purpose, but she just couldn't go around kicking people and get away with it. Amber grabbed the offending foot and wrapped more of the thin nylon rope around the ankle. It was oddly easy, almost as if the woman had paused her struggle in order to allow this further act of abuse from the girl. Amber then sat on Jackie's calves, grabbed her other leg and tied the ankles together.

There was no hesitation in the tipsy teen now. Amber wasn't thinking anything through. If there were any thoughts about possible consequences in the girl's brain, they were quietly drowning in the cheap beer. She flipped the woman onto her front and lashed at her buttocks with the belt again. This time it was sweetly different, the satisfying sound of leather meeting bare skin was electric, and Amber felt the unmistakable wave of pleasure surging within her as she orgasmed, her supple limbs riding the aftershock of the most powerful moment of pleasure she'd ever known as she stood beside her victim, her own plaything, shaking gently as the sensations passed.

Amber knew she was completely lost in the game, just as she wanted. She also knew instinctively that Jackie was as lost as she was, unable to go back.

Raising the belt once more she began whipping the naked butt cheeks, raining blow after stinging blow on the reddening flesh. She owned that ass; it was hers, like the rest of the stupid bitch. Jackie was sucking her socks, it was symbolic, she had signed herself over completely. There was no going back now, not as wave after wave of orgasms rippled through the girl, making her moan in pleasure. The teenager slid her free hand into her panties, frantically rubbing herself while she thrashed her victim, her property, with the improvised whip. She slipped two fingers into her vagina as she began to flail the back of the woman's thighs, working her slim fingers in and out of her pussy. She was really wet, juices coating her fingers and soaking her panties. Then after one last orgasm that rippled through her she collapsed on the bed beside her softly whimpering plaything.

Amber lay next to the trembling body beside her for a

few moments, enjoying the warm afterglow of a sexual frenzy, and then she grabbed Jackie by the hair and turned the woman's face to her. She smiled as she peeled away the duct tape and removed the saliva-soaked socks. She still had two fingers buried deep in her vagina, twirling them gently around. She knew Jackie could hear the squishy sound her pussy made. There was a faint sucking sound as she removed her hand and rolled her panties down her legs, pulling them over her feet, the insides of her thighs soaked. She rubbed them together, feeling them slide slickly, then she lifted her sticky fingers to the woman's face, letting her smell her musky juices. Then she stuck her fingers roughly into the woman's mouth.

'Suck,' Amber said simply, and Jackie did. As usual she didn't say anything. 'I ain't gonna stay in this fucking shit-hole for long,' the teenager said to the woman. 'But until I go I fucking own you. You know that, don't you, bitch?'

Jackie gave no acknowledgement that she understood, but she didn't argue either. Amber removed her fingers and began to run them gently over her handiwork, feeling the ridges and welts, the pretty pink lines across the striped buttocks and legs. Then she untied the woman, pulled on her own jeans and padded barefoot to the bedroom door, carrying her socks. She turned to look at her half-naked whipping toy as she lay perfectly still and strangely content on the bed.

'Here,' Amber said as she threw her soaked panties at the woman, landing damply on her face and falling onto the bed, 'something for you to play with. And I want them back, understand? I can't afford to get new ones.' Jackie just stared blankly at the redhead as she stood in the doorway and sighed impatiently. 'You're supposed to suck them, loser. Jeez, can't you figure nuthin' out for yourself?'

As if she'd been waiting for the instruction all along,

Jackie fed the wet panties into her mouth and did as she was told, sucking the underwear like a kid with a tasty jawbreaker. Amber smiled, shaking her head, then staggered tipsily back to her own depressing trailer.

The rain drummed on the trailer's aluminum roof and water leapt from the small, partly open window like a decorative fountain. It was getting dark, and Amber was bored and broke. As she stared mindlessly at the rain Jackie wandered past, on her way back from the local store, carrying two plastic bags stuffed with groceries. Amber hadn't seen the woman's mother for days, nor had anyone else. She had been asking around, and a crazy old bearded Vietnam veteran in the trailer opposite said she was dead. The man told the curious teenager that someone had found the mother's body slumped in a toilet cubicle in a gas station about fifty miles out of town, something he found hysterically funny. He said the woman was midway through a dump when she had a heart attack. Then he kept rambling on about Elvis and other boring crap until Amber just wandered off, and he hardly seemed to notice she'd gone.

Amber didn't think it was funny, but it was convenient. It had been nearly a week since her last game with Jackie, and her old hag of a mother had been loitering around ever since. She was getting desperate, and she'd been masturbating so much her pussy was sore.

She waited for about an hour then went to Jackie's trailer and let herself in. The groceries were still in the plastic bags on the kitchen counter as she crept to the dingy bedroom and saw Jackie lying on the bed, a hand in her knickers, furiously rubbing herself. The woman froze as she saw Amber standing in the doorway.

'Selfish bitch,' the teenager grinned. 'Why didn't you ask me over to play? I wasn't doing nuthin'.' Jackie slowly slid her hand from between her legs, not answering the brooding redhead. 'Well, I'm here anyway,' Amber continued, 'so we might as well play together, huh?' Amber sidled over to the bed and dropped her backpack onto the floor beside it, opened the zipper and pulled out a length of laundry line fresh from the hardware store in town. It was still wound round the cardboard insert.

She unraveled the cord as the woman lay on the bed looking sheepishly at the opened zipper of her jeans. Then she grabbed her right forearm and lifted the guilty fingers to her nose, feeling excited by the smell of another female's sex. Then, without a word, she began undressing the woman, first untying her sneakers and dropping them to the floor, with a hollow thud as they hit the thin boards. To Amber it felt vaguely reminiscent of getting her six-year-old cousin ready for bed as Jackie passively complied, lifting her legs so she could tug her jeans over her feet. The knickers came off with the jeans and she lay on the bed in her T-shirt much as she had done the time before, but this time Amber didn't stop there. She pulled Jackie to a sitting position then grasped the hem of her top, pulling it over her head as the strangely compliant plaything helpfully raised her arms. Then the teenager unclipped Jackie's bra, pulled it off and flung it across the room. The woman was now quite naked.

Amber pushed her back down on the bed, then rolled her onto her front, and only when she pulled the woman's arms behind her back did she show the first sign of resistance, a weak attempt to pull her arms free, but Amber grabbed her wrists and pushed them up into the middle of her back. Jackie moaned as she was forced into the uncomfortable position, but it was that strange sound again, the one that spoke of silent conspiracy between the two, as both fell into the lie, the one that said Jackie was being taken by the girl against her will, hating every minute of the abuse heaped upon her. Amber was quick and strong, straddling her, holding her down and quickly tying her wrists, laughing as she did it.

'I just felt like playing tonight, loser,' Amber said to the subdued woman beneath her. 'You see, that's the fucking cool thing about owning someone, you don't have to ask or put up with any crap excuses.' The teenager pushed her arms further up her back to emphasize the point. 'Shame you can't get your dirty little fingers in your cunt though, ain't it.' The redhead turned round and shuffled down, sliding over her naked butt, trapping her legs, tying her ankles together. Jackie didn't struggle but she did quiver expectantly.

'Fuck, do you know how many times I've jacked off thinking about this?' Amber moved up to sit by Jackie's head and began pulling her dark hair back into a ponytail. 'Weird the stuff that goes through your head when you're jerking off though, ain't it? I mean *real* weird shit, like stuff that could never really happen.' She held Jackie's newly formed ponytail in her left hand, while she casually wound a length of the cord around it in a tight coil. 'Not much I don't know about knots an' stuff.' The teenager chatted casually, like she was sipping chocolate milkshakes with her friends at the diner, making it last so the owner didn't throw them out for taking up table space. 'Dad used to take me hunting,' she said. 'I used to think he liked having me along until I figured out he was just too fucking lazy to do the roping. He just liked to shoot stuff. So he taught me how to string up a deer real good so it wouldn't fall off the truck. I learned quick too, mostly cos he'd beat the shit outa me if I didn't get it right.'

Jackie's ponytail was now wrapped in a tight coil, and Amber tied off the end, leaving a small loop. 'Never done it on a person though, but it don't seem too different. Except you're not dead and gutted.' The teenager laughed and slapped Jackie on the buttocks. 'Don't sweat, loser, I'm not *that* sick.

'Hey, I got a surprise for you.' Amber reached into the

backpack and pulled out a pair of faded pink knickers that had been worn, dangling them in front of Jackie's face, who instinctively pulled her head back. 'Aw, come on, loser, I wore the fucking things for three days for you.' Amber leaned closer to the naked, tied woman. 'I fucked my fingers for hours every night in them.' She giggled and stuffed the knickers into Jackie's mouth, sealing them in with a strip of duct tape from her backpack, and the woman's reluctance seemed to dissipate quickly.

Jackie lay on the bed, watching the strange redhead as she leisurely stripped off her clothing. She watched as she peeled off her panties, yellow with small flowers on them. She rolled them down her legs and shapely calves, and Jackie stared at the girl's pussy, nestling between lean, tanned thighs, and she sucked.

Using her pocketknife Amber cut another length of cord, tying one end to Jackie's ankles. She bent her legs back and grabbed her hands, tying them together, then grabbing the roped ponytail she pulled hard, forcing Jackie's head back, and tied it to her feet. Jackie's helplessness was now complete. The girl owned her and it was all too late. She could do with her as she wished. Jackie lay bound and naked on the single bed, sucking on her captor's panties.

'That's a good hogtied loser,' Amber gloated. 'Dunno why they call it that though; animals don't bend that way. And they ain't nearly so much fun, either.' Without warning she reached between Jackie's legs and slid a finger into her vagina. 'You see…' Amber pulled out her finger and studied it for a moment, glistening in the dim lighting, 'when you tie an animal it don't really affect its cunt an' stuff. That's all under its tail, and tying don't change much. But people's different. I mean, I could see your bush an' that when you was just laying there, but now it's just out there. I mean, I can see everything, and it's totally easy to get at. Cool, huh?'

Jackie struggled hopelessly against her bonds as the girl examined her sex, prizing her knees apart. With the girl able to probe her virgin pussy at will Jackie's helplessness was total, even more so than the trap that was her existence in this dirty trailer on the edge of nowhere's-ville. Jackie was Amber's, to do with whatever she wanted.

Amber began to tear off little strips of duct tape, using them to stick her captive's labia to her thighs, spreading her vagina open, exploring her most intimate place. She had guessed that with Jackie's mother gone there would be no more alcohol stashed in the refrigerator, so she reached into her backpack and produced a half-bottle of white rum and a carton of pineapple juice. She filled a glass with ice, and then mixed herself a white trash pina colada. Most times it didn't even stretch to the pineapple juice... or a glass, come to think of it. Her and her friends mostly swigged the stolen alcohol straight from the bottle.

She stood looking down at her hogtied plaything, naked, glass in one hand, leather belt hanging loosely from the other. She reached out a foot and pushed the woman onto her side. Jackie clenched her buttocks reflexively, and Amber brought the thin leather belt down with a stinging slap across her breasts. Jackie lurched, the initial sting fading into a warm, delicate glow. She was already getting wet, the huntress was beginning to devour her, and the sharp sting signified the first bite as the attractive girl began to feast. Amber watched a red stripe form in a neat line an inch below the nipple. The teenager looked at her handiwork, smiling, then she downed the rest of the glass and refilled it.

'You're not gonna tell me you're surprised, are ya?' Amber asked, running her finger over the raised welt on Jackie's breast, 'You'd have to be some fucking stupid bitch if you were. Did you really think I was gonna sit in this shitty trailer whacking your ass every now and again, so we could both jerk off about what we really wanted to be doing? That's not me, bitch. You think I don't pay attention? You think I'm like all the other losers around here? If you don't make what you think real, then you're always gonna be a loser.' Amber lashed out with the belt, this time catching her victim's nipple. Jackie squirmed as the pretty predator devoured her breast. 'And I am *not* a loser,' the teenager added.

She downed another two faked pina coladas and began to lash and whip her hogtied toy as she lay on the bed. The belt flicked out at her flesh like the tongue of an angry rattlesnake, its fangs biting into her exposed tits, stinging the pale skin into raised welts. The first time Amber's dad had given her a gun it only took the twelve-year-old half an hour's practice and she was hitting every beer can on the log, and she could catch a baseball as well as any guy. Now she could flick her little whip and bring it down pretty much on target every time, flogging her plaything's breasts so she covered most of the exposed surface. She wanted them both burning red, she wanted to see Jackie's tits covered in scarlet stripes until there was no longer any white skin left on the shapely mounds, so she pulled out more cord, anchoring the struggling woman to the bed frame.

It took yards of rope, but the teenager strapped her down so tight she couldn't even twitch. She looked like she was caught in a giant web, anchoring ropes spreading out from her immobilized body. The spider sat on her stomach, her weight pressing down on her arms and legs as they were twisted and tied under her body. The huntress was consuming her as she lay helpless. She would be swallowed, falling into that divine mouth, sucked between those sensuous lips, sliding down that perfect throat to lay, silently fulfilled, deep within the predator's sublime, soft belly.

Amber was tanked on white rum, but she still believed she could take out those last few annoying white strips of untouched tit flesh. Her body swayed slightly as she raised the belt, trying to focus. Jackie's eyes were shut tight, but the muscles around her mouth seemed to be pulled into a smile, hidden by the duct tape. Amber smiled; the bitch is as weird as her – what a fucking pair.

There was a subtle swishing sound as the belt traveled through the air, then a sharp smack as it hit flesh. But the blow landed on an already swollen nipple, missing its mark.

'Shit.' Amber giggled as she climbed off her prey. There was a wet patch on the woman's stomach where she'd been sitting. 'Have to fucking do… if you'd just stayed still like I told you. All I wanted to do was smack your tits, is that too much to ask?' The drunken teenager began slicing through the web of ropes with her pocketknife, not bothering to untie them. Then she lovingly caressed her handiwork, cupping Jackie's breasts in her hands while her thumbs played over the swollen nipples. She noticed the woman's face was damp with sweat.

'Not finished yet,' she slurred into the face of her plaything, her breath laden with alcohol as she leaned closer. Predator and prey, their noses almost touching. Amber rolled the hogtied woman onto her front, ripped off the duct tape and pulled out the panties. Jackie didn't sob or complain, she just lay there gazing up at the girl. For a minute Amber was confused, then it passed, swept away by a wave of alcohol, there were more games to play.

She moved to the top of the bed, turned and slid her legs on either side of the woman's face. Jackie peered up at the ceiling, her head still yanked back and held by the skillful rope work of the predator. Amber lifted the pocketknife off the bed, flicked out the blade and slashed the rope holding the woman's hair to her ankles. Jackie's head flopped forward against the slimy pink slit between the teenager's thighs. Amber grabbed the coiled ponytail and pulled Jackie's face hard against her sex, her succulent lips parting in welcome. Amber began to rub her pussy against Jackie's mouth, feeling a tongue slide tentatively from between a pair of quivering lips to dab at her pussy. It made her feel so strange, so powerful, so precious. She giggled as the tongue wriggled into her vagina, licking the slippery walls of her tight pussy. Her juices coated Jackie's chin as she pulled hard on the roped ponytail, gyrating her hips so she could rub her clitoris over the woman's face, covering it, marking her territory, her prize.

Eventually Amber flopped back on the pillows, letting Jackie's head fall limply to the bed. 'Yesss… now you got it,' she hissed wearily. 'I'm the hunter, you're my game. Shit, you made me cum like that waterfall down at Ocotillo Creek, just like you're supposed to do. I caught you, now you're mine forever. Got that? Forever.

'Hey, better than shuffling around with bags of crap from the store till they shove you in a home.' Amber laughed. 'What was in those bags, anyhow?'

She jumped off the bed and hurried to the kitchen, rummaging through the groceries. Then she went back to the room and threw a pack of chocolate bars on the bed, took one from its wrapper and crammed it in her mouth.

'Want one?' she mumbled, spitting crumbs in Jackie's face as the hogtied woman nodded weakly. Then she climbed back on the bed and pressed her legs around Jackie's face again. She wriggled her toned bottom, fumbled between her legs, and then a chocolate bar protruded from her pussy lips. 'It's the way you're gonna eat from now on,' she said, stuffing another of the small bars into her mouth, 'just like animals do, rooting for food. Yummy.' Amber giggled at the woman's dazed expression. 'Well, what are you waiting for? Chow down.'

When Amber left that night she didn't untie her prey, it

no longer seemed necessary to allow her catch to have any freedom. She was Amber's totally now. Jackie's brain, still awash with long-buried sensuality, drifted through her fantasies. In her mind she hung from the back porch of the teenage redhead's hut. That's what hunter's were supposed to do with wild animals when they caught them. When Jackie was human she would never have eaten food from another woman's vagina, that's where they pissed from, it was a gross idea. But she was an animal now, and animals didn't care about things like that. Animals didn't care about anything much. The girl said she would come back and feed her from that little pink slit of hers every day, but she also said she wouldn't untie her anymore. Before the girl left she removed the hogtie, binding her prize so its hands were fastened to the top of the bed, her feet to the bottom, but she told her she would be trussed up properly again tomorrow. And the girl had run out of panties, so she used her socks to gag her instead, stuffing them in her mouth before taping it shut. They tasted a little salty, but then animals liked salt.

Amber bent Rainbow Girl over her bed, stretched the young woman's cuffed hands and attached them to the bar that ran all around the bed frame. Just about every piece of furniture and all the fixtures and fittings in the huge house came with various attachments, even the toilets, Amber noted with curiosity. Metal rings, bars, clips, chains, it seemed everything was built with the means to secure someone to it.

Rainbow Girl sniffed back a tiny sob as the metal link from her wrist cuffs locked onto the bar. Amber took extra time with the slave's legs, a little unprofessional but acceptable, she was experimenting after all.

The protégée attached additional cuffs just above the slave's knees as she knelt over the bed. Then she locked them to the bedrail, about two feet apart. Then the tormentor knelt down, unshackled her slave's knees, spread them another foot apart, and then reattached them to the bar. It was obvious the slave was now very uncomfortable, her ass cheeks parted and Amber could see the dark bulls-eye she would be aiming for. But still it would be quite something; a quarter inch off and you had a welt on the cheek, which was unacceptable. The lawyer bitch had managed at least six clean hits, right on Rainbow Girl's anus, no marks on the cheeks. The lawyer hadn't even let the cane extend past the slave's butt crack, so there were no marks on the base of her back. That was precision work.

Amber had thought about taping Rainbow Girl's buttocks apart, giving a wider target area – though it would still take some skill not to overreach – but that would defeat the object of the exercise, and Sabrina, the *Black Glass Bar's* owner, had said the lawyer hadn't done that. She just spread the girl and landed six straight hits, each directly on target. Amber felt like she was preparing to go up against the most deadeye shot in the West, the girl's ass the flesh equivalent of a row of beer bottles on an old fence.

The redhead raised the cane, holding it in the air for a few moments. Rainbow Girl whimpered into her gag as the instrument of pain sliced through the air, then yelped in surprise as the flexible plastic cane thwacked into the bed sheets beside her. Amber dropped the cane onto the bed and sat down beside the tied slave.

'Okay,' she sighed, 'lets get this straight. I don't torture you for fun, and in return I have your absolute loyalty. Got it?' Rainbow Girl nodded frantically. 'If you piss me off, I'll tear you up just like any other slut we own. If you disobey an order, same thing. And if you ever betray my trust, I'll ship you off to China Town so fast you won't have time to blink those pretty blue eyes. You'll end up chained to a bench in a five-bucks-a-bang-booth with some fat slut riding your face while her hag of a girlfriend jams a twelve-inch dildo in your cunt and tries to shove both her fists in your ass…' Amber leaned across to the terrified young woman and unclipped her gag. 'Just say yes, loser.'

The young woman's lips quivered for a second. 'Yes… mistress.'

'Cool, I like that… yes *mistress.*' The redhead laughed. 'It's like being in a fucking porn flick.'

Rebecca showed her usual detached amusement at her protégée's fierce individuality. The Inquisitor knew the dangers of having a maverick in an organization like the Cruza. The cartel was a dark, brooding serpent, utterly ruthless, single-minded and flawless, it hovered above society like a hawk, ever watchful, but this hawk was made of diamond, and like a diamond it could only be marked by its own kind, but it could cut through flesh like a razorblade through a silk handkerchief. Unpredictability was discouraged, with extreme – and usually fatal – prejudice, but then, the girl was hardly unpredictable. She had shown herself to have an instinctive understanding of the Cruza's inner workings, and her respect for the organization was total, but she was not afraid to innovate, and that's what made her so valuable. That she had chosen to turn this particular possession into something resembling a pet more than a slave was an interesting quirk. The girl had spared the slave's body, but held her mind in a vice-like grip. That she allowed her to speak – albeit in a limited fashion – was another curious sparkle of diversity. New blood, thought Rebecca as she sipped her strong, mocha caffeine infusion.

Rainbow Girl knelt beside her young mistress as the girl ate breakfast with the powerful dark-haired woman. Shelly was careful never to meet the older woman's gaze, something she never did with her own mistress, unless ordered to do so. Amber had asked the curators to cover the slave's wrist and ankle cuffs with rainbow-hued silk. The redhead had then asked for a small, tight fitting dress to be made of the same multi-colored silk, which she allowed the slave to wear. The garment had no sleeves, and was practically see-through, and it hung exactly to the slave's vagina. It didn't afford much in the way of modesty, but she was no longer naked like the Cruza's other possessions, and so it set her apart, she was something more, it meant her owner thought she was something special.

Amber grasped the slave's ponytail and guided Rainbow Girl's head between her thighs, parting her robe as she pressed the slave's face against her shaven mound, just as she had seen McKenna do. Shelly pushed her tongue into her mistress's vagina, occasionally withdrawing, pulling it out to flick it across the young redhead's clitoris. The slave felt a glow of adoration as she tasted the girl's juices. She knew she would have died in that basement, but first she would have been beaten and tortured until she went insane. The beautiful redhead had saved her, and now she kept her close, protecting her. Rebecca rose from the table and walked back into the house, Amber by her side, Rainbow Girl shuffling a respectful distance behind.

'Clever,' the Inquisitor said, smiling. 'I think they call it the Stockholm Syndrome.' Amber looked at her mentor, puzzled. 'It afflicts hostages and kidnap victims,' Rebecca continued, 'but the principle can be made to work in a variety of situations. The girl's life becomes threatened, even by you, and her survival instinct kicks in. In an effort to preserve herself she will develop a powerful affection for you, then if you offer her a degree of reprieve… and timing is everything… then she will be bound to you for life.' The Inquisitor turned to face her protégée, a strange look on her face. 'Always trust your instincts, Amber;

they were honed in a place where daily survival was a fact of life. You don't weigh up probabilities, you just act. I've come to trust those instincts of yours, and so should you. Remember, any girl the Cruza takes is like a scorpion's concubine, in a rattlesnake's lair… but it's not unknown for scorpions and rattlesnakes to sting their own kind. Try to remember that.'

Amber lay on her back in the middle of the luxurious bed, naked from the waist down, while Rainbow Girl nuzzled at her mistress's pussy. It was a gentle session, more to help the young redhead relax, a sort of genital massage of the most pleasant sort.

'I had a bitch once…' Amber often spoke to the slave the way people would speak to their dogs, not really caring if they were listening or understood. It was like thinking out loud. 'Even before I came to this place. She was called Jackie, but she was just *bitch*, or *slut*, to me. Had some fun times with her until my bastard of a father spoiled it all.' The teenager looked around at her large, sumptuous room. 'Suppose he did me a favor in the end. Fucker came at me with a baseball bat an' fractured my arm, so I stabbed the bastard in the guts.' Amber smiled like a gladiator recounting a hard won victory. 'He was okay though, it was only a small pocketknife, but they made me go into a shelter cos he'd threatened to kill me for it, an they couldn't put him away cos I'd hurt him too. Shit, I think the lawyers expect you just to stand there and take it just so it don't complicate the case. An' just when things were getting fun with my plaything, too. Things weren't so bad when I had Jackie. Not that bad a life for a high school drop out who'd just turned eighteen. It was like I had my own place. Nothing like this, though.' Amber laughed, gesturing around the grandiose room. 'But I could just use the bitch's trailer whenever I felt like it, an' I kept her naked an' tied to her bed most of the time, so it was my territory.'

Amber moaned and slid down the bed, settling onto the slave's probing tongue. 'I used to love beating her, and I know she liked it too. She was a weird bitch, no doubt about that. Anyway, it felt kinda strange when I had to go to the shelter. I mean, she'd become kinda dependent, laying there on that bed waiting to suck my cunt and get thrashed every night, an' I was getting my kicks that way too. It was fun, but like I said, I was packed off to the shelter before that bastard found me. I didn't fight it cos I knew he'd have one of his guns with him this time, cos I also know for fucking sure the cops didn't find them all. Still, it was a good job I remembered to untie the bitch before I went though, huh?' The teenager's snigger trailed off into a low moan as the slave slid her index finger into her vagina, while still using her mouth to suck the girl's labia. The probing index finger stroked, bringing her to a powerful orgasm. She shuddered as she climaxed against Rainbow Girl's mouth, the flood dribbling down the slave's chin. The teenager tensed her thighs, clamping down hard on the young woman's head, before releasing her grip and flopping back on the thick silk pillows.

'Wow!' she gasped. 'Gotta hand it to the curators, they certainly know how to teach our bitches their trade.'

Swimming in the Dark Fairy Pool

'Why the urgency?' Rebecca strode purposefully along the dark-red velvet-walled hallway with its deep scarlet carpet. It made her think of the medical documentaries she'd seen, a fiber optic camera sliding along a main artery. Not an unreasonable analogy, the hall led to the heart of the building, the command center, and all security control functions were located here.

'As we can tell, there isn't any,' Dakota increased her stride to keep pace with the taller woman. 'Just the way he likes to do things, gives his enemies less time to plan.'

'Well, if the little shit gets me up at five in the morning again he can add me to that list.'

'He's worth the inconvenience; deal's lucrative, safe, and worth about sixty million to us.'

'I'm sure, and please excuse my confusion,' the Inquisitor added sarcastically, 'but didn't you wrap this thing up about two months ago? What's he want? If he thinks I'm slashing my arm so we can mingle blood in some moronic Samurai ritual, then he's going to be a sad old man over breakfast.'

'Not sure he has enough blood left, but I think it has something to do with honor, seeing the head honcho in person sort of thing, and I gather he's proposing some form of cultural exchange, a way for us to understand each other better.'

'Typical Yakuza,' Rebecca sighed. 'Call Amber, have her meet me in the *El Sol de la Mañana* in thirty minutes.'

Dakota dropped back, picked up one of the house phones on a side table and punched in her security code.

The *cultural exchange* stood giggling in the corner of the plush conference room, behind the old man who seemed to resemble the mummy of Rameses III even more in person than he did on video link. Rebecca bowed lightly to the old Yakuza master, and sat down opposite him.

'Time moves on shoujo,' the old man muttered, lowering his head. 'I have seen many changes, I will not pretend to like them, but it is not even in *my* power to change the way of things.' Mr Nakaichirou allowed himself a wheezy chuckle. 'I will never grow used to dealing with women in this way, and time, as you can no doubt see, is not on my side. But I respect you for what you are; we should respect all things, yes? One has to admire the rattlesnake for it is fearless and deadly, and finds prey in the desert where others find only sand.'

'What can I do for you, Mr Nakaichirou? Is there a problem with the services we've been providing your organization?'

'No, shoujo, as well you know. I merely wanted to see the face of the rattlesnake with my own eyes, and not through a machine.' The old man turned awkwardly and motioned to four young Japanese females standing behind him. 'And to ask you to take some of my family into your own.' The Yakuza master turned slowly back to face Rebecca. 'It is our way,' he said simply, 'although I would usually honor you with some of my finest warriors, but your organization is somewhat... unique. In light of this, I hope my choice has been appropriate.' The girls giggled. Rebecca guessed they were barely out of high school, between eighteen and nineteen, and looking younger, as was the way with Japanese girls. They all wore the same neat but tight fitting navy-blue suits, with skirts well above the knee. 'They are my blood,' Mr Nakaichirou continued. 'A great-granddaughter, and three great-nieces, I will leave Jasmine to make the introductions.'

The small Japanese-American translator sitting to Mr

Nakaichirou's left bowed deeply in acknowledgement, as without another word the Yakuza master got up and left, accompanied by his bodyguards, made even more sinister by their garish Hawaiian shirts and sporty sunglasses. Yakuza muscle loved outlandish fashion; it was as much their trademark as the occasional missing fingertip. One of the protectors stood with his thumb tucked in his belt, showing off the decapitated little pinkie on his left hand, a mark of macho pride. Men, Rebecca shook her head as they left; so fucking predictable.

Rebecca sat in the *El Sol de la Mañana* as the dawn sun streamed through the large windows. The aptly named room looked out onto a white stone courtyard, and a breeze ruffled the tops of the seven palms that surrounded the large ornamental fountain in the center, the spray catching the sunlight and igniting a myriad of rainbows in the dry air. Amber sat to the Inquisitor's right as the two watched the slightly ludicrous beauty pageant play out.

The four Japanese girls stood in a line as Jasmine introduced them. Rebecca had known the thirty-something translator for years, and if it wasn't quite friendship they shared, then it was certainly mutual respect.

'Miss Kichi,' Jasmine announced as the girl at the far end bowed, 'Mr Nakaichirou's great-granddaughter, and this is Miss Mayu,' the second girl in the lineup bowed, 'Mr Nakaichirou's great-niece.'

'I think she did it,' Amber whispered, bringing a smile to Rebecca's tired and somewhat bored expression. The image of a police lineup hadn't escaped her either.

'Miss Nyoko,' Jasmine continued, but Rebecca had given up trying to match names to faces, something she was normally exceptionally good at. The girls could be quadruplets for all she could tell. Jasmine introduced Miss Yoshi and the parade was complete. Rebecca shook each of their hands as enthusiastically as she could manage, then handed the problem deftly to her protégée. The Inquisitor had never been given reason to question her judgment of the teenager since she brought her into the family, and as far as she knew, neither had any of her senior officers. In fact, she was finding the girl pleasingly reliable.

'Nan-sai desu-ka?' Amber asked one of the girls.

'I was eighteen two months ago,' replied the Japanese girl in perfect, though accented, English. Rebecca turned and stared at her protégée.

'I had this crush on a Japanese waitress once,' Amber shrugged, and as she headed for the door Rebecca pulled Jasmine to one side.

'The old man called me shoujo.'

'It means girl,' the interpreter replied.

Rebecca paused, then smirked. 'How cute,' she said, then left the room.

Over chilled orange juice in the courtyard, Kichi, Mayu, Nyoko and Yoshi explained to Amber the legend of the Cruza as they'd heard it, and erupted into an excited babble as they discussed the wild sex orgies and other games they were looking forward to.

'Well...' Amber eyed the giggling young women, noting their tiny Asian frames, slender legs and tiny feet, an idea forming in the back of her mind. 'How would you girls feel about putting on school uniforms?'

'Well, duh,' said Yoshi, with an affected south Californian accent, 'we're Japanese; it's like asking if you'd mind wearing jeans.'

Amber laughed. 'Yeah, guess it was a stupid question. Well then, there's someone I want you to meet.'

'Sugoi, Sugoi,' Kichi chirped excitedly, and Amber looked at Yoshi, raising an eyebrow.

'It means *cool*,' Yoshi explained.

Rebecca fired six shots from the Browning DBM 9x19mm at the cardboard outline. The target showed a picture of an angry black guy clutching a battered Uzi; the cardboard had been punctured in the chest, one hole in the neck. Dakota's identical target showed eight neat holes in the face. The lieutenant paused, then took aim again and emptied the remaining seven rounds into the figures crotch area.

'Know how you get amber?' Rebecca asked rhetorically as she flipped the catch, letting the magazine slide into her palm and handing it to her lieutenant. 'You cut a tree, then it bleeds, but instead of its blood drying to dust like yours or mine, something else happens. The more you try to crush it the harder it becomes, until you have something hard as glass and a lot more precious.'

'What level you want her trained to?' Dakota took the magazine and handgun from the Inquisitor, slipping the mag into her pocket and then pulling back the breech to drop the shell in the chamber. She rolled the small brass cylinder between her fingers.

'As high as you can take her, State Girl.'

'Then we're going all the way, Miss R. I recognize talent when I see it too.'

The box was hot and stuffy, and wasn't quite long enough to allow Stephanie to stretch out properly. Lauren didn't keep her hogtied in the toy box, though the slave was still shackled ankle and wrist. The box itself was made of white plastic. It had a lift up lid and was covered in pictures of little yellow flowers. In the center of each flower was a small air hole, cleverly disguised and allowing the captive girl to breathe. Lauren always laid the girl in the box the same way, so her head was at the end that faced the large window where clean sunlight streamed in through gauzy yellow silk curtains. The reason Lauren did this was that the curators had located a small hatch at this end of the box, and the slave had become accustomed to the sound of the little silver latch clicking free and the cover lifting to reveal her tormentor's grinning, over made-up face.

At first the woman's obsession with infantile games had seemed no more perverse than anything else Stephanie had seen in this strange place, just the turn of a coin. Heads: gothic torture rooms, tails: a mock-up of a child's playroom. But time had passed. How much, the slave had no way of knowing, but enough for her to begin to lose her own grip on reality. Part of the reason was that given her position as the woman's personal plaything, she was totally immersed in Lauren's world. Other slaves endured a variety of torments, but at least it *was* variety. Stephanie had been turned into a full size living doll, and she was never allowed to be anything else, never treated as anything else, and everything she saw, every waking moment reminded her of this, reinforcing the idea in her mind.

Stephanie was not alone in the box; there were other toys, too. Some stuffed animals, a pair of roller-blades that dug annoyingly into her hip, miscellaneous items of dirty laundry and several small plastic dolls. They all had names: Cindy, Crystal, Tilly and Sandy were some she could remember. Lauren had perfected her petulant child act so well it was sometimes hard to remember she was in her mid-twenties, and somehow Crystal had managed to piss her owner off, so for her punishment the little plastic doll was currently jammed up to her ankles in Stephanie's vagina. Earlier Lauren had berated the doll as she'd pressed its nylon-haired head against the entrance to the slave's sex, telling the toy how disappointed she was in her, and how *totally gross* her punishment was going to be. Then, without warning, she inserted the doll into Stephanie's pussy, working it in with a corkscrew motion till only the little plastic toeless feet were left protruding.

'And you can stay there till you've learned your lesson,'

Lauren huffed. Then she bound Stephanie's ankles and wrists together and had her replaced in the toy box.

About twenty minutes later the little hatch at the end opened, the slave could see her owner getting undressed, then a hand pushed its way through the hatch clutching a pair of worn pink ankle socks and panties, which were unceremoniously stuffed in the slave's mouth. 'You can wash these as you have nothing else to do,' came the curt command, then the hatch slammed shut.

Amber sat alone on a large, deep, black leather couch in her favorite bar, *The Deadnight Teeze*. Rebecca called the Cruza's desert complex a ranch, Amber would have called it a resort, but if you saw the architectural plans and not just the fancy bars, pools, and stables, paramilitary command base would probably spring to mind. Officially there were two sites combined: one, the *Hacienda de la Escorpión* showed a modest profit – as far as the IRS were concerned – from desert horseback tours. It maintained a half-dozen employees, and everyone paid their taxes. The other site, the *Sonora Desert Botanical Research Center*, was a nonprofit research center, connected to the San Diego Botanical outfit, and as it provided the city based scientists with most of their grant money, it seemed they never felt the need to question the lack of actual research coming from the facility. Rebecca allowed the teenager to roam the base as she wished; she had been given the highest security clearance, which as far as Amber was concerned basically meant, *give them enough rope*... Well, Amber's father had tried to beat her to death on numerous occasions, and a few others she'd run into in the relatively few years she'd been alive had tried to stop the redhead from seeing any more birthdays, and she'd fucked them all one way or another. The teenager had the profile of a survivor and self-destruction wasn't an option. She'd promised *total* loyalty, and that's what she gave.

Another benefit of living on the self-contained base was that Cruza law applied, and it didn't stretch to telling senior officers they couldn't drink alcohol when they were off duty, even when they were underage by state law. Amber took another swig of her lime margarita, and settled back into the couch. *The Deadnight Teeze* managed the seemingly impossible by combining relaxation with a teenager's need to have drip-feed MTV on super widescreens twenty-four-seven, and the spiky-haired peroxide-blonde behind the bar made the sweetest margaritas anywhere. They went down like melted popsicles, and punched like Megan's neat little stun gun.

There were only two other women in the bar, engrossed in conversation in the far corner, at the furthest point from the speakers and screens. Amber watched them idly, switching her attention between them and some purple-haired girl on MTV, dancing on the roof of a Porsche and wearing only a bikini and thick-heeled silver ankle boots. The redhead was seriously chilled, slipping further down into the black leather and waiving her empty glass at the barmaid, and at the very edge of her consciousness she became aware of another sound, a growing babble of excited voices. The sound grew steadily louder, and Amber turned lazily to watch the gang of cute little Asian teens jostling and giggling their way down the hallway. They entered the bar and headed straight for the redhead's little refuge, not that Amber particularly minded, they seemed like fun, and she'd had their number back in *El Sol de la Mañana* – it had taken her all of about thirty seconds. As soon as the five-thousand-year-old Japanese dude in the dark suit and the jerk-offs playing tough guy in the loud Hawaiian shirts had swaggered back to their little island, the true personalities of the toy-geishas they'd left behind came fluttering out like birds released from a cage. Amber could spot competence a mile away, it was part of the survival thing she had going; if someone was a bullshitting bitch then you had better work that out before it got too late to do anything about it, and when it came to playing, the little geisha sluts knew their stuff.

Trixie, Pixie, Flopsy and… Amber grinned, carefully slipping a small piece of card from her pocket and scanning the names: Kichi, Mayu, Nyoko and Yoshi. As they flounced into the bar she realized there was no practical way to ever remember which was which, as they all seemed to have been pre-cast from the same cutesy Asian mold: pretty faces, tiny, perfectly proportioned bodies, and a shy little-girl act that the redhead had to admit, was kinda sexy.

The four babbling teens flopped gracelessly into the vacant chairs around Amber's table, showing the natural ability that most teenage girls had of being able to slouch around like a drunken truck driver, and still manage to look hot enough to scorch asbestos. An image of the chairs branded like cattle with tight little butt marks flashed through the redhead's mind. The spiky-haired waitress reappeared and shoved another margarita into Amber's hand.

'Cool hair!' exclaimed one of the girls.

'What can I get you ladies?' Spiky said, happy to take the compliment.

'What's the boss lady chugging?'

'Lime margarita, with a few psycho additions I made up as I went along,' spiky announced proudly, and Amber raised her glass in endorsement of the highly toxic product, spilling a little down her wrist. The Japanese girl perched on the arm of the couch closest to her leaned forward and licked the green liquid dribbling down Amber's arm. It was slow and deliberate, the little tongue catching the flow then moving up like a salmon following a river, till the tongue slid up the chilled stem of the glass to the rim. The cutesy geisha slut smacked her lips.

'Yep, get me one of those.' She winked at Amber. 'Delicious, huh? Or maybe it was just your skin, boss lady…'

'Yeah,' said one of the others, 'how's she meant to tell, missy? Your skin looks kinda yummy to me.' The teen licked her lips teasingly.

Amber smiled at her. 'What happened to the crappy, *we don't speeky no much eenglish*?'

'Fuck, give us a break, boss lady, I've been living in New York since I was six, so has Kichi. Mayu and Nyoko have been in Chicago about as long. It keeps the old man happy, and he pays for our toys and playtimes. Why, you want fuckky suckky wiv us, lady?' The Japanese girls laughed at the joke, so Amber took back the advantage.

'Yeah, why not.' The redhead put her glass on the table, pulled down her zipper, slid her jeans and panties down past her knees, then picked up the margarita again. There was silence for a few minutes; the only sound the incessant beat from the widescreen. Then one of the girls grinned broadly and got down on her knees, disappearing from view. Seconds later her head squirmed its way up between the redhead's thighs.

'Hi,' said the pretty little face, which caused Amber to giggle, nearly spilling her drink again. The jeans were holding her legs together, so the geisha slut had been forced to do some serious pushing and wriggling to get in there.

'Well get on with it,' Amber said, playfully pushing the head lower, 'everyone else in here thinks I've just fucking given birth.' The girl's soft cheeks slid erotically down the inside of the redhead's thighs as she submerged, then she pressed her face into Amber's shaven mound and shoved her tongue into the waiting slit. The redhead was up for a game, and she *had* regained the advantage, so now she settled back for a leisurely pussy-licking while she sipped her glass of green mind-melt juice.

But leisurely wasn't what she got. The girl went for it

heart and soul, and a little way beyond even that, sucking Amber's pussy lips, twirling her tongue inside the redhead's vagina like a cheerleader's baton, shaking her head from side to side, then up and down, and pressing her face in so hard that Amber thought she might actually *have* to give birth to the girl before the evening was out. Round one to the baby-geisha sex dolls.

The redhead sunk further back into the couch, dropping her guard and deciding this was worth losing a few points for. She knocked back the margarita in one gulp until there was less than a quarter-inch left, then placed the lip of the glass against her pussy mound, tipping it until the green liquid trickled down her labia, dripping onto the frantic tongue, at which point the girl went wild. Amber was sure the tiny tike was going to eat her from the cunt up, which she had to admit seemed like a perfectly wonderful way to go. 'Hey,' the redhead spoke to the unoccupied trio, 'you bitches like to gamble?'

There were three rooms in the hacienda's casino, and the dark wood doors carried descriptive names etched onto brass nameplates. *The Loaded Deck*, *The Straight Cut* and *The Dread Zone*. Amber and the geisha crazies sauntered into door three, catching the slightly acrid taste of dry ice that hung in the air like the heavy mist of a San Francisco summer morning. Electric-blue lasers cut through the swirling fog and stabbed into the gloomy corners of the room, illuminating dark, cruel acts; perpetrators and their victims both caught in the flashes of synthetic lightening. Techno music pulsed from somewhere in the ceiling, the throbbing, hypnotic bass thudding through the silver-tiled floor.

Amber led her tribe through the weird flickering light, towards a shadowy roulette table that loomed out of the fog ahead of them like the Marie Celeste, the varnished shine of the dark wood reflecting occasional splashes of color. At the table's head lay the roulette wheel. It was massive, at least six feet across, its enormous bulk sunk into the floor so it could be seen from the stools at the normal sized table.

As if summoned magically by their presence, a tall blonde in a short tight silver dress and bright-blue wig emerged from the darkness to loom over the apparatus like a sacrificial priestess. As they drew closer Amber could see a young woman strapped to the colossal black and red colored wheel, spread-eagled and naked. There were translucent baby-blue domes over each breast, a plastic tube trailed from each tit vase, fiber optic cable twisted round the tubes like vines round a tree trunk, a pulsating colored lightshow following the rhythm of the thumping techno beat. Between her spread legs the tips of two baby-blue dildos kissed the entrance to her vagina and anus, their bases clamped to elaborate, lacquered-silver pistons.

'You here to play?' The tall woman winked at Amber and the Japanese girls.

'Sure,' Amber replied, 'if we knew how.' She looked at the, for once, silent geisha sluts, their blank faces telling her they didn't have a clue either.

'Take a seat,' the blonde waved theatrically to the stools beside the table, and the girls sat, gazing down upon the woman spread out below them.

'That one of your slaves, boss lady?' Mayu asked, leaning over the wheel to get a better look. 'She don't look like a Latina.'

The priestess laughed. 'No, honey, she's a client, and believe me there's a queue to *ride-the-wheel*. Costs a bundle, so you girls play well for her, huh?'

'I don't have any money,' Mayu said, gazing hungrily down at the centerpiece of the game. 'Well, I mean, I do have money, I have a shit-load, but just not with me.'

The priestess waved away the girl's comment with a manicured hand, silver nails flashing momentarily in a laser trail. 'It's not about money, my dear, just a little competition between the five of you... and her, of course.' The priestess looked down at the naked woman. 'But her prize is already worked out. Why don't *you* decide what the winner gets.'

'Winner gets tongued off all night by the others,' Kichi giggled.

'Which hole?' Amber grinned at her.

'Both, dummy. I didn't mean taking turns. Fuck, what kind of prize would that be? If I win I want one little tongue in my pussy, one coming in through the back door, and the other two can suck a nipple each. And...' the pretty Asian teen ran the scenario through her imagination once more to check the details, 'yeah, and you can switch round every hour. How's that?' The girls looked at each other for a moment. Yoshi shrugged, while Mayu and Nyoko just giggled.

'Okay,' Amber slapped her palm against the dark oak, 'I'll take that bet, but it's gonna be your tongue in my ass, Tinkerbelle.' Kichi stuck her tongue out, also slapping her hand on the table in exact time with the other Japanese teenagers. 'Quit doing that,' Amber laughed. 'You're like a bunch of fucking clones.'

'Well, Caucasian boss-bitch, it might interest you to know you all look the fucking same to us, too.' Yoshi blew the redhead a kiss. 'Okay, so how do we play?'

The tall blue-haired priestess straightened and launched into a rehearsed preamble. 'See the pretty cylinders on her breasts? They're vacuum pumps, basically. Max speed for extraction and release is sixty times a minute, which is one hell of a tit-sucking, girlies.' She leaned over the woman's spread body and jiggled the cylinder on her left breast. 'There's a few that'll orgasm on that alone. How about you, sweetie?' The woman shook her head, mumbling something into her strange gag.

'What's that for?' Amber nodded at it. The mouthpiece

was roughly oval in shape, following the curve of the woman's lips and wedged tightly into her mouth by a black strap. There were six small metal studs sticking up from the outer surface.

'Extra inducement,' the priestess giggled, 'but that's up to her… well, and you, I guess. How about it, bitch?' The priestess looked down at the woman on the wheel, who looked quickly at each of the five teenagers, then nodded quickly at the games mistress. The priestess laughed again. 'Guess she likes you. See the black grips on the side of the table, the ones that look like foosball handles with tubes coming off them? Pull one out.' Mayu did and found a soft black rubber dildo on the other end.

'Okay, honey,' said the priestess, 'the players wear that end, and a gentle suction pump will deliver anything those cute little cunts of yours have to offer to our wheel-whore here.' The priestess was leaning over the roulette wheel plugging five blue light-pulsing plastic tubes into the silver studs on the woman's gag. 'It's harder to hold back an orgasm when your mouth's filling up with teenage cum-juice. I guess she's feeling strong willed tonight. You girls are gonna have a hell of a game going here.'

'Ooh,' squealed Kichi as she unzipped her jeans, pushed them down past her knees and slid the thin black dildo into her tiny Asian pussy, the smooth bumps on the surface exciting the tender flesh of her vagina as the device slotted into position. The rest of the girls inserted theirs, feeling the rush of sexual passion as they became intimately connected to the female on the wheel, the electric-blue tubes connecting pussy to mouth in a deliciously mechanical tongue-fuck.

The priestess resumed her position, poised over the sunken wheel. 'Okay, rules are simple, each time you get the bitch to cum you get five-hundred points. No significance,' the priestess added, 'big numbers are just sexy, right? We have sensors on her body so we'll know the instant she cums, and this…' the priestess pointed to a strobe light above the woman's head, 'will flash when she does.

'Now to the betting procedure. An inside bet, that's one number, direct hit, then she gets the whole works, both breast massagers at sixty sucks a minute, plus both anal and vaginal dildos, both working at thirty-five penetrations a minute. Difficult to fight off that kinda stimulation. You could get a multiple orgasm, and that pays five-hundred points for each one. Split the bet she gets everything at a lower rate, twenty tit sucks a minute, and ten on the two dildos. Street bet…' The priestess looked at the confused faces gathered round the table, and sighed. 'Let's just say you can lay bets in a line, and if you get a hit on any of those she still gets the works, but the per minute level is low, and as it only lasts two minutes your chance of getting her to cum is pretty slim, but hey, who knows? Still with me, girls?' The priestess perked up at the sight of the eager nods and devilish grins on the faces of the eighteen-year-olds.

'You can also play an outside bet. That means you choose black or red, or odds or evens. Better chance of scoring so lower return, and the computer does a random thing so she'll get the medium hit on *either* the tit suck, or *one* of the dildos, good for warming her up, but I doubt you're going to get her squirting juice like that. You get seven tokens each. Okay, let's play.'

Excitement getting the better of their judgment, the girls all went for a single number inside bet, and lost. The roulette girl spun giddily as the priestess leaned over and set the near frictionless mechanism that moved the great wheel in motion. The silver ball dropped into black four, all bets lost. The girl's head had been positioned directly under the zero, her hands held at red twenty-one, and seven, her legs spread obscenely wide at black thirteen and thirty-one. The enthralled onlookers had reflexively gone for the numbers that lay beneath the female's genitals, where the two torpedoes waited like a couple of nukes on full tactical alert. The priestess smiled.

'C'mon, girls, think a little. We all want to see the bitch squirt, but how about we work our way up to the grand slam?'

This time it was a sure thing, so the five teens went red, black, odds, evens. The wheel spun and the ball dropped into black seventeen, a hit for Mayu and Amber. A monitor at the foot of the table showed the computer doing its random thing, the screen displayed a picture of a naked female, blue circles flashed on the figure's breasts while two long cylinders flashed between the cartoon-woman's legs. The blue patches flashed faster and faster, and then suddenly stopped, blue circles illuminating the breasts. The brat pack stared at the girl as the tubes on the breast pumps glowed brighter, suddenly there was a hissing sound, like a flat tire, and the young woman's breasts were sucked into the cylinders, filling them with pink flesh, then just as quickly they flopped back to her chest, then sucked back into the clear domes again. The woman moaned behind her gag and the players' insertions began to vibrate.

'Oh shit, that's nice,' Yoshi said breathlessly, rubbing her groin. The woman on the wheel struggled to hold back while the pumps worked on her breasts and six tubes trickled teenage cunt juice into her mouth.

'Fuck, look at her tits,' Mayu squealed excitedly. 'Hey bitch, you're getting a workout,' she giggled as the woman struggled to distract her mind.

'I feel like I'm working in a gas station,' Yoshi panted, 'look at this.' The geisha slut held up her tube as it sucked juices from deep in her pussy, the humming stimulator sending ripples of pleasure deep into her cervix, little bubbles of cum slithering along the blue conduit as the micro-pump delivered the liquid directly into the mouth of the sweating form writhing on the wheel.

'Wow, fill her up, girlfriend,' Mayu clapped her hands gleefully.

There were two more disappointing misses, followed by another display of mechanical breast sucking, then Kichi got a hit on the vagina torpedo on an outside evens bet. Mayu leaned so far over the wheel Amber had to grab the back of her T-shirt, fearing she'd fall in. The breast tubes went dark, while the blue dildo poised at the entrance of the woman's vagina began to glow, a soft blue radiance like a child's nightlight, while the other stayed dull and unlit. The woman's thighs clenched as the lubricated missile slid forward, pistons hissing, pushing aside her labia, inexorably entering her body, filling her with its thick girth until the wide rubber base squashed against her, flattening her clitoris. There was a brief pause, then the pistons suddenly pulled the blue shaft back out of the woman's body, exposing six of its full twelve-inches, then it plunged back into her, then again, and again, pumping hard, working her cunt to a state of ecstasy. The woman's ankles pulled hard against their restraints as her knees tried to move up to her stomach, erotic reflexes kicking in. Her butt lifted off the wheel and for a moment she welcomed the thrusting, glowing shaft, drawing it into herself. Kichi was already counting her points when the wheel-woman went limp, the low moan escaping from behind the rubber gag the only sign of her struggle to hold back.

'No points, bad luck girls,' the priestess announced.

An hour or so later they'd hit all three devices on low levels, and the spread-eagled woman had resisted them all. Mayu was ahead on the number of hits, even if the points were all in the wheel-woman's favor, then the horny little micro-slut hit the jackpot, inside bet, one number. The wheel slowed gradually as the silver ball hopped from slot to slot, dancing to the techno beat, then it simply dropped into black eight. It took Mayu and the rest of the teenagers a second or so for the win to register, then they all hung over the wheel, breathlessly waiting for the big one.

All the devices glowed, the double torpedoes' blue luminescence lending a ghostly pallor to the five expectant faces that gazed down on the naked figure, the hoses running from the breast pumps pulsing with brilliant blue light as the shackled human Christmas tree prepared to fend off a full-frontal ecstasy assault. The missiles slid powerfully into the woman's body, Mayu watched as the lower of the thick blue shafts push its full eight-inches deep into the woman's anus and the teenager's stimulator vibrated, sucking juice from deep within the lithe body and squirting it directly into the wheel-woman's mouth. All five tubes bubbled and gurgled as the naked woman swallowed continuously, struggling to keep up with the flow. Then the equipment went into overdrive, the pumps sucked and released with dazzling speed while the two torpedoes thrust into the bound body like jackhammers The girls could feel the rim of the wheel vibrating as the woman was assaulted by the devices as they ravaged her sweat-soaked body. A jackpot lasted five minutes, but the wheel-woman only lasted seconds under the full weight of the assault, the electric-blue strobe flashing across her squirming, writhing, sweating body as she relented, allowing the orgasm to ripple through every inch of her naked, bound body.

'Wow, fuck!' was all Mayu could manage. The priestess was all smiles, watching the players moan as they climaxed in sympathy with their adversary, all five tubes full of cum, pumping into the wheel-woman's moaning mouth in such quantity that the juice seeped around the edges of the gag, trickling down the woman's chin as she swallowed and orgasmed.

'Congratulations, girls, you hit the big one. That's thirty-thousand points to the young lady fucking herself with the stimulator.' The priestess winked at Mayu. 'Don't worry, honey, I can turn up the vibration if you want. Little unfair on her…' she pointed at the limp, exhausted form spread out on the wheel, 'but as I'm the final judge and jury here, I say it's okay.'

The next low-grade hit was an outside bet that set off the breast pumps, but the wheel-woman was beaten, she lost control and orgasmed from just having her tits fucked, the extra vibration sending her opposition into orgasms of their own, filling the spread-eagled woman's mouth with sweet tasting cum. The breast pumps stopped, but the fresh flood of sexual juices seeping past the gag onto the woman's cheeks drove her into another swallowing, gulping orgasm. Even the princess was impressed, awarding five hundred bonus points to each of the girls.

Half an hour later, amidst heated accusations of cheating, which the priestess put down with a scornful look, Mayu hit another jackpot – red three. The delighted Asian nympho was granted the honor of ripping the slimy gag from the wheel-woman's mouth, and grinding her teenage pussy directly onto the bound woman's face as the devices pounded her for another five minutes. Mayu pulled out her stimulator, kicked off her jeans and panties, leapt down onto the wheel and flung herself across the gasping mouth.

'Cool, cunt juice lip-gloss,' laughed the Japanese girl as she lowered her pussy onto the waiting mouth. The devices kicked in, sending the woman into a convulsive fit of multiple orgasms. She bucked and writhed as the tiny Asian rode her face like a rodeo star on an unbroken mount. Her four friends looked on, feeling their own excitement built through the buzzing stimulators between their thighs.

Alice had slipped through the looking glass, hadn't she? And she'd got out okay in the end, but then, it had been a journey. The parts were every bit as strange as Stephanie's looking glass world, though not nearly as awful, but the girl had been moving, traveling through the strange land until she reached the end. Stephanie wasn't actually going anywhere; she was quite firmly stuck in this strange world with its casual cruelty. She was sure she was still a person, but less sure than she had been. *Why would a person live in a toy box*?

But then, Alice had only gone through one looking glass, so it would be easier to find your way back, wouldn't it? It must work like doors; if you just went through one then it was easier to get back than if you'd been through twenty, or thirty. Then another looking glass lost its form and sucked her through. The lid to the toy box opened and sunlight from the golden window streamed in, strange little faces peered down at her, Asian faces with golden skin, little noses and pretty dark eyes like black buttons. The faces were smiling... no, not smiling, grinning. There was a difference, a very big difference Stephanie had come to learn, and as her eyes adjusted to the light she saw hunger in those faces, behind those brilliant white-toothed smiles. Four fairies, tiny-framed, small-breasted fairies, with pretty faces, dressed in pink ruffled skirts and pink silk vests, like little ballerinas. Slender arms and delicate hands reached into the toy box and lifted the living doll out, the fairies giggled; they wanted to play with the doll. Stephanie wondered what kind of games fairies played, and then one of them laughed and lifted up her tutu, revealing a hairless pussy nestled between slender Asian thighs. The fairy's private place was shiny, noticed the slave, shiny because it was wet. Then she guessed what games the fairies were going to play.

The fairies carried the doll along a narrow hallway leading off the back of Lauren's spacious bedroom. It was not the way to the playroom; Stephanie had been there many times before.

Further down the rabbit hole.

The fairies took the toy to a strange room, a place where fairies lived. The walls were covered in shiny metallic paper, like expensive wrapping, and they glowed from the sparkling light of a thousand tiny lamps that hung from the ceiling on silver tassels. Like sparkling flypaper to trap fireflies, a million of them, stuck fast and flashing their distress. In the center of the room was a huge bed, bigger than any bed Stephanie had ever seen or imagined. Its width was three times her height, and its thick mattress stood more than three feet from the floor. The fairies placed the toy on the bed. If her arms had not been bound to her sides Stephanie would have put her hands over her ears to drown out their constant giggling and unintelligible excited babbling. The noise, the strange lights and the colors only served to heighten the surrealism of the world this deep in the rabbit hole. One little fairy leaned close to the slave's head, Stephanie could smell the tiny creature's perfume, and her breath washed over the toy's face like a summer breeze, carrying the unmistakable scent of bubblegum. The fairy whispered in the toy's ear.

'Osoroshii kangae nimo osoware mas.' The words spilled from the delicate ruby lips like peach blossom falling from a tree, and for a moment Stephanie wondered what magic they might contain.

Perhaps an incantation to open the mirror that would take her back home?

Then another fairy leaned close to the toy's other ear and blew in it gently.

'She says her mind is full of evil thoughts,' the second fairy said, running a hand across the toy's breasts, 'and what we think, we should do. Don't you agree, toy?' The fairy gently gathered loose strands of golden blonde hair from the toy's face, tidying her blonde ponytail.

Stephanie lay back against the cool silk sheets; large,

scarlet pillows lay all around her like sandbags ready to ward off a pixie-dust attack. The fairies also surrounded the naked young woman, giggling and bouncing on their knees, clapping their hands and touching each other, slipping fingers inside pink tutus, rubbing each other's tiny breasts.

In a strange gesture they introduced themselves to their plaything in rapid succession, each fairy pointing a slim finger at her own chest in turn as she spoke the unfamiliar name. Kichi, Yoshi, Nyoko, Mayu. Fairy names for fairy girls.

Then as soon as the last proudly spoke her name she suddenly jumped on top of the supine blonde, sitting across the toy's belly. The fairy Mayu pulled up her tutu and wriggled her little tush, getting comfortable, and Stephanie could feel her wet pussy on her skin. The girl leaned forward, grabbed one of Stephanie's breasts in each of her miniature hands, and began to knead them like she was making pizza dough. The fairy hummed to herself, shaking her head from side to side, long dark hair swaying like silk drapes.

Perhaps she had been lied to when a child. It wouldn't be the first time. Fairies were supposed to be kind and gentle, and they never seemed to do much except fly around on their gauzy wings, chasing butterflies and lounging on flowers. But then perhaps Stephanie should have guessed there would be other kinds, after all, everything in life seemed to have a light or a dark side, and this was obviously true of fairies. These were bad fairies, Stephanie knew that now.

The fairy became quickly bored with kneading the toy's breasts and the bad little fairy grabbed both of the toy's nipples in her delicate fingers and twisted. Then she leaned back smiling and pulled hard; the bad little imp obviously felt she'd been given two water-filled party balloons to play with. Stephanie watched the fairy laughing as she let go, feeling her abused bosom flop back into place, then the young blonde felt a sudden stinging sensation as the fairy began to slap her breasts, the tiny hands delivering stinging blow after stinging blow.

'Mayu, Mayu, Mayu.' Stephanie's tormentor called out her own name as she whacked her tits. Despite her small stature the fairy was strong and she was playing rough. Stephanie let her discomfort show in her face as the girl rolled, pulled, stretched, flattened and slapped her breasts, and the other fairies noticed. 'Aw,' said Mayu, 'don't you like playing with us? But you are our very special toy. Missy Lauren said we could play with you,' the fairy announced sulkily, pouting prettily. 'She said we could do anything we wanted with you.'

'Yeah, and we want to do lots of fun stuff with you… well, fun for us, anyway,' Yoshi giggled, and the rest of the fairies joined in the private joke.

One of the other fairies clambered off the bed, its sheer size emphasizing her small stature. She lifted up a big silk bag, as big as the girl and brightly colored, emblazoned with thousands of tiny glittering orange flowers. The others grabbed it and hauled it onto the bed. Then they shook it out, spilling the contents onto the bed like a group of excited children on Christmas morning.

Stephanie felt the pull of the rabbit hole as she fell deeper, a vague dizzy feeling where remembering even simple things became difficult. There were just so many things a fairy needed to be able to play, strange things, all colors and sizes and shapes. The odd assortment of objects spilled across the bed and the bad fairies grabbed at them. One by one they pulled off their tutus till they were all quite naked, their olive-skinned bodies lithe and strong, surrounding the helpless blonde as she began to drown in the bad fairies. They closed over her like a pool of warm, scented water, swamping her till not an inch of her remained above the surface, their skin touching her skin, their hands slithering over her bound body like a nest of baby vipers, newly born and hungry.

Nails dug into her flesh, petit hands grabbed, testing and exploring everywhere and everything. Stephanie felt the fairies move inside her, fingers wriggled into her mouth, her vagina, her anus, it really wasn't that bad, and for a moment she felt she would be okay; the fairies would grow bored with her and then go away.

For a mere moment a gap opened in the wall of young flesh, and Stephanie saw one of the creatures donning something. *A magic sword belt*? The slim young woman was strapping something black around her waist, the straps held a triangular leather patch over her groin, and Stephanie noticed the shiny silver ring at the center as it glinted in the room's twinkling lights. Then the rest of the fairies climbed off their plaything and did the same. Stephanie tested her restraints again, a whispering voice in her head telling her she should run, and run fast, this was deeper in the rabbit hole than any good girl should ever come. But then she hadn't been a good girl, which was probably why her restraints held her fast.

For a while the bad fairies knelt silently around their sacrifice, translucent, pastel-colored swords protruding from their groins. The swords looked soft and round-ended, but Stephanie was still afraid, perhaps because this far in the rabbit hole size was distorted; the fairies were so little and the sword things were so large, as large as their skinny arms. Then they were upon her.

One fairy lay on top of the struggling blonde, her hips digging into the toy, a hand slid down her belly, between her legs, grabbing the sword and guiding it into her body. The blonde's pussy lips moved aside to accommodate the lubricated tip, then it slipped inside. Stephanie's labia closed over the slightly bulbous end, gripping the shaft.

No, please... A whispered plea for mercy, inaudible over the raucous noise as the girls giggled and chattered excitedly in their fairy tongue. The fairy lying on Stephanie's belly reached up to grab her slave-collar, strong fingers locking under the thick leather, and then she pulled hard, driving the thick shaft deep into the writhing plaything's vagina. It was huge and the girl was so much stronger than she looked, her arm muscles working like powerful hydraulic pistons, pulling her slender torso up the larger girl's body as the shaft drove into her, the tip of the magical sword pressing deep. Stephanie bit her lip, and noticed another fairy fluttering near her head, the huge sword protruding from her groin looking like a hardened stick of strawberry pink jello. The fairy slid her hands under the blonde and turned her onto her side. Stephanie lay with her flushed cheek against the cool sheets as hands moved round her face and pushed a red silk scarf into her mouth, and when it was full, her cheeks bulging, the hands looped another scarf around her head, gagging her.

The first fairy clung to her, casually sucking and chewing on one of Stephanie's nipples, her jello probe still buried deep in the slave's body. The blonde was then aware of another of her tormentors sliding against her back as she lay on her side. The fuzzy feeling in Stephanie's head had gone, leaving crystal clarity in its place. What was going to happen next was utterly predictable and utterly frightening, but there really was no escape. Her wrist cuffs were strong enough to hold a horse, and they were clipped to her waist belt with a sturdy steel ring. Nor was anyone going to come and save her. Perhaps if she'd been a good girl they might, but she hadn't and they wouldn't. The creatures that clambered over her like ants that had found a juicy fat caterpillar were in total control of her fate. The fairies were pretty and cute, just like fairies were supposed to be, but they were also cruel and hurting naughty girls like Stephanie was what they did best.

The young blonde felt several strong hands grasp her buttocks, pulling them apart, the tip of the magic sword pressing against her anus. The fuzzy feeling was back and Stephanie abstractly wondered what color the jello-like thing was that was about to violate her. She had seen a pretty blue one, the strawberry-red one, a yellow one, and one that was a lovely shade of lilac. The plaything felt her anus being forced open as the shaft slid past the opening and made its way into her rectal passage. Feet dug into Stephanie's thighs as the fairy climbed her, like a koala bear after eucalyptus leaves, the shaft penetrating deeper and deeper into her body.

Once in place the two fairies, one clinging to the front of her collar, the other to the back, began to gyrate their hips, those tiny Asian pelvises sucking the thick jello-poles out of the toy's orifices, then plunging them back again. They were fucking her. The pretty, little, bad fairies were fucking her. Stephanie endured the ordeal for what seemed a lifetime, as the remaining two fairies licked her face and taunted her in fairy talk she couldn't understand. Then they slid down to join their companions, each lying next to one of the fairies violating her. Stephanie was still in her dizzy place, but she could feel the fairies shifting position, moving aside so that their companions could squeeze in close beside them. The young blonde felt the tips of the other two magic swords at the entrance to her vagina and anus and they began to press against the already full passages, impatient to be allowed in.

More scrabbling, fingers gripped Stephanie's slave collar as the two other bad, bad fairies pulled and pulled trying to force their own jello-poles alongside the others. Stephanie's mind screamed at her body not to allow it, but her body betrayed her, the dizzy place became a sleepy, fainting sort of place as her vagina and ass surrendered to the evil fairies and two more slick, fat, jello-shafts pushed aside her flesh and began their journey deep into her helpless body.

Dakota slammed five shells into the dummy the minute it sprung from behind the fake door at the back of the range. Chunks of foam rubber, blasted from the target's face, floated gently to the ground like confetti. State Girl handed the Browning DBM to Amber, keeping the barrel pointed down range.

'I know where you come from, Amber. In fact I know a lot about you, and I know you've handled plenty of guns in the time you were in that godforsaken little shit-hole you called home, but what we have here is something that's a whole lot more expensive, and a hell of a lot more accurate than daddy's old Colt, or the Saturday night specials the local macho boys were letting you play with for a chance to get in your panties. It'll hit hard, and it'll hit accurately, if you know how to point it. It won't jam, and you'll be able to reload the mag in under three seconds when I've finished with you. With me so far?'

'Fuck Dak, didn't know I'd joined the marine corps.' Another target popped up and Amber pumped six bullets in the direction of the foam figure, landing one in the head and three in the torso, while two sunk harmlessly into the back wall.

'If I didn't love you, sweetie, I'd let you whack shells into the wall all day, but then I'd have to watch while some coked-up pimp put another hole in that cute little body of yours, and then I'd have to kill him twice and miss you for the rest of my life.'

Amber blew a kiss at the Cruza lieutenant. 'Ooh, Dak, I love it when you talk about my holes.'

The woman laughed. 'C'mon, bitch, get your little tush in gear and let's get this right, security check's only a week away.'

'What we looking for?'

'Nothing much, sweetie. Some jerks have been hassling one of our delivery teams, nothing the girls can't handle, but I'm just curious. I don't know if they have any idea what we're bringing in, or if they just reckon anything coming into a neighborhood like that has gotta be worth something. Either way, if we don't move them on pretty soon the cops will, and *that*...' Dakota replaced the Browning's magazine clip, '...we don't want.' The lieutenant emptied the clip into a moving target board crossing the back wall like a fairground duck shoot, and the center circle exploded into a mass of holes, not a single miss. Dakota then unloaded and checked the pistol and replaced the black and bluish-silver chunk of metal back in the rack. She then pulled out something that Amber thought wouldn't have looked out of place in a sci-fi flick. Not much bigger than the pistol the gun was a curious sculpted shape, speaking of hidden danger and power that belied its size.

Dakota grinned as she pressed a button on the range control, loosing another foam assassin. The alluring woman seemed to absorb something from the weapon in her hand, feeding off its dark intent and potency. Looking younger than her thirty-one years, her dark eyes glistened and the young redhead looked on, quite captivated. In her old world guns had been the preserve of white men riddled with paranoia, or young punks out for trouble or to impress, but never anything like this.

The goddess of destruction raised her weapon in a smooth arc as the foam figure leapt into her view, propelled at lightening speed by the gas ram it was attached to. Her gaze never wavered; dark-brown eyes sparkling and alive tracked their target. The weapon spat fire and noise, blasting the head clean off the dummy, the rapid burst of metallic death finishing the job in seconds, leaving only the ear guard-softened echoes to soak into the shielded walls and the cloud of debris to drift slowly to the floor. Dakota lowered the weapon, retracing the identical arc of motion as if her arm were some smoothly oiled machine running on a shaped track. Her movement stopped, the weapon resting on her fatigue-covered thigh.

'Uzi pistol; small, light and deadly, especially if you're using titanium tipped shells.' Dakota's gaze stayed resolutely ahead, as if the machine arm had infected her somehow, spreading the mechanical efficiency throughout her body, seeping into her brain, producing a very beautiful cyborg of death. 'We *always* use titanium; vests are so available now you never know if some punk's wearing one. They'll rip right through your average two-hundred dollar flack-stopper.'

'Can anything stop them?' Amber ignored the gun, staring intently at the dark-haired goddess and feeling glad she was on her side.

'Highest-grade vests maybe, but they're heavy. If you come up against one then they knew you were coming, and they're not going to be street gangs. That's why I, and only I, carry a little something extra for emergencies.' Dakota pulled a mag clip from her vest pocket. It had tape wound round it, yellow and black like on police hazard warnings. She held it up in front of the girl. 'Depleted uranium. Nothing stop's this shit.'

'Then why don't we use it all the time?'

The machine melted back into a human being as the woman chuckled. 'Be like writing your name, address and social security number on the wall in ten foot high letters, sweetie. This shit's rarer than unicorn piss. Like I said, for emergencies only. Here.' Dakota passed the tiny angel of messy death to the girl. It ain't neat, but then that's not what you're here to learn, is it, darling? We have people that do neat and tidy very well. I am just making sure you know how to protect that very cute and very tight little butt of yours.'

Amber giggled as she held the gun in her hand. 'If you give me a good grade, Dak, I'll let you kiss it.' The redhead flickered her eyelashes at the woman, doing her best bad little girl impression.

The redhead extended her tongue. *Contact. Huston, we have an airtight seal, proceeding with entry to the module as planned.*

Amber tasted the girl's sweet wetness, sucking it into her mouth. Spiky appeared with a fresh batch of blue margaritas in a jug and pressed the lip against Yoshi's muscular stomach, tilting the glass pitcher until a river of blue wound its way down the girl's torso, spilling into her bellybutton then trickling down over her shaved pubic mound, dribbling into the pink gash and finding Amber's mouth. The redhead drank down the heady brew of azure-blue alcohol and sweet pussy juice, chugging down the liquid passion as Kichi joined the other two geisha sluts between her legs, the three mouths fought over their soft, pink wet prize like a pack of hungry coyotes snapping at a kill. The redhead moaned in pleasure as another orgasm welled in the pit of her stomach, then rippled outward to flood through her body and mind.

Stephanie lay on the floor beside the giant bed, wrapped in red silk and sobbing quietly to herself. Surely even bad girls didn't deserve this. Nobody could ever deserve this. The fairies had played their horrid game with her body for hours, and then dressed in very un-fairy like clothes, just regular jeans and T-shirts, and wandered off, leaving the blonde lying strewn on the floor with all the other toys that were carelessly scattered about. Like bratty teenagers they hadn't even bothered to pick up after themselves.

A long time passed when she heard footsteps, and Lauren sauntered into the room and stood surveying the mess. Rather than being angry the woman seemed pleased, as if surveying the remnants of a fun game her beloved kid sisters had been playing. Stephanie's owner walked to the dresser and pressed a blue button next to the phone, and within minutes the silk-wrapped mummified blonde heard more footsteps. It wasn't the fairies, she knew that, because they always giggled, always, and these people were silent. Several maids entered the room. They weren't slaves but well-paid assistants, and they stood confidently beside their employer staring at the fun time carnage with looks of mild amusement.

'Can we get this place cleaned up, Debbie? I want the girls to be in bed as soon as they get back, and...' Lauren walked over to Stephanie and nudged her with her shoe, 'can you clean this up to? I'm going to let them take it to bed with them. They're such little cuties, don't you think? And so full of fun.'

Stephanie moved back into her dizzy place at those words, as two of the maids cut away the silk and dragged her off to the bathroom.

Being forcibly washed was a surprisingly humiliating act; it made her feel like a *thing* perhaps more than anything else. Things get used, and then have to be cleaned and put away after. The two maids had reinforced this by chatting idly to themselves while they soaped the blonde down, bending her over so they could insert soft foam nozzles into her vagina and anus, flushing out the lubricant that smeared her inner walls. They washed her long blonde hair, dried it, and then pulled it back into a ponytail. Stephanie was then dried, moisturizing lotion was rubbed into her skin and she was carefully perfumed. Then her restraints were replaced. Stephanie never even considered trying to get away during wash time; the maids were strong and they carried electric prods, and besides, where would she go? She was so far through the looking glass that she had no idea of the way back.

When they had finished and the toy was properly clean and secured, they walked her back into the strange fairy room. It still glittered like a million stars had been snatched out of the sky and scattered across the ceiling, and now it was dark the effect was even more magical.

Stephanie realized, as the maids lifted her onto the giant bed, that it had not been an illusion of her dizzy place. The maids, struggling to get her into the center of the enormously exaggerated bed were normal sized women, and it still looked vast. Stephanie was laid between the scarlet pillows in the center of the bed, and arranged carefully so she looked her best. One of the maids ran a silver chain from the slave's collar and attached it to the head of the bed so that she didn't drift out of position. Her ankle cuffs, removed the day before, were replaced and clipped to a spreader bar so she couldn't close her legs. Now her owners would be able to see her freshly shaven vagina, lying invitingly between her obscenely spread thighs.

Lauren walked ahead of the fairy girls like a schoolteacher on a field trip, ushering them into the fairy bedroom. The fairies were now dressed in identical light-pink, long T-shirts that fell about a half-inch below their pussies. Each fairy had her name printed in dusky pink glitter across the front of her T-shirt; the words clear, undisturbed by having to deal with much in the way of breasts. Kichi came bouncing in first and stood beside Lauren, then Mayu, who followed the first fairy. Nyoko sauntered in like an arrogant teenage brat, and jumped up to sit on the edge of the giant bed, Yoshi came in last and looked as sulkily brooding as her predecessor. Kichi took a running jump and leapt onto the bed, clambered over to the blonde conveniently laid out for them, and whispered in her ear.

'Ooh,' the fairy said, giggling, 'you are in so much trouble. Yoshi and Nyoko have been drinking, and they get really mean when they do that. But I like it ...' the girl confided in the bound slave, 'cos they're really fun to watch when they get like that. But you're not gonna like it. No way. When they're tight they bite, for sure.' Kichi laughed and lay back on the pillows.

'Okay, time for bed, girls, you jump in while I get your toy ready.' Lauren clambered over to Stephanie, unclipped her chain and pulled her to the edge of the bed. The fairies climbed into the blood-red silk sheets, looking lost in the exaggerated bed. 'Now, my little toy, I am going to put a magical fairy strap on you so our friends can play with you properly.' Lauren held out a leather harness for the slave to see, and for a moment Stephanie thought it was her ass-worship brace that Lauren usually made her wear when they were in bed, but as the blonde looked closer she could see differences. The older woman slipped the leather brace onto the bound slave, sliding the straps over her head. It seemed a simple affair to Stephanie and nothing covered her face at all. There was a headband and two straps that came down the side, tucking behind her ears, which then clipped to her collar, and it wasn't until Lauren reached behind her head that she understood. The strap that ran down the back had a thick rubber handle grip in the center. It was as simple as that; her owner had attached a sturdy handle to the back of her head.

Lauren then produced a number of delicate chains from her pocket and began to attach the tiny clips to the slave's piercing rings. Four were attached to each nipple ring, Stephanie was slipping back into her dizzy place, but the significance of the number didn't escape the helpless girl. Then Lauren moved down, working between her spread legs, attaching four chains to the toy's clitoris ring. When Lauren had sent Stephanie to the curators for piercing, she also specified that the girl's soft pussy lips have four rings inserted, two each side, upper and lower, but Stephanie's owner also had the slave's labia majora, the fleshy area either side of her vagina, pierced. This was unusual, and thankfully the curators had used anesthetic; something they hadn't done for the minor piercings. The labia majora rings were two large circles of steel, one on each side that disappeared deep into the relatively thick flesh. Their purpose was more than decorative or for improving access to a slave's vagina; they were a sturdy implant. Lauren had once dragged the bound slave across her bathroom's shiny tiled floor using thick chains clipped to the toy's labia majora rings. It had not been particularly painful, but reinforced Stephanie's mental picture of herself as a utility, dissolving some of the last remaining shreds of human identity the girl still possessed.

Lauren attached a single chain to each of the four rings on either side of the slave's vagina, and then produced four of the much thicker chains, attaching two to each of the large rings that pierced the blonde's vaginal mound. The mass of chains lay in a pile between the slave's spread legs, while others dangled like tinsel from her breasts.

The fairies threw back the red sheets and one of them lifted a shapely foot on the end of a slender leg and pressed it gently to Stephanie's lips. The young blonde thought back to her storybooks. They'd said nothing much about such things but she was pretty sure fairy feet were like sugar candy, not horrid at all, and the neat toes did look like cherry drops with their red nail polish. Stephanie felt the toes pressing against her lips, sliding in to touch her teeth, and she surrendered her mouth as she had done so many times before. She slowly parted her lips, the toes wriggled inside, and she sucked them. They didn't taste of sugar candy, they were salty, but the initial taste soon faded to a bland nothing as the slave sucked on them. The fairy lent forward, grabbing a nipple chain from each breast, then pulled as she forced her small foot deeper into Stephanie's mouth. The blonde slave slipped further away into her dizzy place, it was for the best, she knew there was so much more to come. Stephanie didn't know about good fairies, but bad ones were such copycats; if one did something then they all had to.

One by one the slave sucked the toes on each of the eight feet in the large bed, and she could hear Lauren laughing as she did. Then the woman stood up, obviously bored with the show, and pushed the naked, bound slave into the mass of wriggling legs on the bed.

Stephanie fell into the olive-skinned limbs and they began to wrap around her. She felt like a doomed fish that had wandered into the waving, stinging fronds of a lurking sea anemone. The lithe thighs gripped her tight as the fairies pulled the silk sheets over their prey, plunging her into a squirming darkness. She felt their hands reaching for her chains, and felt the slight tugging on her nipples, labia and clitoris as they found them.

Stephanie's night in the deep dark pool of the bad fairies was just beginning.

Night was very dark beneath the waves and Stephanie couldn't see the stars anymore. Like all naughty girls who swam in the deep, dark pools late at night she had been seized by a monster, caught in its hundreds of arms and legs as they squirmed and writhed like a pit of snakes. Hands scuttled down her body; reminding her of the fiddler crabs she'd seen on a Caribbean holiday, clutching at the mass of chains that dangled from her. Like a mermaid, fronds of bright green seaweed waving in the breeze while the crabs ran over her beautiful body, pinching and snipping.

One of the chains on her left breast pulled taught, followed by the chains attached the rings on the left side of her labia, Stephanie wriggled on her belly like a snake trying to answer the summons from the cruel fairy, but it was difficult, her arms were bound to her side and her legs held uselessly wide apart.

The tugging continued and the blonde slithered to its call, aware of the muted sounds of distant voices, giggling and laughing above the surface of the scarlet ocean she swam in. The chains pulled her between the strong legs of one of the fairies, guiding her face toward the tiny mouth between the soft thighs. Stephanie couldn't see the genitals as she slid inexorably to them, but she could smell the musky perfume, then she felt the moist lips kiss her own. The mermaid slid her tongue into the dripping hole, licking the wetness. The hands released her chain and grasped the handle at the back of her head, pulling her deep into the slit. The rustling of silk sheets accompanied the fairy's knees as she pulled them up to her chest so she could place her little feet on the mermaid's shoulders, then the fairy pulled on the handle with all her might, wriggling her pelvis, driving the blonde girl's face deep into her smooth, wet pussy.

Luckily the fairy was just too small to drown Stephanie, the blonde's mouth was buried in wet flesh, jaw muscles aching as she pushed her tongue deep into the hole, working it round and round, but her nose was clear, pressed to the little clitoris. The fairy danced a special fairy dance on the mermaid's face, forcing Stephanie to drink fairy juice, and the blonde was not thirsty at all, but the fairy had so much juice, and the mermaid had no choice but to drink it.

It was a long night. Stephanie had been forced to put her tongue into so many of the wet little mouths, shutting her eyes, even though it was dark, and pretending she was kissing a handsome prince in the backseat of his car. Big, wet, kisses, as the prince dribbled all down her chin. She was bound and helpless, and the spider web of chains controlled her completely, which was the mad princesses idea all along.

The fairies held Stephanie's head in place with their strong thighs while they used her mouth, only releasing her when they finished their dirty little games. Stephanie lay in the darkness, in the depths of the fairy pool, where the tiny feet and wriggling toes swam restlessly all night like shoals of fish.

One by one the fairies had fallen asleep, leaving the mermaid in the gloom where the strange taste of fairy juice lingered in her mouth. Stephanie was frightened; they were changing her, working fairy magic. She licked her lips, savoring the strange taste, and finding it… *pleasant.*

The Delivery

A passing servant had entered the room where Juana and another slave were mopping the floors, shuffling awkwardly, naked and barefoot, moving their leg braces with care along the expensive tiles. Both girls showing exemplary concentration as they held the mop handles awkwardly between hands that were manacled at the wrists. The woman pointed at Juana.

'You. Curator's office, now.' Then she promptly turned and left. Juana made her way carefully towards the service elevator. The servant made no effort to check if the slave had obeyed her orders; that was so unlikely it didn't warrant further consideration. The small box elevator transported slaves from the curator subterranean levels to the main house, or vice versa. There were chains, rings and metal cuffs attached to the walls. A young woman had been attached to the back wall, spread-eagled upside down, she looked like she'd been pasted there as a decoration, which could quite possibly have been the case. Or she may have simply been forgotten, while whoever put her there attended to more urgent matters, like taking a piss perhaps. If so then the girl was lucky, Juana mused. It was not unknown for staff to use the girls for such purposes if they were any distance from the nearest bathroom, or sometimes just because they got a kick out of it. The girl's soft brown eyes looked through Juana as if she wasn't there; the unfocused daze was a trick the mind used to shut out the humiliation. *If you're not looking at them, then they're not looking at you.* A trick borrowed from childhood, Juana used it too – often.

The doors slid open and Juana turned from the human décor and began to shuffle out of the elevator when two sets of strong hands reached in and grabbed her, pulling her out with a swift, practiced motion. The porters were both black women in their mid-thirties, and they handled their human cargo like meat packers running gutted carcasses through the packing plant. They oozed rehearsed competence and blasé indifference to the *product*. One dragged over a two-wheeled trolley, the like of which Juana had seen before at her father's factory, the men using them to move and stack boxes. The other porter bent down, unclipped Juana's ankle bar and bound her legs tightly together. The young Latina was then strapped in a standing position to the trolley and wheeled away.

The porters left her in a corner for more than an hour, people came and went while the girl waited, and eventually she was taken to a workbench and lifted off the trolley. One of the black girls dropped a large case onto the bench, white plastic, like a picnic cooler, but much larger. As big as it was it didn't look large enough to hold even a small person, so when Juana suddenly realized they meant to put her in it she panicked, suddenly jerking upright and pulling at her bonds. A woman stepped from nowhere and pressed a rubber oxygen mask over the struggling girl's nose and mouth, except that the acrid chemical gas hissing from it was not oxygen. The porters held her shoulders as her vision blurred, the room span and faded into darkness. Had her mind not been losing its struggle to remain awake Juana may have been embarrassed. Did she really think she was the first girl to have panicked at being packaged? Maybe they all did…

The gas evidently had a very temporary effect; Juana's brain struggled back to consciousness before they had even closed the lid of the box. It took a few seconds for the throbbing pain to hit, and then she felt it in her twisted joints. The slave had been bent double, laying on her back in the deep cooler, her torso had been strapped to the base, a thick Velcro belt around her waist, one across her chest just above her breasts, and another low across her lap. Her arms were pinned to her sides by her usual wrist cuffs, but the porters had grabbed her legs while she was out, folding her in two so that her feet were now crossed at the ankles behind her head. Juana was fit but she was no gymnast and her hips screamed at her to move and release the pressure, but she was held fast. The porters then produced a clear plastic hose, Y-shaped at one end. They clamped the single end in the slave's mouth, then ran the tube down her belly, inserting one Y-piece into her vagina, the other into her anus. Juana looked like a self-contained waste recycler, and she understood this was just marketing, fancy packaging, all part of the service, like having her bent this way so her sexual organs were on display as soon as the box was opened. No slave would ever evacuate her bowels or bladder if they were wired into her mouth, and it would never travel that far anyway, but she didn't doubt the device must look amusing. As always, her tormentors' pleasure seemed to rise in direct proportion to her own discomfort and humiliation.

The lid of the box slammed shut and the girl was engulfed in darkness. She felt the box being lifted, then dimly heard the vehicle's engine and felt the sensation of movement. She was being delivered.

Dakota drove the metallic-gray BMW an inconspicuous distance behind the delivery van, *Banquette de Plata* written in large colorful letters on its side. In the high-class neighborhood of La Jolla, the Beverly Hills of San Diego, quality catering firms flourished, running back and forth as they supplied the appetites of exclusive dinner parties, the up-market equivalent of the pizza delivery guy. The van pulled a right and cruised to a stop outside a large, red tile roofed one story house, and Amber could see the arc of light thrown up by the patio lights at the back of the property, while reflections from the surface of the pool shimmered against the trunks of the palms and bougainvillea trees.

Dakota pulled their car into the adjoining road, making sure they had an uninterrupted view, and within seconds of the lieutenant pulling on the parking brake a small red car swung round the curve and parked a short distance from the van. The interior light went on and Amber could just make out a woman struggling to fold a large map, looking around in puzzlement. The redhead glanced enquiringly at Dakota.

'Megan,' the lieutenant said simply. 'Always set a potential target in crossfire. Our girls in the van are armed, so if the scum arrive as planned we have three-way crossfire if we need it.' Dakota sighed admiringly as she watched Megan wrestling to fold the map. 'Always nice to watch a real artist at work.' Amber smiled, thinking about poor little Megan all lost and alone. *Lions and tigers and bears, oh my... Bang. Bang. Bang. Better run mister wizard, the yellow brick road's got some icky red stains on it now.*

The lieutenant's radio crackled into life. 'State Girl, target sighted, over.'

Dakota lifted her handset to respond. 'ETA?'

'Five minutes to your location, they just passed us, black Merc entering residential area.'

'You catch that little-girl-lost?'

'Right in the pitcher's mitt, all set here.' Megan's voice was calm and focused, as always.

'Outfield, this is State Girl, any sign of law enforcement?'

'Negative, State Girl, you have a clear stage.'

Dakota lifted the Glock 18C she was carrying from its holster, screwed in the silencer and checked the clip, then repeated the operation, sans silencer, with the Uzi. Behind the back seat a Fabrique Nationale P90 was locked into its holding clips on the car's floor panel. Grade one military hardware, emergencies only. Amber wondered if that was where the depleted uranium shells were loaded. She checked her own hardware, as instructed. Dakota had told her that things were much harder once, women's fashion and serious weaponry a difficult fit. But now? Modern clubbing fashions were a cinch. Amber wore black jeans and army boots, black T-shirt and a long coat, light enough for the hot nights of southern California, good enough to conceal the Uzi pistol.

The black Merc cruised round the corner, pulling up opposite the truck. The occupants, four men, sat and watched as the two women unloaded a large, vacuum cooler food container from the back of the van, and closed the doors. As they placed the heavy box onto a delivery cart the men stepped out of the car, three white guys, one black, jeans, T-shirts, light jackets, bulges at the top left corner pocket.

Amber watched, waiting for instructions. The men spotted the little red car almost immediately, its brightly lit interior and flustered single female occupant. Two wandered over while their companions started towards the van, and the next thing Amber knew Megan was winding up the car's windows and shouting fearfully at the two men in her best panicked voice. The other two gatecrashers turned to look.

'Now.' Dakota issued the simple command as she opened the car door and jumped out. Amber followed, coat flapping in the soft breeze she followed the lieutenant. The men were streetwise, spotting the trap almost instantly, but they hesitated. One of the delivery women had pulled a pistol, so had the frightened female with the map, now two angels in black coats were advancing purposefully from their rear. Dakota pulled out the Glock in that same fluid motion Amber had seen before and punched a silent bullet into the nearest guy's thigh. His partner moved for his gun, but Dakota's pistol never stopped moving and now pointed straight at his head. The Glock could spit a shell straight through his skull before he could twitch a finger, and he knew it. With her other hand Dakota removed the Uzi from her belt. Amber did the same, excitement coursing through her veins. Oh yes, this was real fucking power. These jerk-offs had been bullying and scaring people like her all their lives, now look at them, all wide-eyed and scared, and shitting their fucking pants. Dakota had left no room for confusion about who was in charge.

'You guys hungry? Be a lot easier to phone out for Chinese, wouldn't it?'

'There ain't no food in those boxes, lady.' The guy's hand, which had paused midway to his breast pocket, twitched but stayed where it was.

'Really? Well that's going to ruin the party a little. So why don't you tell me what you *think* is in there?'

'Big for drugs, unless you're planning on supplying the whole west coast.' He watched Dakota's reaction, and saw none. 'Hey, if we fucking knew then we wouldn't be taking a little look now, would we, whore?'

Megan appeared, camera in one hand, Uzi in other. The camera's flash fired as she took pictures of the four men.

'What the fuck?' the guys arm jerked for his pocket, Dakota's Glock spat hot metal, burning a hole through the middle of his hand. The bullet passed through and lodged in his breastbone, he went down hard, cracking his skull on the road. She raised the Uzi.

'Get the fuck off our turf. Now.'

The two uninjured thugs dragged their companions back to the car, spitting threats as they went. Dakota never took her eyes off them, even as she spoke to Amber beside her.

'Okay, listen up. They're running on the universal law of live to fight another day, but they'll be back as soon as they patch up the fallen and get some bigger hardware, which means later tonight.' Dakota motioned to Megan and the woman handed Amber the digital camera and a business card. 'Take the beamer, go to that address, ask for Shadow Stalker, she'll know who you are. Tell her I need the clean up by midnight. If she asks about costs tell her double fee if she gets it done in the timeframe. Wait at her place, she'll be expecting you to, then report back to the hacienda. Drive fast when you're on the freeway, but walk back to the car. Got that? *Walk* back to the car.'

'Okay,' confirmed the redhead as she turned and made her way to the BMW, every muscle screaming to be let off the leash. *Walk*, she repeated to herself.

Light flooded into the case as the lid was lifted, and the bizarrely bound girl blinked as her eyes adjusted, seeing several blurred faces gazing down at her. Three women, seemingly in their mid-fifties, wearing too much make-up smiled down at Juana. Not smiles of happiness, or even concern for her condition, something else… anticipation, maybe.

One reached in and unhooked the recycling tubes, allowing them to fall to the bottom of the box, while another released the girl's wrist and ankle clips from the bolts on the packing case, then they dragged the stiff-limbed Latina from her temporary sarcophagi, watching as she swayed uneasily on numb legs.

Mariana De Vesille glided though the kitchen door like a large, attentive bird of prey, hovering above the slave as though she were a sparrow caught in the open. Although Mariana was the same age as her friends she had weathered life's storms a little better and could pass for an attractive thirty-five, her light-brown hair brushing tanned shoulders was one of the paradoxical aspects of her looks and personality that Mariana enjoyed. She held the slightly curly, blonde-streaked hair in place with pink grips, and she sported two plaits at the front in garish teenage beads, little drops of soft pastel glass that swayed in rhythm with her body's movements, graceful, like a dancer. All a stunning contrast with the woman's almost black eyes, which stared out from the pretty face in arrogant contempt. Her soft lips could also switch to a frighteningly cruel sneer that would often catch the unwary. Mariana was a delicately crafted, expensive exercise in contradiction, a living enigma. The hostess looked at the girl.

'Pretty.' Mariana's friend nodded at her observation. 'In fact, my dear…' the hostess lifted Juana's chin to look into her frightened eyes, 'quite beautiful. Which is of course essential. My parties are legendary, my guests always expect something new, and I? Well… I aim to please.' Mariana gently tugged on the silver chain that ran from the slave's collar between her small but shapely breasts, to finally slither across her toned stomach where it snatched hold of her clitoris like a hungry snake.

'Do we have time to train her properly?' one of the women asked.

'She doesn't need it, do you, sweetie?' The hostess gripped the young woman's chin a little firmer. 'I am certain she will be *completely* compliant.' Mariana led the girl into the next room, a grand, high-ceilinged affair, decorated in Roman-Greek style with sumptuous couches in secluded corners. The centerpiece of the room was a large pool; the tiles lacquered gold, and yellow lights were set beneath the waterline so the water itself seemed to be the precious metal in its liquid form. The twinkling, sparkling reflections from the pool's surface pervaded the room, and even in Juana's apprehensive state she had to acknowledge the effect was stunning. 'I will give you an hour to wander the party room and familiarize yourself with the layout. Pay particular attention to the couch alcoves. Your duties will be threefold, but all very simple. First, you will ensure that a constant supply of champagne is delivered to our all female guests, the bar is located over there, behind the statue of Isis. That should require no thought whatsoever, however, you will need to concentrate on your second duty. I do not want you to appear reluctant, it will reflect badly on me.'

The hostess fixed the naked Latina with a stare that surpassed any language barrier. 'The party room has no bathroom, primarily because I see nothing less elegant than women standing in line waiting to take a piss. Totally crashes the flow of things, my dear. So… to twist the law of gravity to my own purposes for a moment, consider the human body like this; what goes in, must come out. So your main function will be to deliver one liquid to the guests, and relieve them of another. You look like a smart girl, so I am no doubt making myself perfectly clear.' The hostess raised an eyebrow and the slave nodded weakly.

'Good. Oh… and the third duty, you will perform any – and I mean *any* – sexual act the guest wishes you to. They have all been instructed to limit this to three minutes otherwise you'll end up trapped in some corner being pawed over all night, and I didn't lay out serious cash for you to be a private whore. However, my staff will regulate the timing in a discreet manner, and you are *not* to pull away of your own accord, understood?'

Juana nodded. She understood only too well.

The apartment sat over a liquor store in a rundown neighborhood. From the outside it looked jaded and dingy. Amber climbed the stairs, fingering the Uzi nervously. The initial excitement had faded and the eighteen-year-old was feeling decidedly out of her depth. An attractive blonde woman answered the door, ushering the anxious redhead inside without asking questions.

'Shadow Stalker?' Amber asked, a little breathless.

'Yes, my dear. That's for me I assume?' The woman reached out and took the camera from the girl. 'You're Gemstone, I take it?'

'Yes.' First Amber had heard of her handle, but it made sense. The woman plugged the camera into a laptop and hit print.

'Timeframe?'

'Midnight, tonight.'

"Mmm, interestingly tight. Fee?'

'Double,' Amber replied, trying to place the woman's accent. New York; she was from New York. The young redhead placed it by running TV shows through her head.

'Acceptable...' Shadow Stalker held up the four photographs, 'and achievable, the same four losers I've been scouting for three days. It's nice not to have too many surprises from the client side of things in my line of work, Gemstone. I get enough of that from the targets.'

The woman showed Amber into the plush lounge. The outside of the building was a façade, literally, and inside the apartment reeked of money. Shadow Stalker led the girl to a comfortable couch and placed a strong vodka-martini in her hand. 'Plenty more in the cabinet, my dear.' Then she left the room.

When she returned she was dressed a little like Amber in black fatigues, and carrying a black unmarked sports bag. She was also leading a pretty Indian woman by a leash attached to a collar. The martini had bounced off Amber's empty stomach and landed straight in her brain. *Acceptable*, she thought, internally mimicking the strange woman's voice.

'I carry her with me for entertainment; there can be a lot of waiting around in my line of work.' Shadow Stalker handed the naked slave's leash to the young redhead. 'Something to help pass the time. Don't worry about marks, but just don't break anything, okay?'

Amber nodded, feeling pleasantly woozy. The blonde picked up her bag and headed out of the door.

Shalyn picked up her cell-phone as she drove. One call to a primed junior doctor with a gambling habit and target one was off the list. She had delivered the sodium pentothal and potassium chloride to the nervous young man from Taiwan personally, and he'd tucked the deadly phials in his pocket, clutching the brown, cash-filled envelope nervously. Shalyn made it clear that he could expect another envelope if the target received the contents of the phials in A&E, or a bullet to the brain if the target walked. Shadow Stalker liked simple choices; they suited the simple people she had to deal with. Another phone call told her that targets two and three were together, one wounded, while target four was at his girlfriend's apartment.

Amber relaxed, it was all going to be okay. She had an overwhelming sense of confidence in the assertive blonde, and she'd done her part exactly as outlined. The teenager pulled the Indian woman down to her knees, and she sat there, brown eyes looking through the girl holding her leash.

Amber popped the stud on the waistband of her combat jeans, pulled down the zipper and slid them down to her ankles, while the slave remained frozen in place. The redhead pointed a little drunkenly to her cute little panties, with the sparkly pink heart on the front.

'Like these?' The teen tugged the leash and the slave nodded. 'Yeah, me too. Fuck, when I remember what I used to have to wear when I was with my dad in the trailer. I even stole stuff off washing lines. Can you imagine that? Stealing underwear off washing lines cos your dad was a shit-face drunk and thought the tinkerbell panty an' sock set mom got me when I was ten would "do just fine girly, you ain't no woman yet".'

Amber laughed at her own impression. 'Well these are fucking class, probably cost more than the old man's trailer. She slipped the prized panties down her shapely legs, pushing them on top of the black jeans. She drained the last of the martini then shuffled over to the drinks cabinet, panties round her ankles, and giggled at herself the whole way there. She poured a martini, two-thirds vodka.

'Well...' the teenager looked over at the slave, still impassively staring at the vacant couch, 'it's either a sleepover or I'm getting a cab home.' Amber giggled then thought for a while. 'They'll probably send over a limo if I ask.' She took a swig from the strong drink, shaking her head. 'Y'know, life can turn around real quick sometimes. A limo... fuck, who'd have thought?'

Shalyn knocked on the graffiti-covered door in the dingy apartment block, leaning in close so her face would fill the spy hole.

'What you fuckin' want, whore?'

'To suck your dick, big boy. Danni give me fifty bucks an' says go round an' do Lazy-T, so I'm here.' Shalyn heard the latches unclip.

'No Lazy-T here, bitch, but I got a dick if you're looking for somethin' to suck...' the last two latches disengaged. 'If you can fit the thing in your mouth, whore. This ain't no fuckin' pencil I'm holdin' in my...' the door swung open and he stared at the Navy issue MP5, custom silencer, in the blonde's hands. He fell silent.

'I know, messy really, but then this job's all about speed. Have to sacrifice a little finesse, right?' The machine pistol emptied twenty-five rounds into the man's chest before his brain could even register what had happened. The body fell heavily to the floor.

Shalyn moved confidently into the apartment. She found

the corpse's wounded companion in the back room, tugging frantically at the rear fire escape door. The MP5 tore open his back, shedding lung and heart tissue into a fine pulp that splattered over the worn, paint-flaked door.

Amber settled back onto the couch, lifted her legs and placed them over the Indian woman's head, so the slave now lay inside the zone marked at the rear boundary by the redhead's jeans, at either side by her taught thighs, and at the front by her shaven pussy. The teenager reached clumsily forward, grabbed the Indian by the hair and plunged her face against her waiting sex. Definitely not a virgin cunt-licker, thought Amber as the woman's tongue wormed its way deep into her already lubricated vagina, flicking from side to side as it descended into the girl's tunnel of joy. Amber rummaged in her jacket pocket, pulling out a small pair of silver-plated pliers, a gift from McKenna. The teenager unfolded the delicate implement then reached around her own left thigh, groping for the woman's breast. After a few seconds of drunken fumbling she found it, roughly pulling the pert tit to the side so she could see it past her leg and the bobbing head as it worked away on her dripping pussy.

Well, thought Amber, this ain't gonna break anything, and the drunken girl guided the pliers to the dark nipple, slid the jaws either side of the small bud, then squeezed. The slave jerked, losing her momentum for a moment, but she recovered quickly, lapping at the teen's cunt like a kitten at its first bowl of milk. Amber smiled to herself and closed the jaws of the pliers, squeezing the slave's nipple, who increased her efforts proportionately, driving her twirling tongue deeper into the young slit, pressing her face into the vagina, moving from side to side.

'Mmm, not bad,' Amber murmured. 'Know what I like? Close your mouth round my hole. You're gonna have to get in real close though, then like, totally suck on it, like you're trying to turn me inside out an' have my guts in your mouth.' Amber giggled, spilling some of the martini on top of the woman's head. 'Hey, that sounds gross, doesn't it? Feels pretty cool though. Okay, let's see how you do.' The drunken teen gripped the slave's nipple and began to twist it, turning slowly clockwise and stretching it outward away from her breast. The reaction was immediate and the woman had evidently been listening intently. She jutted out her lower jaw, forcing her mouth between the girl's labia so her lips closed around the vaginal tunnel, her small nose pressing against the girl's urethra. The slave sucked and Amber moaned, forgetting the night's tension.

'More,' she ordered, twisting the tortured nipple and yanking hard. The slave's chest heaved as she sucked frantically, gulping down air, drawing the teenager's labia into her mouth, swallowing the girl's juices, trying desperately not to choke on the flood. 'Yessssss...' Amber flopped back into the soft scatter cushions, she felt her vaginal fluids being sucked from her and imagined them seeping down the slut's throat, an orgasm creeping upward from her genitals, hitting her brain like an electric shock, and as the teenager writhed in the throes of a multiple orgasm she wrenched hard on the nipple imprisoned in the silver jaws, a hostage to her continued pleasure.

The second apartment was virtually indistinguishable from the first, apart from the fact that the graffiti on the door contained some legible words, meaninglessly scrawled obscenities. The door was helpfully ajar. Shalyn squinted through the small gap, and seeing nothing she eased the door open with her foot. It swung wide silently and the assassin smiled; only a truly arrogant bastard would leave his door open in a neighborhood like this, and Shalyn loved arrogant bastards. They were so easy to kill. If someone wasn't watching their own back it was easy to put a bullet in it.

She clung to the shadows following the voices from the second floor. A male was shouting, a female trying to argue back in between stifled sobs. Rounding the corner the assassin could see clearly into the bedroom. The man stood, arms waving, a powerful handgun clenched in his right fist as he ranted at a cowering girl in front of him. A disheveled, brown-haired girl, her pretty face spoilt by lines of mascara that flowed down her cheeks following the tracks of tears from a pair of attractive green eyes.

The assassin couldn't get a clear shot without hitting the girl; if she hadn't been attractive she wouldn't have hesitated. Shalyn paused, a risk, but possibly worth it. She clipped the MP5 to her belt and silently slid off her small backpack. Reaching inside she pulled out a black disk, roughly the size, shape and color of a hockey puck. The device had a single small switch recessed into a groove on the puck, two positions, forward or back, timer – fixed five seconds – or pressure activated. Shalyn set the mine for timer, and then slid the taser-anti-personnel-munition into the room.

It came to a halt between the man's legs and he stared at it for the remaining three seconds before it exploded, sending out darts carrying a disabling charge of fifty thousand volts. The assassin moved swiftly into the room, the occupants twitching convulsively on the floor. She moved quickly to secure her unexpected prize, pressing duct tape over the young woman's mouth, using the girl's own T-shirt to wipe away the vomit residue; taser side effect; loss of bowel, bladder and stomach control.

Cable ties had the girl secured in seconds. Shalyn grabbed the waistband of her jeans, dragging her across the room, pausing to press the MP5 against the skull of the twitching male. She squeezed the trigger, mingling his blood and brains with the pool of shit and piss he lay in.

Shalyn slung the girl in the back seat of the innocuous red pickup. 'You better be worth it when you're cleaned up, bitch. The police can put an MP5 down to a gangland hit, but taser mines are a little special.'

Juana slumped onto the plastic chemical toilet, discretely hidden behind a curtain beside the bar. She noted wearily that urine passed though her system as quickly as cheap beer, and she had to empty herself every time she returned for more champagne. The slave dabbed her crotch with a soft towel, grabbed another silver tray of bubbly fun-juice and headed back into the babbling crowd. She ducked into an alcove, finding a woman with a girl, who was all giggles while the woman played with her exposed breasts. Juana placed the tray on a side table and poured two glasses.

'You need to pee, little sweet thing?' the woman asked the apparently mindless giggling blonde. Juana felt sure it was an act, something the older woman got off on. 'I'd love to watch.'

'Okay then,' was all the girl said, slipping down her panties.

Juana wasn't sure if anything more was expected of her and hesitated, but the woman grabbed her arm and pulled her down across the low marble table before the couch. The giggling thing crouched over her and worked her way up the supine slave's body till she was straddling the Latina's head. Juana knew what was expected of her, and opened her mouth and allowed her mind to drift away.

The teenager groped drunkenly at her vagina, pulling the lips apart clumsily, then a look of intense concentration fell across her face, exciting the older woman. A squirt of warm piss splashed against the slave's cheek, the blonde giggled and adjusted her aim, and then she was on target and a surprisingly forceful stream of perfectly clear pee bubbled and frothed into the slave's mouth. Juana gulped it down. The life of a slave forces a reassessment of priorities; once she would have been fighting and screaming – but now? Well… actually it wasn't that bad; she had no ego that could be humiliated anymore, the teenage blonde, all giggly squeals and oversized tits had been drinking heavily, and all Juana tasted was warm, slightly salty water.

The older woman was visibly turned on by the display. She dragged the slave from the table, pulling the Latina between her own legs, and began to empty her bladder into the waiting mouth. Since Juana was forced to lick spillages from the floor she had quickly learned to keep a tight seal, but the woman was cheating, getting round the three minute rule by masturbating on the slave's face while her piss gushed into her mouth. Juana felt a strong hand grab her hair, holding her head in place between the plump thighs while the woman rubbed her pussy over her face. Urine glistened on the Latina's cheeks and forehead, soaking her hair and dripping from her chin to form a puddle on the floor. The flow stopped to be replaced by a trickle of sex juice, and having stolen the illicit orgasm the woman then used her *official* three minutes by having the vacant blonde press her fist into Juana's pussy, while the slave knelt on all fours licking up the puddle of piss.

'We only have three minutes, sweetums,' the woman told the grinning airhead, stroking her soft, hair maternally, 'no time to be gentle.' The teenager jammed her hand into Juana's vagina causing the slave to wince in discomfort, but she continued lapping at the pee-puddle like a kitten with a bowl of milk while the blonde, seemingly unsure what she should be doing, rummaged around inside the Latina as if she were digging in her purse for a set of lost car keys.

Humiliation's Daughter

Amber wasn't sure how it got this way with Rainbow Girl – it just sort of happened. The two fell into the relationship naturally; owner and slave shifted slightly, like the foundations of a house after one of the San Andreas quakes, becoming mistress and servant. It was subtle, Rainbow Girl still wasn't free and she still had sexual duties to perform, like tonguing Amber's pussy every night till the teenager drifted off to sleep, but the redhead treated the woman with an unusual courtesy. She didn't hurt Rainbow Girl, even though she was her property, nor did she unnecessarily degrade her. Amber even allowed the young woman to speak, if she was given permission to do so, and in the deep recesses of Rainbow Girl's mind, her mistress, Amber, had rescued her from an unthinkably hideous fate in that basement. As a result the young woman was fiercely loyal to her mistress. The relationship suited both of them, but it meant something was lacking from the teenager's life, a proper toy she could play with as she pleased.

But today was her nineteenth birthday, and she'd pretty much got the hint from Dak that Rebecca was planning to give her a toy. Not that Amber was expecting anything as special as a blonde, which would have been fantastic, but she knew she'd surpassed every one of Rebecca's expectations – and the Inquisitor didn't play for low stakes – so she'd probably get one of the really pretty Latina's McKenna pulled in last week. Amber had been down to the curator's levels taking a sneak peek at the four wide-eyed, olive-skinned young Mexicans, like a kid in a toy store the week before Christmas.

The redhead's personal favorite was number 7466. She looked so scared she'd probably piss herself and faint if Amber so much as gave her an order. Breaking *her* in would be exquisite, as the little bitch would loathe every minute of the miserable existence the redhead had planned for her. So consequently Amber was a little disappointed to see the young thing being shipped out two days later, but one of the others would do fine. They were all pretty.

Rainbow Girl gently shook Amber awake at seven. The family ritual was to bring gifts to the birthday girl's room in the morning, reconvening later in the day for the celebrations. The redhead liked the idea, but then she would have liked any idea. Birthday celebrations had not played a major role in her life to date, and some she would definitely like to forget.

She was wearing nothing but a pink thong, so she slipped her robe on and took the coffee Rainbow Girl handed to her.

The knock on the door came at exactly seven-thirty, as expected. Rebecca, Dakota and McKenna hugged the birthday girl, while Lauren hung back doing her shy thing, but that was okay. Amber respected someone who could play like Lauren, there was never any downtime, she'd been doing it so long now that her real life and fantasy worlds had become one and the same thing. Nice work if you can get it, the birthday girl thought as the world's greatest fetishist stepped forward and gave her big/little sister a hug.

Then the fun part. In came the big box, wrapped in silver paper with black ribbons and bows, and it sat on the floor in front of Amber, beckoning her forward. But the redhead waited, savoring the surprise, squeezing everything from the moment she could. In a way this was a symbol, it said she'd made it, she'd dodged all the shit that had been thrown at her and come out the other side kicking hard. And more than that, not only had she escaped the world she hated, she now had the power to go back and bust its fucking balls for messing with her in the first place. But then Rebecca had said that thing Amber had heard before, in a movie or something, *revenge was a dish best served cold.*

The redhead leapt forward and began tearing the wrapping. She got three fingers under the lid and yanked it off. It sailed slowly through the air in a flourish of silver paper, landing on her bed. Amber peered in, expecting to see a pair of pretty Mexican eyes looking back.

'Oh fuck!' Amber jumped back, excitedly squeezing her hands into tight fists. 'Yes!'

'Like it?' Rebecca wore her usual *I'll always be one step ahead*, smile.

'Like it?' the birthday girl squealed. 'It's fucking awesome!' She clapped her hands. 'Jenny-fucking-Moyse, shit, last time I saw this bitch I fucked her over a toilet seat after taking weeks of her "I run this place trailer-girl" crap. Well hi, Jenny, been a while, and guess what?' Amber gestured to the large bedroom suite, 'I run *this* fucking place.'

'It was McKenna's idea,' Dakota said, patting her colleague on the back. 'She looked through the file we had from that shelter. Took a while but we eventually found her in LA, just getting her life together I guess. She had a shitty little job and a cheap apartment.'

'How d'you do it?' Amber couldn't take her eyes of her former adversary.

'The things we do for you, sweetie.' Dakota shook her head. 'How shall I put it? The little slut won a trip to Jamaica, collected the tickets, told everyone at work and her landlady, then we snatched her. We had a look-alike board the plane and get off the other end. So, last thing anyone knows Miss Jenny Moyse was in Jamaica, and that's where they're still looking for her. Though not too hard, I suspect. No family, no one to make a fuss, and what with the FBI as overstretched as it is.'

Amber laughed. 'Cool. You guys are fucking awesome.'

'Well...' Rebecca leaned forward and kissed the birthday girl on the cheek, 'gotta go. See you tonight, and have fun.' Dakota and McKenna both kissed Amber on the lips, and the birthday girl giggled when McKenna slipped her tongue in.

'Hey!' she cried in fake indignation.

'Sorry, honey, but you'll be the boss one day – might be the last chance I get.' McKenna turned to leave. 'Well, have fun playing with your new toy. Bet she's gonna love every minute.'

Rainbow Girl touched her fingers gently to her lips, a little like the signal for shush, except that in the slave's case it was a request to speak. The packaging had been cleared away and Amber had the bound and totally naked Jenny Moyse lying on her back in the middle of the floor, while she sat on her captive's stomach diddling with her nipples.

'Go ahead,' said the mistress, seeing the request and granting permission.

'Do you like her, mistress? I thought she was mean to you.'

'Like her?' Amber echoed. 'It's the only way you can like a fucking bitch like Jenny Moyse, butt-naked, tied nice an' tight, an' completely in your power. Ooh, I got goose bumps then, Jenny, how about you? Yeah you did, I can feel 'em.' The redhead ran her hands across the blonde's breasts. 'Oh, Jenny girl, are you ever in the biggest fucking trouble? I mean, everyone here knows how I love to humiliate an' hurt slaves, an' I've never even met any of 'em before I lay into the bitches. But fuck... someone I actually *hate*. Wow, that's gotta be good.' The young blonde thrashed around under the birthday girl, struggling against her wrist and ankle cuffs, hollering into her gag. 'Rainbow Girl.'

'Yes, mistress?'

'I don't think we're gonna have much luck humiliating little Miss Moyse here until we teach her how to behave, do you?'

'No, mistress.' Rainbow Girl kept her head respectfully bowed, but there was no hint in her voice that she resented the submissive pose. In fact she seemed delighted that her mistress had asked her opinion. 'I think she'll need a ton of training before she's any good to you, mistress.'

'Think you can handle it?'

'Yes, mistress, I can do it for you.'

'Okay, you can have some fun with her while I'm at the gym. I want Jenny here to be occupied pretty much twenty-four-seven, so I'm gonna leave that task up to you, Rainbow Girl. I'll give you some extra privileges to make sure she's treated right.' Amber winked at the struggling blonde, though she knew her victim had no idea what was actually in store for her. The blonde bitch was a very special birthday treat and the first time was always the best, so Amber planned on taking her time, subjecting her victim to acts of degrading humiliation at a leisurely pace. It wasn't as if Jenny Moyse was going anywhere. 'Start by warming her ass, like we did with that little Brazilian slut, Elzira.' The blonde had gone quiet and seemed to be listening to her abductor's conversation, and Amber rubbed the young woman's nipples between her fingers. 'Elzira,' the redhead repeated, 'she was fun, huh, Rainbow Girl?'

'Yes, mistress, you trained her till she was crying like a baby.'

'You see, Jenny, a lot of women don't like to let the sluts have names, they think it makes it worse for 'em, y'know, like they're just stuff. But I always make 'em tell me their names. So much easier to tease someone when you know their name, right? I mean, you did it all the time in the shelter, an' I bet you did it at school, too. But I know your name, don't I, Jenny Butt-Fuck Moyse, an' I bet you remember what I did to you last time.' Amber wriggled her little tush on the blonde's stomach, trying to get a reaction from the young woman who had gone suddenly still and quiet.

'Well, things are gonna be different now. I'm not interested in *that* end anymore. I'm going to let Rainbow Girl have those bits. Nope, I want the other end.' The redhead gazed into the blue eyes and saw no response. 'Shit, you're a stupid bitch. Duh, the end with the tongue, loser.'

That got a reaction. The blonde arched off the floor trying to throw her rider and shouting into her gag, but Amber just clung onto the girl's tits and laughed at her pathetic attempts to get free. 'So now you have a new name,' she said to the bucking blonde, 'Miss Jenny Butt Licker Moyse. Got a ring to it, don't you think?' The blonde started to sob, thrashing her head from side to side in an exaggerated *no*, but Amber just laughed and turned to her kneeling assistant. 'You can play with Jenny whenever I don't need her, Rainbow Girl. You'll be her keeper, and I guess she might as well sleep on the floor in your room. I'm going to the gym for a couple of hours, then I'm having lunch with Dak. Oh, and teach her the rules while you're at it.'

'Yes, mistress.' Shelly smiled to herself. The mistress really liked her now, and she'd like her even more if she treated the slave with total contempt. The young woman had to be evil, why else would the mistress have had her captured? Why would she dislike her so much? The door slammed as Shelly's teenage mistress left for her workout, while her assistant hummed happily to herself as she rummaged in the closet looking for the thin cane.

Shelly dragged the blonde across the carpet and into the small room beside the closet. It was tiny and had nothing in it but a single bed, but it was hers; mistress had given it to her. Shelly shoved the bound slave forward so she fell to the floor on her knees, torso flopping limply onto the bed, then she locked her wrist and ankle cuffs to the base rail. Jenny Moyse's naked torso now lay facedown on her keeper's bed, arms splayed to the sides. She began to struggle again but Shelly just ignored her, still humming as she clamped the slave's restraints in place and removed her gag.

Jenny Moyse began to whimper and complain, begging Shelly to let her go, but the slave's keeper just smiled then brought the cane down sharply across the blonde's exposed buttocks. Jenny Moyse squealed like a smacked puppy, which only served to make the girl disciplining her laugh as she stepped forward and landed another blow close to the first. Shelly moved around the base of her small bed raining blows down upon the reddening butt cheeks, ignoring the blonde's frantic pleas and grinning to herself in a smugly superior way. Only when the blonde fell silent, finally figuring out that her whining and pathetic begging was simply prolonging the torture, did Shelly lower the cane.

'Finally,' the mistress's assistant said, mimicking the arrogant tone she'd heard her own superiors use. 'Well, it's probably okay that you're a little stupid, the rules really aren't that complicated. First thing you have to remember is that everyone is going to use you anyway they want, and you'll have to perform any disgusting, degrading task they think up, and it won't matter a fuck what you think. So complaining will just earn you punishment, not reprieve. Oh...' Shelly suddenly lashed out with the cane, thrashing the blonde's already red ass, 'and sometimes they might just want to punish you for the fun of it,' the slave's keeper added.

Shelly climbed onto her single bed and pulled up her flimsy silk dress, sliding down until Jenny Moyse's chin rested on her shaven pubic mound. Shelly looked down at the blue eyes peering over her flat belly; the blonde was now in the position she herself enjoyed with her mistress most evenings, but instead of the intense sense of affection and pleasure that would threaten to overcome her when she was pleasuring her young mistress, the blonde began to sob, tears dripping onto Shelly's pussy. The slave's keeper sighed, shaking her head in a condescending way.

'All you have to remember is, firstly, I take care of the mistress's pussy, and you take care of mine. Secondly, you take care of the mistress's ass, feet and… well… pretty much anything she wants, really.' Shelly giggled. 'It's going to be real fun finding out what she's gonna make you do. She really doesn't like you, you know. Anyway, for the minute you're mine, so…' she raised her pelvis off the bed, sliding Jenny Moyse's face between her soft thighs till the slave's mouth rested against the opening to her moist vagina and the blonde's nose gently brushed her clitoris, 'lick me.'

Nothing happened, Jenny Moyse lay with her face buried in Shelly's pussy, mouth tightly closed, bright-blue eyes staring wide and terrified over the other's mound. Shelly picked up the cane and sat upright, squashing Jenny Moyse's face between her legs, the blonde crying and slobbering into her keeper's wet cunt as she struggled to draw air past the soft folds of flesh. Shelly brought the cane down upon the blonde's abused butt, lashing her with six rapid stinging blows. Jenny Moyse cried out as the cane kissed her ass once again, but with her face jammed so tightly in the woman's sopping vagina all that came from her was a squelchy noise as she spluttered. Shelly found the whole thing hysterical as she instructed the blonde to get her tongue in there, and Jenny tentatively licked the fleshy wetness, leaving her tormentor less than impressed. Shelly leaned further forward, and grabbing her own ankles she held the position, watching the blonde pull frantically against her bonds as she suddenly realized how difficult it was to breathe in this position, every lungful of sweet air being drawn via the other female's genitals, tasting the sticky juices that flowed into her mouth with it.

Shelly let go of her ankles and flopped back on the bed. 'Look, you'd better get your tongue deep in my cunt and suck and lick at it like it was the sweetest thing you'd ever tasted in your whole life, or I'll quit wasting my time and do something useful, like paint my toenails.' Shelly looked down at the gasping face between her thighs. Jenny Moyse's mouth hung open, as if she were afraid to close it and accept the sticky sex juice that coated her tongue and lips. 'And your face is staying exactly where it is while I paint every one of my pretty little toes. Ooh...' the slave's keeper rolled her eyes, 'and it takes me forever to do.' She winked at the blue eyes. 'Hope you're getting this, blondie.'

Apparently blondie did, for Jenny Moyse's tongue stiffened visibly, her keeper seeing this pushing her pelvis down onto the trapped face, accepting the tongue into her body like an overdue guest.

Since she'd been abducted Jenny's mind had been busy telling her this was a nightmare, that she would wake up back in her apartment, or at the very least the hotel in Jamaica. As she had gazed up into the terrifyingly familiar face of the redheaded slut, while it grinned down at her, she tried very, very hard to wake up. Then something in her brain clicked and she fought back to reality. If she was going to escape the sudden horror that had descended over her for once bright world like a dark shroud, then she had to think – and think hard.

And she was still thinking, with increasing desperation, as she found herself tied naked to a bed with her face buried deep in another female's cunt, sucking and licking while the obviously demented bitch writhed and moaned in pleasure. The thighs suddenly clamped her head tighter and she felt the female's body judder as she struggled to free her head from its slippery prison. She tried to lift her head, willing to break her own neck to escape, then from somewhere buried deep in her brain a survival function clicked in, doing a reversal of policy a politician would be proud of, so she lay there, telling herself it was all just a nightmare after all.

Mistress had freed Shelly, freed her from that unspeakable dungeon, but what mistress didn't know was that she had also freed her from a life of sexual abstinence. Shelly had never been able to accept her problem, she never spoke of it, not even to her closest friends, and only once did she get up the courage to visit a doctor. The doctor politely told the shy, embarrassed student that it was all perfectly normal, her G-spot was considerably larger and more sensitive than average, and thus more easily stimulated than in most women. The doctor also seemed unconcerned when Shelly sheepishly told her that that whenever she masturbated to an orgasm it was just like being seven again, when she had her other problem, the hot wet flood, pouring from between her legs to soak her panties, her jimmy-jams and the sheets. When she had an orgasm it was like wetting the bed. And just like when she was seven, she would leap from the covers staring in horror at the rapidly spreading stain as it soaked into the cotton sheets, like a diagram of a river delta she'd seen in a book at school – except this wasn't pee. The doctor reassuringly told her it was a harmless condition, that she was even *lucky*, that some women spent years trying to have a G-spot orgasm. Shelly didn't feel lucky, she could never let another soul be there when it happened, so she went to bed every night lying on a thick towel, never had a boyfriend, and became a compulsive masturbator. But now, well, now everything was different. The deliciously probing tongue and soft lips between her thighs didn't belong to a person, not really, just a big sex toy, one she could play with whenever she wanted. Shelly was no more ashamed that the toy was getting some very close up experience of her condition than she had been about her vibrator collection back home. Besides, her new toy could no more speak about it than her favorite purple dildo could.

Jenny's mind reeled back from the horror of what was happening to her. For a moment she thought the horrid slut had pissed in her mouth, but the fluid that poured from the sex her mouth was forcibly closed around wasn't pee, it was coming from the slut's vagina for one, and all women knew where their pee came from, even if guys usually got confused.

Shelly felt the warm liquid trickling from her pussy hole. The blonde was gulping like mad, her tongue, still buried deep in her cunt, was acting like a fleshy little aqueduct, guiding the cum directly into its owner's mouth. Only the tiniest trickle seeped from Jenny's lower lip, a little rivulet slowly moistening Shelly's anus. Shelly decided she would have Jenny lick that clean after. Mistress wouldn't mind, after all, mistress hated a job half done. She would want her assistant to make the bitch do it; she hated her.

As the terrific buzz of the first orgasm anyone but herself had ever given her dissolved into a pleasurable throb in her groin, Shelly dug her elbows into the bed and pulled back slightly from her toy's mouth, but as the tongue slid out of the sopping hole it lay in the sensation unexpectedly triggered a second orgasm in her. Shelly was as surprised as her new masturbation aid was about to be and a convulsion juddered through her pelvis and thighs. Reflexively she clamped down on Jenny's head once more, slipping her feet under the slave's chains, using them as leverage to pull herself even more firmly onto the squirming face, clamping her pussy to the shocked mouth. She reconnected the drainage channel just in time, for a second flood burst from inside her into Jenny's mouth. Shelly knew she had the blonde clamped to her cunt even tighter than last time. It was a fit the engineers at NASA would have been proud of; Jenny's mouth and her keeper's pussy sealed so tightly, the two females resembling some strange elongated beast from a bad sci-fi flick.

Shelly could feel Jenny swallowing desperately, gulping, then as the orgasm evaporated like a spent force she released her foothold, allowing the slave's face to slide slickly back from the genitals that had trapped it. Jenny gasped for air, craning her neck, filling her lungs.

After resting for about ten minutes Shelly pulled away from the face that had given her so much pleasure. She knelt on the bed before the breathless slave and grabbed her ponytail, lifting the limp, unresisting head. 'Cool,' she said, smiling broadly as she examined the dry sheets, then she jumped off the bed, pulling down her flimsy silk gown. As she made her way to the suite's internal phone she made up her mind to use one of the privileges the mistress had lovingly bestowed upon her.

Shelly could feel the woman on the other end of the phone smiling as the quasi-servant explained what she wanted to know. For the second time in her life she found herself explaining her condition to a doctor, but this time she felt no shame, and when the Cruza's chief medical officer actually called it a gift, she felt positively elated.

'You see,' the doctor began, a little patronizingly, 'vaginal fluids are mostly water, but there are other components, none of which are harmful, but with your gift, well… the body is forced to produce large quantities at short order, so the percentage of water goes up. No worse than living on soda.'

Shelly replaced the receiver, all smiles, and skipped back

into her little room. She lifted Jenny's limp head off the bed again and looked into the bewildered blue eyes. 'The doctor says you'll be fine,' she told the female. 'She said if all you ever got to drink was my cum you'd be perfectly okay, so it's a done deal. Mistress says I am in charge of feeding, watering and keeping you clean, so from now on you'll drink nothing but my cum.' Shelly hummed contentedly to herself as she unclipped Jenny from the bed, preparing her for cleaning, and as she lashed the blonde's hands behind her back she remembered what else the doctor had told her and made a mental note to drink plenty of water; she didn't want to dehydrate herself. She dragged the blonde upright and marched her to the bathroom, annexed off her own little room.

'Guess I just have to figure out something fun to feed you now, huh?' Shelly giggled as Jenny began whimpering and sobbing again.

It was mid-afternoon when Amber got back to her room, her gray sweat-pants and white T-shirt still damp with sweat. Her workout had been hours ago but Dak had taken the birthday girl for lunch on the broad patio outside the *El Sol de la Mañana*, and although the colorful parasols kept the fierce sun off them the air was hot and dry, and even the discretely placed fans seemed unable to stir it. But the birthday girl didn't want to cool off; she had plans for an afternoon of entertainment, so she instructed a surprised servant to turn off the air coolers around her. While Amber chatted with the lieutenant the air drifted lazily over her, superheated by the reflected sunlight bouncing off the lemon-yellow bricks that made up the patio floor. It felt a little like when her mom would open the oven door when she was baking cookies, releasing a momentary blast of fiery dragon breath.

The birthday girl's toned body produced more sweat, and she felt it trickle in rivulets from under her arms and down her spine, collecting between her legs. She reached over and poured herself another glass of fresh lemonade, downing it in three or four gulps. She was still wearing her athletic shoes with the pink trim, and her feet felt like they were baking in the oven with mom's cookies. Her white ankle socks were soaked and she wriggled her toes in the dampness, like she did when she was a little girl after she'd jumped in the wading pool with her sneakers on. She smiled, recalling how she'd have to run like fuck when her daddy saw her and came roaring out of the trailer like a crazed animal.

When the pleasant lunch ended the birthday girl took her sweat-soaked body back to her room, smiling to herself as she contemplated having some fun before a nice long soak in the tub.

Rainbow Girl had done a good clean up job on Jenny. Her eyes were red and puffy, but she'd been washed and smelled nice, her blonde hair had even been brushed through and pulled back into the neat ponytail all Cruza slaves wore. Rainbow Girl had even added a black ribbon to the ponytail, a nice touch, Amber concluded. The redhead sat on the bed with Jenny Moyse kneeling before her, imagining what it must be like to be knelt there like that, naked, hands and feet tied, not daring to look up into the eyes of the brat you used to hate, who now owned you.

'Jenny, Jenny, Jenny,' Amber said in a singsong voice, 'betcha don't know how much I love this, do you?' The redhead laughed. 'Probably about as much as you hate it, huh? Anyway, I went to a ton of fucking trouble for you.' The teenager plucked at her damp T-shirt, letting it fall limply back to her breasts. 'I've had to sit in this gross stuff for hours, just for you. And it really is all for you, Jenny Moyse. I'm not going to let anyone else have a single drop, not even Rainbow Girl. Every tiny, teeny, itsy-bitsy little weenie drop is just for you. How cool is that?'

Jenny had been crying since Amber sat down, quietly, but the birthday girl could see the tears running down her cheeks, being diverted to the side of her face by the gag. The redhead motioned to Rainbow Girl and the young woman came and knelt behind the blonde, unclipping the gag and pulling it out of the slave's mouth, wiping the drool from it with a pink towel. She then ran the towel around the slave's face, removing the tears like a mother with her messy infant.

'Well...' said Amber, placing her athletic shoe on the slave's right shoulder, 'where do we start?' The teenager winked at Shelly, who smiled back coyly at her mistress, then the mistress's assistant reached forward and untied the teenager's athletic shoe, holding the heel while Amber slid her damp foot out. The white sock looked like a wet rag and Shelly carefully removed it, then took hold of her mistress's pretty little foot and held it lovingly in the palm of her left hand, while with her right she grasped the slave's jaw, pulling down firmly, opening the young woman's mouth. Jenny was no rocket scientist; she didn't need to be to figure out what was happening, but the session with the cane had done its work well and she sat perfectly still as the assistant moved her mistresses foot closer to the waiting mouth. Shelly knew the young woman would be screaming if she dared, but she didn't, she had to sit in compliant silence while the degrading ritual continued. The toes slid into the gaping mouth before them and the assistant stopped pulling on the jaw. She pushed upward, closing the mouth around the foot. Soft lips closed on mistress's instep and sole and Shelly leaned forward, placing her mouth next to the slave's ear.

'Suck,' she said simply, then when nothing happened for a second she added, 'or do you want to come and play with me and my little cane again?' Shelly felt the blonde's jaw move and saw her cheeks pull in. 'Now use your tongue.' The jaw, which Shelly still held gently, began to move from side to side as the young woman played her tongue over the goddesses foot, being granted the gift of her sweat.

Amber pulled over a large silk beanbag and leant contentedly back into it, wriggling her toes in Jenny Moyse's mouth, feeling the bitch slurping at them, then the blonde's soft tongue wriggled its way between her tootsies, knowing her assistant must have instructed the slave to do it. Then Rainbow Girl grabbed her mistress's heel with her left hand, clutching the slave's ponytail in her right, and began to fuck Jenny Moyse's mouth with the foot, siding it in and out of the sucking, tonguing hole like it was cunt, saliva instead of cum soaking the wriggling toes. Amber moaned in delight, winking at Rainbow Girl. The relationship was working out very well indeed... unless you were Jenny Moyse, of course.

Rainbow Girl had taken over an hour to complete the well thought out ritual, much to her mistress's pleasure, but then there were two feet to contend with. Amber examined her freshly sucked and licked left foot, now clean and fresh and free from its oven-like prison. She wriggled her toes in the cool breeze from the air-conditioner, and thought about shoving them back in the bitch's mouth; as much as this was supposed to be about humiliating the young woman, having your toes sucked was actually very enjoyable in its own right. The teenager ticked off a mental note to make this part of her daily routine from now on.

Jenny had slipped into a state of shock, and kept smacking her lips like a kid who'd just finished a tasty lollypop. She could probably still taste Amber's feet, and her mind was struggling to come to terms with what had just happened. The birthday girl was about to carefully reiterate to the dazed blonde her place in the hierarchy of the bedroom suite when she realized the time. She had to get ready.

'Rainbow Girl, please explain to the new member of our little family what her place and duties will be, please,' she said. 'Just hit the bitch with it. I don't want you wasting your time being gentle.' Amber skipped happily off to the bathroom. 'Oh…' the teenager peered round the doorframe, 'and I'll only be a few minutes taking care of, um, business, so perhaps you'd better start now.'

'Okay,' Rainbow Girl said, grinning down at the kneeling blonde. 'I've already told you it all, anyhow, but you seem a little stupid so perhaps there's no harm in going over things again. Mistress is the most important thing in the whole world, got that? The whole world. You have to live in this suite, and in my bedroom when she's not playing with you, and you don't get to go out like I do. You stay in your restraints, and mistress wants you naked all the time.'

Jenny Moyse just stared blankly at the floor, and Shelly had to repeat several times that the mistress now owned the young blonde woman totally, that there was no set time to serve, no parole, no reprieve, this would never end, not even if the mistress grew bored with her, she would just be passed on to someone else. The blue eyes blinked as her phased brain slowly absorbed the mind-shattering concept, and when she finally got it the blue eyes opened wide, blinking back tears.

'You're gonna have to get sharper than this,' Shelly sighed in an exasperated tone. 'Now like I told you, I get to take care of mistress's pussy, because that's important, you get to take care of her ass. And you better do a good job of it too, cos my little cane and me will be keeping tabs on you.'

Amber knelt on the bed, head on her silk pillow, ass stuck up in the air. She pulled up her robe exposing her tanned buttocks, and then she spread her legs slightly, opening the valley a little. Rainbow Girl clambered up the large bed to her mistress, dragging Jenny Moyse by her collar and leash. The birthday girl looked round and saw her assistant taking a firm hold of the whimpering blonde's ponytail, then she laid her head back on the pillow. On a tripod beside the bed the red light on the video camera winked on and off. This was something she wanted a record of, like an important family event.

The hand on the back of Jenny's head pushed her towards the buttocks that loomed before her, and she descended into the crevice. The buttocks engulfed her face like a soft pillow. The other strange female in her nightmare pressed on her head, pushing her further until she was struggling to breathe and her lips touched the trailer-slut's anus. Then Jenny felt something cold and hard close on her clitoris, something metallic... pliers perhaps. The implement squeezed gently, so Jenny thought of nice things, pretty things, like flowers and golden beaches and butterflies, and then she stuck out her tongue and pushed it into the redheaded brat's ass, and began to lick.

Part Two – Coming of Age

Gray Steel Under Dark Skies

Amber wore black fatigues, multi-pocketed with Velcro straps at the ankle, calf and thigh, while her long black coat hid a lightweight armor vest and two Browning rapid fire pistols, holstered just behind each hip. A lazy drizzle drifted in from the sea, covering the dockside in a clinging, heavy mist, but inside the cargo ship it just pushed the humidity uncomfortably high.

Amber walked casually behind their informally dressed Russian host, the short, dark-haired woman dressed in jeans and T-shirt, her large breasts looking like they were struggling to break free from their white cotton prison. Amber envied the woman as they pushed on through the dank air inside the ship, but she was on Russian mafia turf now, so the vest and pistols seemed the minimum acceptable precaution. Dakota walked a few paces behind, similarly clothed, while McKenna and a veritable private army waited on the quayside. If the two Cruza females didn't reappear unharmed in one hour the stinking hunk of rusting steel would be stormed and then sent to the harbor bottom. McKenna had brought enough plastic explosive to sink a fleet.

Amber enjoyed her nominal role as a senior player in the organization, even when she was little more than a kid playing with the grown-ups, but since she'd turned twenty-one things had been a little different, as different in many ways as the girl herself. No longer just a pretty red-haired teenager with a sadistic streak, the lucky genes hadn't let her down, producing a stunningly beautiful young woman with a razor-sharp mind and reflexes to match. Nor had time tamed her cruel streak, merely accentuating it, mixing the sadistic, occasionally violent urges with a growing sophistication, producing a lethal combination that made her the most powerful and popular women in the San Diego Cruza next to Rebecca, and though she was both loathed and feared by those outside the organization, she was also grudgingly respected.

Nina stopped by a large metal door with the familiar wheel mechanism, perfectly normal for a cargo ship, except for the iron bar that prevented the wheel from being turned from the inside. Nina slid the bar loose, spun the wheel, and with a little effort pulled open the hatch. The smell of sweat and piss belched from the opening and Amber wrinkled her nose, but was careful not to overreact. The Ice Angel, as she had affectionately come to be known, stepped over the raised base of the hatch following Nina inside, while Dakota remained outside, fully alert.

Around twenty young Eastern European females were arranged around the walls of the otherwise empty room. The metal chamber reminded Amber of a giant pressure cooker, the pungent air made worse by the heat. The females were lying on the hard metal floor, wrists and ankles shackled in crude chains, looking miserably wretched and filthy. Amber pulled on a surgical glove, and then grabbed the nearest girl by her lank hair, lifting the tearstained face for a moment before letting it fall limply back. She was busy taking stock of the sorry looking cargo, noting that under the grime the girls were fairly high-grade – pretty and slim with fair skin, a number even blonde – when a previously unnoticed ceiling hatch suddenly grated open and three men dropped through, whereupon the Ice Angel snatched both pistols in one fluid move, thrusting one against the lead man's head and waving the other two back with the second.

'Whoa.' The lead man raised his hands, waving to his

henchmen who were moving slowly to their belts. The guy going head-to-head with the 9mm knew his goons had no chance of retrieving their weapons before he lost a piece of his skull.

'You get within one inch of those pistol grips, macho boys, and the first shot will leave you picking his brains out of your eyes, while the next dozen will tear holes in your chests we can put that fucking hatch in.' Amber smiled her best Ice Angel smile, never taking her eyes off the man in front of her. 'Sure hope you understand English, or things are going to get messy around here in about three seconds.'

'They understand, no problems lady, everything is cool, right?' The man with Amber's pistol pressed to his forehead gave a gentle flick of the wrists and the other two stood down, bringing their arms up and folding them across their chests. 'Nice pistol,' he added, looking at the female holding it. 'Pretty, like you.'

'Know what the most powerful handgun in the world is, dumb-fuck?' Amber asked, and the man stared blankly as her frustrated sigh filled the silence. 'Whichever one happens to be pointing at you.' The Ice Angel twisted the barrel against the sweaty forehead a couple of times before she lowered it. 'Which part of "no fucking surprises" didn't you understand, exactly?' She saw the men's eyes look past her and knew Dakota had moved closer to the hatch. The fact that procedure meant she wouldn't enter the room probably didn't make the P90 look any less threatening. Nina, silent until now, stepped in to calm things.

'This is Vladimir, head of… security… on this ship,' the Russian woman explained. 'He didn't mean to break with our agreement, he was just, well, enthusiastic to greet our American guests.'

'Consider us introduced, now get out,' Amber motioned to the door, past her backup with the serious firepower.

Vladimir muttered to the others in Russian, but he left anyway, slipping arrogantly past the business end of the P90 to swagger away deeper into the ship. 'What did he just say?' Amber stared directly at their guide, and noticed the small woman swallow anxiously.

'Nothing, he's just being Vladimir.' She attempted a smile. 'Bit of a maverick, likes to think he's more important than he is, it's best to just ignore him.'

The redhead pulled a slick two-way digital radio from her pocket, signal boosted to cope with the metal sauna they'd entered. She'd left it switched on in her pocket. 'Mac?'

'Here.'

'What did he just say?' she asked.

McKenna turned to the translator beside her in the truck. 'Basically that you'd never get off the ship alive, some stuff about no bitch talks to him like that, and some other stuff we couldn't quite get.'

'Okay, hold position, we can handle this.' Amber nodded at Dakota, who flipped up the safety on the P90 and slipped it into the holder in the small of her back. She then calmly removed her faithful Glock and screwed in a long black silencer. Nina stared openmouthed as the woman moved stealthily along the gangway in the direction Vladimir had taken. Nina went to speak but Amber looked at her and held a finger to her lips, gesturing for the small Russian to remain quiet.

'Well,' said the Ice Angel, 'I suggest we continue with the inventory check.'

They checked on several similar chambers to the first. The girls were in poor condition, but cleaned up would be an unusual infusion of around two hundred fair-skinned additions to the stable. A host of interesting ideas could be built around a catch like this. The male crewmembers had been told to keep clear of deck six, so Amber, not realizing there were female crew on Russian ships, reacted when she saw movement in the corridor ahead, a pistol slipping reflexively into her right hand. A large muscular woman, her dark hair cut short, stood smoking a cigarette a short distance away, leaning against a bulkhead.

'Don't you know that's bad for you?' Amber lowered the gun a little.

'Not as bad as that,' the woman gestured to the pistol in the redhead's hand. 'You come to shoot me? If so, let me finish this first, it's my last one.'

Amber smiled and holstered the pistol. 'It's okay…'

'Olga.'

Amber nodded. 'It's okay, Olga, women have permission to be on this deck.'

'So you're the lady come to take our toy away, huh?'

'Perhaps. What toy would that be?' Amber felt herself relax; she liked the woman's attitude, though the sailor was a little dykey for the redhead's tastes. Olga gestured to the cabin door she was leaning next to. Inside were four bunks, two against each bulkhead, and a table in the center. Lying naked on the table, wrists and ankles tied to each corner, was a small-framed fair-skinned woman. The cabin was a mess, dirty clothes on the floor, and the whole place stank of sweat and unwashed pussy. The girl looked like the late night dregs of a wild poker game; there were playing cards on her belly, a couple of dice, and between her legs an assorted jumble of makeshift sex toys.

'They let us have one,' explained Olga, 'for the voyage, one of the older ones. The men get one too. Lucky for our bitch there are only four women on the ship, but then, as there is little to do but play with her, well…' she shrugged, 'perhaps not so lucky.'

Just then Olga's companions came off duty, wandering into the cabin, releasing the Velcro on their coveralls, stripping down to their gray sports underwear. Olga offered her colleagues a quick explanation in Russian, while the women nodded at Amber in turn. They all looked strong, one was tall like Olga, the other two shorter, one stocky, one wiry. 'We were going to have our last goodbye playtime before you took her,' the Russian sailor said, 'but I guess we were a little too late.'

'Maybe not,' Amber said, reaching for her radio. 'Mac?'

'Online.'

'State Girl checked in?'

'Yes, mission accomplished. She's waiting near the main gangway.'

'Okay, I want you to extend my arrival time by one hour.' The redhead replaced the radio in her coat pocket. 'Hope that's long enough for a goodbye, girls.'

The four Russians stripped naked and untied the woman from the table, two strong hands pulling the slender, mousy-blonde's arms behind her back and securing them. Olga and one of the shorter sailors began strap homemade leather harnesses to their waists, the thick girth of a rigid shaft protruding from the triangular section that fitted between their legs.

Olga patted the shaft she was wearing. 'Police batons, we cut off the handle and attached to the belts. Clever, huh?'

'Very,' Amber admitted, genuinely impressed at the improvisation.

One of the dykes grabbed a small breast in each calloused hand and lifted the woman off the table, her slender frame made to look even more pitiful by the size of her playmates. The others grabbed her legs and they stood there with their toy, holding her entire body in the air as if she were no more than an inflatable doll. Olga opened a tub of grease and smeared it along the shaft, her colleague doing likewise, then the big dyke positioned the remodeled baton at the entrance to the woman's ass and shoved it in.

Amber was impressed as toned muscles drove the black tube into the petite anus in one smooth motion, never pausing until it was buried to the hilt in the woman's body. She began to whimper and moan, mumbling in Russian, at which point the captor holding her breasts lay her head on a chair and promptly sat on it, cutting back the sound to a muffled sob.

They twisted her sideways, allowing the second dildo assassin to plunge into her vagina with equal determination. The two dykes worked the captive woman with remorseless determination, their timing perfect. As the stout shaft pulled out of her stretched anus, the one in her vagina was driven in hard so the leather base slapped against her pussy lips. The fourth woman straddled the slender waist and lowered her mouth to the small breasts, biting and chewing on the woman's nipples, then kneading them like dough in a baker's shop. The face-sitter brought her legs up, placing them on the edge of the seat, then she grabbed the arms of the chair and used her powerful biceps to drive herself down onto the mouth that, from Amber's viewpoint, appeared to be licking desperately at the dyke's ass, the sailor's thick black bush of pubic hair resting on the woman's chin.

After about ten minutes came a reshuffle of near military precision, and it was obvious this ritual had been played out on the hapless woman every long, boring night of the two-month voyage. All the dykes were hairy, which intrigued Amber as the fashion in the West had been for shaven pussies for years. As the new set of powerful buttocks swung over the quivering mouth Amber watched the dyke sailor wriggling as she located her asshole over the unwilling mouth, and a wave of pleasure wash over the dyke's dark features as the soft tongue finally penetrated and found its mark, sliding into the sailor's anus.

The Metalworker's Daughter

Everything seemed as chaotically noisy as always, but it was the words that were silent, the shouted insults and usual zoo-like babble at the Guadalajara Female Penitentiary were… different. Another of those strange secrets that visited the collective women occasionally had come, it stalked the hallways like a silent ghost, dampening the usual insatiable curiosity and love of gossip with the certain knowledge that to know this thing was to die from it.

Everyone inside the razor wire-topped walls knew that Rosario Hernández had stabbed and killed Maricruz. She took the opportunity while the two were walking single file along the narrow, strip-lit, bare brick hallway that led from the grubby, festering mold pit laughingly referred to as the shower block. Everyone knew, and no one cared. Maricruz had it coming; she'd been threatening Rosie for a while and something had to give. Nor would anyone shed tears; Maricruz was a viscous murderer, she'd killed her own kids along with almost everyone else in her sleazy little life she considered baggage. It was perhaps a little more mysterious why Rosie never got shoved through official channels; after all, she'd done for an inmate, and not a favored one at that. But no, she got shoved down a flight of steel stairs instead, while handcuffed, dieing from head injuries several hours later. Usually you only got that for attacking a guard, or an informer, but the dark secret didn't stop there. Somehow Maricruz was resurrected, living with the secrets like a ghost as the body in the morgue became Angelica Pérez… while Angelica Pérez herself was walked quietly out of the large gates to disappear into the hot, cicada filled night.

The blonde American drove Angelica to a small motel just outside Caliácan, told her to shower and clean up, and gave her a change of clothes and a new name. The blue passport with the gold eagle on the front declared that she was now Angelica Ramirez, and a United States citizen residing in Phoenix. The strange blonde looked at Angelica intensely, moving beyond the ex-prisoner's brown eyes into her soul.

'I need an artist, one who understands things like you do,' the American woman had told her.

Angelica just nodded and picked up the towel and clothes. 'I knew you would come one day,' she replied simply as she went to remove the filth of her confinement with a bar of lilac-colored soap.

Angelica's father had been a metalworker, but deep inside him had lived an artist, the artist that would come out to teach the eight-year-old Angelica how to make metal dance, twisting into fabulous shapes in the soft glow of the oil lamps. When she was twenty-one Angelica's father died, leaving her his tools and his gift. She moved to a place of her own and learned how to work with new metals, ones her father had not known of. Her favorite, titanium, had something unspeakably beautiful hidden in its flat gray tones.

One day her cousin, Aimara, had come to stay with her friend Erendira. The two nineteen-year-olds were making their way south along the coast looking for work, or a husband. Angelica made rice and beans and during the simple meal Aimara – tall, elegant Aimara – picked up a piece of Angelica's sculpture and, opening her blouse, pressed it against the soft golden skin of her belly. The girl giggled that it was so cool and smooth, but Angelica saw how the dull gray of the metal became alive against the girl's flesh, how the two were always meant to be one, and the artist saw the beauty of the angel's sign and knew what she had been born to do.

Angelica took the teenagers in their sleep, moving stealthily to the unconscious forms, gagging and binding them so quickly they had no time to cry out. Then she moved them to her workshop. Angelica placed the struggling Aimara on the workbench and removed her clothes, revealing the girl's wonderful body for the first time. Then she placed the naked and tied girl in a chair and watched as the moonlight reflected off the sheen of sweat that coated the struggling teenager, saw the stark outline of the chair, and received her second revelation.

Angelica worked hard, shaping the metal, making it smooth like never before, matching its crystalline curves with those of her living subjects. Slowly the frame of the chair took place, a thing of beauty. It took three weeks and the artist labored hard and long, suffering the annoying distractions of caring for the captive girls and telling distraught relatives that they had never arrived at her modest home. But now the chair frame was ready, its gray form crying out to be made one with the perfect bodies it had been designed to hold. It was a magical night, clear and cool and moonless, and by the light of the oil lamps she still used, Angelica laid Aimara's naked form onto the bare metal, laying her on her back, arched in wonderful symmetry as the molded chair accepted her. Angelica moved upwards from the girl's shapely ankles, buckling the leather straps that held her struggling form in place, fastening a strap across her belly, under her breasts, gently across her delicate throat, moving to the band that ran across her forehead, attaching her head to the flat plate. Erendira formed the back of the chair, her torso the main section, with her legs folded back on themselves at the knee, her head, bent forward, lay next to Aimara's, where the two pretty faces would form the seat.

Angelica marveled at her creation for some time before removing the girls' gags, stripping naked herself, and taking her place on the living throne. The artist stroked the smooth curves, loving how the metal seemed to flow as it followed the girls' forms and enjoying the way her own weight pressed her excited, sensitive genitals down onto those wonderful faces, the very seat of the throne.

It was how the police found her. She had been sitting on her beautiful chair for two days, feeling those young faces between her legs as she pondered the problem of how to care for the girls without removing them, when the law officers burst in. They took her beautiful creation and sent her to prison. The attorney told Angelica to say she was mad, which was of course ridiculous; she was an artist, and anyway, one day the angels would send for her so she could continue her work.

Now the angels had sent their messenger and Angelica could begin again. The artist towel-dried her hair, smiling to herself. She had no regrets, she knew why the angels had let her go to that place… after all, it was there that she solved her greatest problem.

Paying the Devil Her Dues

The Pacific spat itself into the heavy winds that carried the moisture to the land, laying the thickening drizzle across the stony-gray dockside in sheets. Amber paused at the base of the wide gangplank, noting the position of her vehicles and watching as the large removal trucks filed into the harbor. The first had already parked close to the ramp at the ships stern; the distant figures carried the cheap wooden crates with their precious living cargo down from the floating hulk like ants raiding a rival nest. Nestled between a large immobile rusting winch and a dull concrete storage bunker sat a dark car, motor gently idling. Amber pulled her long coat about her and walked towards it.

Shalyn smiled pleasantly as Amber climbed in the passenger seat and closed the door. The Shadow Stalker turned down the CD player, allowing Wagner's dark harmonies to blend into the soft rain that fell noiselessly onto the vehicle. Shalyn watched the cargo being unloaded.

'I didn't think Rebecca would go for it,' the assassin said as she lit a cigarette, opening the window an inch to blow the smoke out into the fine mist.

'It was a close call,' Amber acknowledged, loosening her coat and letting the car's air blow over her skin, 'but there were many considerations. The Russian cell is newly formed and the FBI was breathing down their necks, so what do we do? We leave them to sink and we have the biggest scandal in decades on our doorstep, or we risk working with amateur thugs.'

'Tough call.'

'Luckily it wasn't mine to make.'

'Not yet,' the assassin smiled, then placed the cigarette between her dark-pink lips and drew another lungful of smoke.

'Rebecca's still young; I don't want that weight on my shoulders just yet.' Amber looked at the assassin, who just shrugged. 'Rebecca wouldn't give them money, so we offered them a little start up opportunity. We clear the family currently running the northeast drug supply, they move in. Minimum entanglement for us.'

Shalyn thought for a moment. 'Krohonas family, Greek. How many to topple it?'

'Three. I'll take out the old man. We want you to handle the son and the old man's second, a guy called Pallas. The son's a jerk, typical playboy, never got hardened on the streets like his old man, but Pallas is dangerous. If he slips us he'll go to ground and become a problem.'

'So we do it all in one night?'

'Thursday. Gives you three days to prepare. You okay with that?'

'Sure,' the blonde assassin drew the last wisps of life from the cigarette held gently between her lips, which shifted into a cruelly amused smile, 'why not?'

XTC touched up her gothic make-up and adjusted the pendant that hung between her breasts bearing the letters of her snappy stage name in archaic black script. She smiled as Alexander Krohonas sauntered into the room. XTC felt no emotion; the slender young Greek was a regular customer, but only because he found the petite girl easier to hurt, playing out his macho fantasies on her tiny Asian frame. Basically he was an asshole. The strange blonde woman had paid her three months' wages for this one small favor; XTC dimly remembered lying on a table, drifting in and out of sleep as the dose of tranquilizers pleasantly numbed her brain. She lay on the table breathing heavily, her body limp. The woman had said it would be quite painless, well... for XTC anyway, but it was important she did not move. 'So why take unnecessary chances?' the blonde had said. XTC felt the gynecological spreaders slide into her vagina and she giggled a little because it felt nice. Then the woman released the spring, opening her up, and that felt strangely pleasant, too. XTC felt a little like Sleeping Beauty, hardly stirring as her sex was readied. The woman was careful to make her a full partner in the process, telling her how important it was that she knew what to do, but it hardly mattered to the sleepy girl; Alexander was a prick, he had it coming.

The blonde smeared surgical glue onto the flat side of the spiked strips, then carefully inserted them into the girl's gaping sex, sticking one either side. The woman had shown the dreamy Korean girl the strips with their needle sharp points and the plastic covers which formed a protective barrier over the deadly, poisoned metal teeth, angled sharply downwards so they posed no threat to the girl with the covers off, so long as she lay still enough. The plastic covers themselves were attached to a tough nylon thread, which dangled from XTC's vagina like a tampon string.

As usual XTC lay naked on the bed while Alexander undressed. As he turned his back to her to hang up his expensive Italian suit she pulled gently but firmly on the string, sliding the shallow strips of plastic from her vagina. A strange feeling came upon the girl; sessions with Alexander were always tinged with fear, each time was more violent than the last, but you didn't say no to Alexander. Now the Korean girl lay back on the bed, aware of the power she carried within her small frame, like a diamond-back rattler, ready to strike.

The leering Greek mounted her, grabbing her breasts with both hands, twisting them like he wanted to tear them from her chest, smiling at the pain that flickered in her eyes as he did. His erect penis was poised at the entrance to her vagina, then one hard thrust and the blood-engorged organ drove into her.

Almost immediately he yelled, leaping back from the girl, clambering from the bed to stand, staring in confusion at the flecks of blood on his dick. Anger and fear welled in his eyes as he moved to pounce on the slender girl like a furious wounded animal.

'You fucking whore-bitch!' He staggered, the look in his eyes changing. 'I'll… fuck you…' then he slumped heavily to the floor.

'Great last words, asshole,' the Korean giggled as she lay naked on the bed.

XTC lay quiet and still on the dingy, sweat-and-semen-stained mattress, Alexander's body in a lifeless crumpled heap on the floor. After a few minutes of silence Giorgio opened the door. The big fuck always waited just outside, listening. It was some kind of joke between the two that when XTC was too mauled up to be of interest to Alexander, the grinning giant would be thrown the leftovers. He used to look at her like a hungry dog and she could almost feel what was going through that thick skull and it would make her shudder. Now he just stared at the body on the floor, frozen by his own stupidity into inaction, then something else went through that thick skull, a slither of metal that wiped out all thoughts of what he would do to the slender Korean girl, taking a large part of his face with it. The blonde woman stood in the doorway and slowly removed the black silk hood she was wearing, allowing XTC to see her face.

Bad sign. Bad, bad sign. See face then they kills ya. The Korean whore knew enough to know that.

'Said you wouldn't hurt me. Did what you want… thought you was straight player like XTC.'

'Perhaps you're just too trusting, my dear,' said the

blonde, a smile breaking across her attractive face like dawn cutting down a very dark night. 'Or perhaps you're just a lot smarter than you let on.'

'Me plenty smart, big fucking smart, you know that. Why else you trust XTC?'

'I'm not going to hurt you, but then you already guessed that. Like I said, smart. You're coming to work for me.' Shalyn nudged the bodyguard's lifeless form with her boot. 'Sorry, but I guess I'm just not used to asking.'

'That okay, lady, XTC not used to being asked.' The Korean girl spread her legs wider. 'So we get this snake teeth outa my cunt now, huh?'

Spiders in the World Wide Web

The disjointed dream that had begun with the overweight Greek drug baron trying to tell his long-dead mother that he couldn't help papa with the boat because he had his own boat now, had leapt to his private yacht, where he and Alexander were hauling in bulging nets. The catch of the day was premium grade cocaine and not sardines, but Alexander and he were pulling the bags out and gutting them just like they were fish, choking white powder clouding over them. Then he was in Paris with Idalia, his girlfriend, the one his wife didn't know about, and she had her sister there, but this time instead of looking at Krohonas like he was dog excrement she was interested, so the three of them slipped into the warm bubbling hot tub and Idalia's sister reached out to…

The internal phone reached into Mr Krohonas's subconscious, where he was about get Idalia's sister's pouty lips around his dick, and yanked him back to reality with all the subtlety of a slap in the face. There was a moment of disorientation and a little annoyance, when the unlikeness of anyone paging him at this hour struck him; it had to be urgent. Krohonas picked up the phone.

'Mr Krohonas, it's me, Pallas.' The man sounded hesitant and Krohonas could just smell the bad news on the breeze, just like the fish on papa's boat before it docked. 'We have a big fucking problem, and I mean big, but I don't want you havin' no heart attack or nuthin'. Our fuckin' A team is on the way, and I got those tech guys comin', and Gabby.'

'What the flying fuck is going on, Pallas? What the

fuck we need the tech-nerds for? And Gabby? She's a detective, Pallas, she detects things.' Krohonas had thrown off the covers and was dressing as he spoke, hopping on one leg as he tried to pull his pants on, breaking off to say soothing things to his stirring wife: *it's nothing, go back to sleep, just a little accident with one of the cars, Pallas is just overreacting*. Problem was, Pallas never overreacted. The man was only capable of just enough emotion to stay the sane side of psychopath.

'Meet me in the tech room.' Mr Krohonas gently replaced the handset in the cradle.

The tech room was an annexed office, inland from the villa, hidden from the house's broad ocean-facing sundecks by a line of waving palms and ground spreading aloe vera. Mr Krohonas kept a team of hackers, and some other tech types, mostly for listening in on the police and the competition. Krohonas was calm when he walked through the door, panic was like a circle, you moved from calm towards losing control, but if you were pushed far enough, well... you found yourself back at calm again. Gabby sat by herself, looking acutely aware that she'd given her make-up far less attention than she would have liked. His two most senior tech guys were also in the room, the heavies having been told to wait outside. Krohonas had passed them, all tooled up and twitchy, like they got when they knew something big was going down.

'Go.' Krohonas slumped into a seat pointing at Pallas. Either his number two and lifelong friend had gone over the edge or something had got really fucked up.

'Okay,' Pallas surveyed the other three team members with a menacing glare, 'you all know you don't get dragged out of bed in the middle of the night just to piss-ass around.' The short, middle-aged man with the receding hair and expanding paunch pulled out an Uzi and pointed it at the tech guys and Gabby in turn. They all flinched, color draining from their faces.

For one brief second Krohonas's heart skipped a beat; maybe the old fucker had flipped.

But Pallas gave no sign of being anything other than deadly earnest. 'If any of you ever repeat anything you see or hear tonight I will personally ensure that you are silenced. I won't be listening to any explanations – you talk, you die. Everyone clear on that?' Silent nods. 'Good. Mr Krohonas… they got Candiss.'

'What?' Krohonas jumped up from his chair. 'Who's fucking got her? Where's Sly?' The girl's bodyguard was as tough a son-of-a-bitch as you were ever likely to meet, and professional too, ex-military, not one of them street punks. Where Candiss went he went. Simple.

'Dead. Found him with the car. Look, Mr Krohonas, that's why we're all down here, because we ain't got it figured out yet. Sly was stabbed in the fucking heart. Now you know as well as me, Mr K, we don't know no one who could get close enough to Sly to use a blade. It don't make sense. Then we finds a CD taped to his chest, not the music kind, a computer thing. Mr Vaughn here tells me it's a fucking web address or some Internet crap. I'm telling you, Mr Krohonas, this is weirder than shit.'

'Put it on.' Krohonas sat stone-faced. Someone had his twenty-two-year-old niece, and that someone was either very smart or just lucky. Either way they would be dead by morning. Mr Vaughn, the bleary-eyed tech guy, went to say something, but Krohonas cut him short. 'I said… put… it… on….'

Mr Vaughn's mouth shut and he switched on the large computer screen.

Amber grabbed the Greek girl's jaw and turned the olive-skinned face toward her.

'It's a party, honey, that's all. Except that, one, you get to stay with us when it's over, and two, a few people are going to be watching.' The Greek girl was strapped naked to a crude wooden table with her feet in stirrups. The table and surrounding area bristled with web cams, all of which were pointed at the helpless bitch, showing her private bits and pieces in fully digitized, enhanced color, high-bandwidth glory.

Hidden from the main stage, and the camera's view, two Cruza technicians ran the whole video feed through a thirty second editing delay before pumping it straight to the web address. At the moment several thousand anonymous individuals who'd drifted onto the site as they randomly surfed were watching the proceedings.

As far as the Ice Angel was concerned they were very welcome to the party. The tech people had allowed unrestricted access for authenticity, but all that mattered to Amber was that the girl's uncle was watching.

The Ice Angel watched on the big screen as the cameras panned in on Mayu and Nyoko's dazzling white smiles beneath the cat-woman masks as they busied themselves shaving the Greek slut's snatch. When the two masked girls had finished they showed off their handiwork to the cameras, one of several positioned between the Greek girl's legs, zoomed in for ultra close-up as Mayu and Nyoko spread her vagina obscenely wide. Mayu grabbed a handheld camera and almost shoved it in the pink hole, and the net audience numbers began to grow as they tuned in to a gynecologists eye view of a young Greek pussy. Amber spoke freely into the mikes, everything fed through a sampler where voice patterns were changed.

'Hi boys and girls, hope you're enjoying the view. But stay with it because we're going to be seeing a lot more of the little lady in a minute.'

Amber picked up a thick black strap-on from a table and held it up to a camera, trusting the tech girls to edit for effect. 'Now this... this is really neat, folks. If you look closely you'll see we've had tiny cameras inserted into our little toys. Cool, huh? And we're going to go split screen, so you can see my girls here fucking the bitch, and you'll also see just where these monsters are going.' Amber moved to the Greek girl's head. 'Her name's Candiss, or canned-piss, or some Greek shit. Anyway, wonder how it feels to have a perverted gyno exam broadcast live over the net, Candiss? Knowing how many copies are being made, knowing that this is going to be recycled for the rest of your life.' The Greek girl shouted behind her gag as Amber continued. 'I guess you're just as excited as everyone else, huh? Okay people, let's play.'

The Japanese girls burst into immediate action. Mayu pulled the Greek girl onto her side and began stuffing her cunt like she was preparing a Thanksgiving turkey. She fed the monstrous black rod into the slut's freshly shaved slit, the girl's vagina stretched wide to accommodate it. The wall screen showed the live net feed. One half was the little masked Mayu wearing a strap-on almost as thick as her arm, clambering over the Greek victim as the black shape disappeared into the struggling girl's body. On the other half of the screen the spectators saw the dildo's miniature camera light wink on, illuminating the fleshy pink tunnel ahead of it.

Nyoko, wearing a similar sex weapon, unceremoniously grabbed the Greek girl's buttocks, pulling them apart, and thrust the shaft against her victim's anus and began to push, the left of the screen showed the two abusers filling their victim with hard rubber, while the right side split again, horizontally, giving everyone a glorious color view of Candiss's rectum as the black beast drove deeper into her.

Yoshi and Kichi were starting work on the girl's face, ripping out the gag and climbing on like excited kids on a fairground ride. The network of cameras found it hard to cope, so Amber grabbed a handheld. Yoshi climbed on the girl's face with her back to Mayu and Nyoko, who were working the girl's lower half, while Kichi climbed on facing Yoshi. Candiss found herself smothered by two shaven and extremely wet little slits. The Japanese girls embraced, giggling, and began to kiss passionately, writhing and masturbating on the Greek girl's face.

Amber held the tiny web cam by the cable and dangled it between the two face-fuckers' slender bellies. There were occasional glimpses of the victim's eyes as Kichi slid back, and equally rare glimpses of her mouth. Mostly all the camera could see was her prominent Greek nose, sandwiched between the pubic mounds of the girls riding her face.

A masked technician wandered over carrying a bundle of cables, which hung limply in her palm like dead snakes.

'Micro cams and fiber optics,' she explained simply, then proceeded to kneel beside the strange scene, poking the cables into the writhing, squirming mass. The technician looked up at her boss. 'You said you wanted maximum impact from visuals, ma'am,' she explained, and Amber nodded and smiled encouragingly.

The screen suddenly switched image, and it took a few seconds for Amber to realize what she was seeing. One camera was lying on Candiss's lower lip, illuminating Yoshi's pussy as it brushed and ground onto the mouth beneath it. The visuals were excellent, showing the shiny wet glean as the Japanese girl's juices smeared the Greek girl's lips and chin, then the screen split to show a tightly closed pair of eyes, and the sloshing, wet, pink pussy that was busy smearing its trickle of cum over the face beneath it. Forehead, eyebrows, eyelashes, cheeks, all coated in a glistening sheen, then another camera showed the unfortunate victim's nose as it seemed to be passed from pussy to pussy like a bizarre game of tennis.

The various images, including the ever-onward journey of the oversized black dildos, alternated on the screen at five-second switch intervals. Amber decided to go for broke and called up two extras, waiting patiently in the background, and set them on Candiss's breasts. More cameras were hurriedly brought up as the two women began sucking, chewing and squeezing the Greek girl's tits, slapping them, grabbing the nipples in their teeth and stretching them, covering the olive skin in hickeys and playful bite marks. The writhing mass looked so erotic that Amber had to pull her hand out of her panties and her mind back to the real purpose of the abduction and abuse. Okay, she thought, now the hook line. If this didn't bring them running nothing would.

'To all our viewers out there in cyber land, hope you're enjoying the show, but don't forget, at four in the morning pacific standard time we up the pace. The bitch gets strung up and whipped… then we're all gonna use her as our own little potty-mouth toilet. How very Internet, Amber thought, smiling coldly as she walked to the technical desk. 'Okay, hook lines gone out, how did we do with subliminals?'

'All as planned,' the tall Indian tech specialist said, never taking her eyes from the monitors that flashed on the desk in front of her. 'We got most of them in the early stages. These warehouses were originally used for smoking fish, if they're observant, and we're assuming they will be. There are only two locations where they're still found.'

'So how will they know?'

'Too many upright beams.' The Indian woman pointed at the wooden pillars that ran the length of the warehouse. 'They're what's left of the smoking rack supports. The Krohonas family were fishermen back in Greece, and that's how they started out when they came to the United States, until they realized cocaine was a better paying catch than fish and they had all those boats out there doing nothing. So now they know we're in one of two locations. Any less than that and they'd smell a trap. But the drugged-out gang of crazies on a wild sex trip act was very convincing. I think they'll bite.'

Dakota had seen them scouting the old wooden sheds. They would have spotted the out of place satellite transmitter early on. To make sure they didn't find any additional back up, there wasn't any – just Dakota. *Just you and them State Girl, and by now they've figured that out.*

The black limo roared up the small access road as Dakota leaned against the faded splitting wood, smoking a cigarette. As if living in some hyped up teen action flick the driver braked at the last minute, skidding to a halt in a dust cloud in front of her. The driver, his face just visible through the windshield, grinned at her. As expected they were going to sit safely in their bulletproof cocoon until they were one hundred percent sure she was alone. Trouble was, this wasn't an action flick where everyone showed their hand for the audience, and told their diabolical plans in detail before carrying them out. This was real life, and about as real as it gets. Dakota dropped the cigarette and in one fluid action removed the P90 and swung it to face the car. The driver's expression showed little surprise and no concern; they were going to wait, catching her on the reload.

What happened next was never in Mr Krohonas's script. The depleted uranium shells tore through the car's thick steel and ceramic plating like it was tissue paper. Unbreakable glass broke, impenetrable steel perforated, and toughened ceramic shattered like grandma's best crockery. The inside of the car turned into a meat grinder and a cloud of razor-sharp fragments caught in the hail of radioactive shells shredded the occupants.

Just like that. No talk, no revelations, no nothing.

Whatever fury was raging in Mr Krohonas's head as he cradled his own weapon and thought of the unspeakable atrocities being committed upon his virgin niece, was now smeared around the interior of the limo, along with his brain.

Dakota watched the Cruza's tow truck approach in the distance, a small dust cloud coming closer. *Depleted uranium*, she ground the still smoldering cigarette stub into the dirt with her boot, shaking her head, *now that's gonna take a professional clean up job.*

Mr Krohonas and his cronies would be buried at sea as they had always planned, though being immersed in a twenty ton block of concrete, still in their limo then dropped into the deep ocean, probably wasn't exactly what they had in mind.

The clean up crews pulled in just as Amber was leaving in the SUV. The Japanese girls sat in the back pulling off their masks, but not bothering to put on any clothes. The side door opened and the Greek girl, still naked and bound, was flung into the vehicle, landing on the geisha sluts' laps.

Candiss knew the score; she was raised in a family at constant war; you won some, you lost some, and the spoils went to the victor. Her captors' demeanor clued her into the fact that her side had lost, and now she belonged to the bitches who had abused and humiliated her all night. Even though she had no gag she kept quiet.

Mayu sat at the far right near the door, the Japanese girl wriggling around trying to push the Greek captive's head into her lap, both hands pressing down on Candiss's mane of jet-black hair as the girl sank between the slim thighs. The rest amused themselves with whatever body part was closest.

'She's a dead weight, girls, and she knows it. Too risky to sell her out. So… how do you fancy a new plaything?' Amber watched wicked grins light up the pretty Asian faces, and she smiled.

It was a time of new things. Stephanie had noticed the new doll as soon as she was thrown into the fairy pool. It wasn't the same one that lived at the bottom of the toy box, it was a new one altogether, although it had the same dark skin. This doll was tied in a strange way, her ankles strapped behind her neck, which looked uncomfortable, though her vagina did look nice all open like that.

One of the fairies pulled Stephanie's head down to the soft silk sheets and slid her tiny fairy foot into the blonde's mouth, but she told her not to suck it. The foot wriggled around in her mouth for a while until it was wet with her saliva, then the fairy took it out and placed her toes at the entrance to the new doll's vagina. One tiny toe slid inside, then another, then another… then the fairy pushed and half her foot slid into the pink hole. The new doll moaned and mumbled to herself but another fairy sat on her mouth so Stephanie couldn't hear her anymore.

Stephanie was just beginning to feel left out when a fairy grabbed her and pulled her off the bed into the deep ocean trench. She'd been here before, deep, deep down where the strangest games were played. The fairy slithered under the bed, a mysterious cave in the depths. Her small but strong hands reached out, grabbing Stephanie's breasts, then they pulled her into the cave. Up above she could hear bouncing and laughing as the new doll was put through her paces, and she found herself hoping that the new doll was boring – like the one in the toy box – and that the fairies wouldn't want to play with her much. After all, she was dark, not golden like Stephanie. She was missy's and the fairies' favorite toy.

The blonde was pushed onto her back and the fairy squirmed on top of her, opening the slave's legs wide and clipping them to the underside of the bed. Stephanie new this fairy and she knew here little secret. The fairy began to delve into the blonde's vagina, probing fingers going deeper and deeper while the fairy's pussy wriggled into place on her mouth. The blonde began to lick the sweet hole, savoring the taste all the while knowing what was to come. The fairy began to grind herself onto Stephanie's mouth, the movements getting faster and faster as she approached her climax, then she let go her little secret and the blonde felt the warm pee trickle past her tongue, filling her mouth, and the toy gulped down the salty flood, not spilling a drop.

Once the fairy had only used Stephanie's mouth for her little secret every now and then, but now she did it every time she was sent to visit the fairies, when the others didn't see. Now the fairy liked to play her secret game a lot more, sometimes coming to Stephanie's toy box when missy wasn't there and opening the little laundry flap. The fairy would then press her pussy to the hole, and the toy, knowing what was required of her, would press her mouth to the moist slit, licking it until the pee came. Stephanie didn't mind because the game was secret, and that made her special, very special. The blonde licked the drops of pee from the fairy pussy pressing against her mouth, and then buried her tongue in deeper.

Dawn's Blood Edge

Pallas had the driver slow as they approached the wooden shacks. He would be careful – he was always careful – but instinct was nagging the edge of his mind, telling him they'd missed the target, which meant Mr Krohonas was riding into the zone right about now. Pallas muttered silent curses to himself; he'd wanted to be the angel of death to the fuckers that had Candiss, but also Mr K was walking into a situation with zip self-control and his closest friend and bodyguard thirty minutes drive away.

'Beck,' Pallas snapped at the driver, 'get Mr K on the phone and tell him his location's live, so to be careful, right?' The driver nodded, reaching for his phone. Molly sat back in the leather seats looking disappointed. Pallas always took a young woman on hits; he got so high he had to have pussy on hand. Pallas climbed out of the limo, drew his handgun and walked carefully towards the quiet warehouse. It was as still as death.

Shalyn waited until the small man stepped into the shadow, a luminous, fuzzy figure in her night vision sights. She squeezed the trigger and saw the figure slump forward, further into the shadows. It took her three minutes to climb down from the water tower and reach the car. By luck it happened to be exactly the same time the goons were getting worried about Pallas. They emerged from the car slowly, with practiced, wary movements. Shalyn dropped silently into the dry grass. The sniper rifle in her hands spat through its muzzle three times in rapid succession. She dropped the weapon and ran, halfway to the vehicle before the last of the bodies had slid down the car and into the dust, leaving a wet stain on the polished paintwork. A woman's scream broke the night, but the driver was no fool. He slammed the car into reverse and screeched into a turn. He would have made it too, Shalyn mused, but the female was too stunned to close the rear doors, which swung wildly like the wings of a giant beetle. The assassin slipped her pistol from its holster and sent a burst of shots through one of the open doors and into the back of the driver's seat. The car rolled slowly to a halt as Shalyn radioed the Cruza clean up unit, which by her reckoning gave her less than two minutes to investigate her unofficial bonus.

Molly was sitting in terrified silence watching the blood ooze from beneath Beck's chair, when a black figure leaped from the shadows into the limo. The girl's hands flailed in self-defense, but her wrists were grabbed in strong hands and twisted behind her back till she thought her shoulder sockets would pop. Cable ties bit into her flesh, duct tape slapped against her mouth stifling a half scream, then the gangster's pet was flung unceremoniously onto her back while her ankles were bound.

Molly lay sobbing silently in the trunk of Shalyn's car while the assassin stroked her new acquisition's blonde curly hair, watching the Cruza's clean up crew at work.

'Took a really big chance on you, honey,' the Shadow Stalker twirled a lock of the girl's hair distractedly around her trigger finger, 'but then, you were left for me. Everything is meant to be… did you know that? I have some interesting plans for you, sweet-thing. Some very interesting plans.'

Life in the Toy Box

In some unexpected twist of fate, like the one that brought them together, the way in which they had both grown and matured over the last few years bore a greater resemblance to the complex relationship between siblings than mistress and servant. There was, of course, the ever-present pecking order.

Shelly would always be subservient to her mistress – but then, few were not subservient to the powerful redhead – and like siblings as they had grown in confidence and stature, they had invariably grown apart. Shelly saw little of the mistress these days, but just as that relationship had slipped quietly into the background another blossomed in its place, one that the mistress approved of and seemed keen to encourage.

Lauren had taken Shelly under her wing and made her a most special and favored playmate, which suited Rainbow Girl in a number of ways as Lauren generously shared her many toys, and Shelly had grown bored with Jenny Moyse after the girl surrendered herself. So Rainbow Girl sat happily in the brightly colored room, combing Beach Barbie's golden streaked hair while one of Lauren's toys nuzzled her between the legs, sending gentle waves of pleasure through her belly.

After an hour or so Shelly grew bored with the olive-skinned Latina slave, and opening the large toy box she replaced the girl in it, shackling her face-up to the metal rings at the bottom. The box's usual incumbent, the pretty blonde, was off somewhere playing with her mistress. Shelly smiled, enjoying the security of her new life's rigid hierarchy. Even the toy box had a queen, and she would be back soon.

There was another real doll in the toy box with Stephanie. She'd been there two days now, underneath somewhere. Yesterday Stephanie had lifted a fluffy purple teddy out of the way with her teeth so she could see the doll's face. Her eyes looked frightened, and she had a gag in so she couldn't talk. Stephanie replaced the purple teddy, but later she got bored so she moved some other toys and junk out of the way and found the doll's breasts. She burrowed down and bit a nipple, making the new doll wriggle and kick her tied legs, which was fun, but Stephanie got bored with that game after a while.

Now Stephanie lay in the toy box wondering what had happened this morning. Something had gone very badly between the little plastic dolls and missy. The woman had opened the lid of the box in a very bad temper, shouting at the three dolls, and now they were being punished the real doll under her now had two of the little plastic girls buried deep in her vagina, and one in her butt, and missy hadn't been very gentle about it either. Stephanie saw it all quite clearly because after the first day missy put the new doll in the box the other way around, her legs folded back under her, and she was lying on her back like before, so now it was her crotch that was under the purple teddy and not her face. In fact, the new doll's face was somewhere much more interesting, roughly below Stephanie's groin.

Stephanie found she could dig her way down with her knees, pushing toys out of the way and piling them higher at the sides. Eventually her knees sank quite low and she felt the other doll's face touching her pussy, which was even more fun than biting her nipples. Missy hadn't played with Stephanie for a while and the blonde had done all the laundry; a little pile of sucked clean socks and panties lay near the small hatch, so now the blonde amused herself by masturbating on the new doll's face. Stephanie had tried pleasuring herself before but she could never find anything suitable to rub against and the smaller toys just slid around, but the new doll's face was perfect. The blonde found the best way was to wriggle the dark-skinned girl's nose into her pussy and rub on that.

When missy got them both out the next day she didn't seem to mind that the new doll's face was all sticky with Stephanie's cum. In fact things got even better. Missy wouldn't always tie the blonde before putting her away, and this was one of those times. Stephanie watched as the new doll was thrown roughly into the box and the plastic dolls reinserted, and this time missy didn't put the new toy's gag in, but she was tied very tight as always. Then Stephanie climbed obediently into the box, and missy shut the lid. The blonde worked her knees down as before until the other doll's face was between her legs. She rubbed a little on the nose, and then sat her pussy on the dark-skinned girl's mouth, but the other doll just lay there, perfectly still, even when the blonde rubbed against her lips. Stephanie was sure the girl understood, but she was just being selfish and boring, so the blonde decided to make use of her freed hands.

Stephanie cleared away the loose toys so she could see between the other doll's legs The little plastic dolls were buried up to their waists in the girl's holes, and the blonde grabbed the one in the girl's ass and shoved it in deeper, so just the little plastic feet were showing. The other doll wriggled and kicked like when the blonde had bitten her nipple but she still wouldn't play, but Stephanie had plenty of time and she was sure she could make her. Besides, she was far too excited to give up, and pretty sure tonight was the night she went swimming in the fairy pool. She always dreamed that one day the fairies would keep her so she could swim in the pool forever, down with the tiny toes, like little fish, sliding between fairy legs to kiss their special fairy mouths, that tasted so nice. Stephanie had got herself all worked up over fairy night, so it was quite important that the other doll got the message. She had to shove all the plastic dolls in up to their ankles, then she shoved some other stuff in as well, but it seemed the pinching was what worked. A little tongue sneaked out and licked her, and from then on it was easy, it just took a lot of pinching, grabbing the girl's pussy lips and squeezing them between her fingers until she was licking properly, just like the blonde did for missy and the fairies.

Parting Gifts

The rusting ship looked less oppressive in the fierce southern Californian sun, but also more decrepit, even fragile, leaving Amber to wonder if it would make it back before winding up as an insignificant sonar blip on the ocean floor. The Ice Angel's driver pulled the sleek car alongside the gangway like a slither of black obsidian, the sun reflecting from its gleaming paintwork.

Amber stepped from the car, followed by Dakota and Megan. The solitary sentry at the top of the wooden ramp had been gazing into the water with bored disinterest, a half smoked cigarette dangling from his lips, but as the women emerged from the car, their clothes as black and sinister as the vehicle they appeared from, he jerked to attention staring dumbly at his radio as if expecting it to offer useful advice.

Moments later a black van pulled alongside the car, and two women in coveralls followed the dark trio up the gangway, carrying a wooden crate between them. The lone sentry stepped aside, a nervous smile spreading across his face, memories of Vladimir's fate still very present.

Amber gave the man a cursory nod, and then moved purposefully into the ship's bleak interior, descending through the warren of passageways and hatches until she reached Olga's quarters.

The Russian woman was in residence, along with her three comrades. The women lay in various stages of undress on their bunks, looking bored and hot as a pathetic little fan screwed to the far bulkhead struggled to move the thick, humid air around the cramped cabin. Amber stood framed in the doorway, hands on the metal hatch frame. Olga spotted her first.

'My friend.' Olga jumped up, moving towards the redhead. She paused for a moment, then sensing approval hugged the young woman. 'You come to say goodbye, I am touched. I always want for a woman like you,' she shook her head earnestly, 'pretty like painting, and tough like steel.' The Russian thumped the bulkhead for effect. 'Instead I have these ugly bitch whores. Terrible, no?' Olga's comrades laughed and jeered her in Russian.

'I brought you a present,' Amber said, signaling her two helpers to bring in the crate. 'Least I could do after I took your last toy.' She had their attention now, and one by one the tough looking women jumped up from their bunks.

One of the women in coveralls levered opened the crate to reveal the naked form of Jenny Moyse, freshly scrubbed and delicately perfumed, her tousled blonde hair framing her pretty face. At the base of the crate was a smaller section that held a dozen bottles of the finest Vodka San Diego could provide. The women gazed into the crate, while a pair of nervous blue eyes stared back at them.

'A little something to keep you entertained on the voyage.' Amber gestured to the open crate with a theatrical sweep of her arm.

'For keeps?' Olga asked, stupefied.

'Yep, for keeps. Sell her or keep her when you get back home, your choice.' The cabin fell into silence, but Amber could sense the underlying excitement. She clapped her hands together. 'Mind if I stay and watch you play for a while?'

Two of the women grabbed the girl's legs and tied her ankles to her thighs, and then they pulled her knees to her chest, tying them to her torso with more rope. Jenny's arms were then secured behind her back and she was thrown onto a sheet of thick yellowing canvas, which had been cut and sewn into a crude bag. There was a round hole at one end and a small slit at the other, both trimmed with tan-colored leather. A row of brass eyelets ran along the center. To Amber it looked like a particularly severe straight jacket, only missing the long sleeves.

The leather-trimmed hole was pulled around Jenny's neck, while the rest of her was folded into the bag. The women then threaded rope through the eyelets and pulled the bag tight, turning the blonde into a laundry bundle with a head.

One of the sailors grinned at Amber and pulled open the small slit, revealing Jenny's tight little ass, which in her neatly folded position stuck out prominently, literally inviting use. Canvas straps were then buckled tightly around the bag and the brass hoops sewn into them were used to suspend the plaything from the underside of the sturdy wooden table, at which the four women sat, laughing as they arranged a deck of cards and glasses of vodka. Olga leaned under the table and set the bagged slut spinning.

The muscular Russian shrugged at Amber. 'Always add a little chance to everything,' she explained, 'like spices to a meal, it will be all the sweeter for it.'

Jenny slowly came to a halt in one of the four possible positions, hanging like the needle in a compass, and was immediately grabbed by the two women she hung between. One snatched greedily at the canvas sack and slid the thick strap-on she was wearing into Jenny's ass. She began to hump the little bag of entertainment, driving the thick shaft so vigorously into the girl that she knocked the table spilling some of the precious vodka. But oblivious to her companions' protests she drove into the blonde, pounding her rear mercilessly. Jenny would have cried out but a similar black rubber strap-on was thrust into her mouth, two strong hands holding her hair and pulling her onto the thing.

Both of Jenny's abusers came quickly, growling in Russian as they reached orgasm. The woman working on the girl's ass pulled out and flopped back into the chair shaking slightly, while her companion held Jenny's face tightly as she quivered. Olga banged the table in satisfaction and held up two fingers, which seemed to signal to the women that they should down two glasses of the potent clear liquid in quick succession, and then she leaned under the table once more and set the bag spinning again. Jenny twirled inches from her new owners' knees trying to catch her breath, while the drunken women chanted and clapped their hands.

The Seventh Day

XTC sat semi-naked on the thick black carpet, feeling the soft pile tickling her butt. She was wearing nothing but a small pink strappy top, with the words *Fuck You* in silver across her small bosom. Her left hand toyed playfully with one end of a leather leash, while her right rubbed gently at her moistening pussy. The Indian woman on the other end of the leash knelt before the Korean, head bowed. Angelica padded barefoot into the room and sat cross-legged next to the Asian girl.

'So when do I get to see it?' XTC yanked the leash, pulling the blindfolded slave girl a little closer.

'Not really up to me, *poco falta*, you know only she can allow that; *ángel oscuro*, she will say if it can be so, yes?'

'You think she let XTC have a go?' The Korean began to draw in the leash, hand over hand like a fisherman pulling in a large net.

The woman shrugged. 'Who can say? It seems you are in favor, but tread carefully, little one. *Pisada cuidadosamente*… tread always with care.'

'Wanna see her do her trick?' XTC slid her index finger into her wet vagina and wriggled it around.

'*Sí*, why not?'

The Korean girl giggled, removed her wet finger and dabbed little patches of her own juices on her body, one just above her navel, one on her left breast, then leaning forward, one on her left ankle. 'Shadow lady says she keep her blindfold so little princess get good taste and smell. It's like she only dream of pussy now, all time.

Watch.'

The Korean girl pulled the slave between her parted legs, and the Indian woman sat on her haunches sniffing the air, then she bent down, smelling the Korean girl's body. The slave moved her head slowly to XTC's hand and began to suck her finger. 'Hey, easy bitch, you gotta do better than that.' The slave suddenly twisted her body, hesitated for a moment, then began to lick the Asian girl's ankle, then moved to her belly button, and finally her breast.

'Okay,' said the Korean whore, mildly impressed, 'guess you get your prize now.' XTC shoved the slave's face between her thighs and clamped her ankles behind her back, pulling her in.

Angelica laughed. 'Perhaps it is my imagination, little one, but you have been here three days and this one...' the artist reached out and slapped the Indian slave on the buttocks, 'has been between your legs the whole time.'

Angelica had placed the chair – a near perfect copy of her original inspiration – in front of the living bed. The new work was draped in a blood-red silk sheet ready for the unveiling ceremony. Of course, Angelica had known all along that the Korean girl would be needed to complete the bed, just as the Indian slave had been needed for the chair. Materials were in short supply but she felt no guilt; she did not decide these things. But then, the little whore had been very interested in this new creation; perhaps it was interesting then that she now found herself a part of it.

Shalyn swept into the room, her billowing black bathrobe giving the grace and sinister intent of a vampire. The assassin sat in the living chair, wriggling down onto the two upturned faces and lashing out twice with the crop when the dormant tongues did not immediately set to work. Shalyn smiled, leaning into the girls' soft flesh, feeling the warm tingle as the now active tongues probed her lower orifices.

Angelica did not care much for over elaborate ceremonies, so she grabbed a corner of the silk sheet and whisked it away in one move. The beautiful curved lines of the bed's frame snaked away in every direction like the twisted legs of a giant metallic spider, and in the middle of the divine chaos lay a recognizable mattress, covered in sympathetic silver fabric. A single strand of titanium tubing wound in a spiral to form the head of the bed and the support for its living components. Three girls lay side by side, their legs raised over the coil, secured behind it at the ankles, their knees, kept slightly apart, forming a living balustrade above the metal. The girl's buttocks rested on the mattress, where pillows would normally be placed, three shaven vaginas smiling back at any onlooker. Their torsos disappeared abruptly into the mattress as if it were quicksand, the lithe bodies tightly strapped to the underside of the structure. The slave's heads reappeared halfway down the mattress, sticking up out of holes in the silver fabric, making them look as if they had been laid in a mold and set in lead. Angelica took a deep, respectful bow, apologizing to her employer, the dark angel, for the use of gags on two of the girls.

'I did not want to spoil the effect by allowing these ungrateful wretches to voice their simpering complaints,' she explained to her employer. 'I have not had time to train either the Asian girl or the blonde you brought me a few days ago, but then, perhaps it is something you would enjoy, madam.' The artist bowed again, noting the approving smile spreading across the face of the dark angel as the woman gazed upon the glory that was now her bed.

That night Shalyn used her bed, unable to suppress a contented smile as she peered within the intricate framework at the three bumps beneath the black sheet. The bed was a marvel, but sadly incomplete. Twists and turns in the frame indicated where another living monument to Shalyn's power should have been placed, but she had used all the slaves she had... but her artist, the strange, twisted genius, was not the only one to have visions; the assassin had been granted one of her own. An entire skulking ship, full of human modeling clay, and she knew where that clay was currently being stored.

Shalyn pulled back the sheet and smiled coldly at the three faces, and sliding her naked body onto the cool mattress she chose the middle face, the little Korean whore. She leaned down and removed the girl's gag, clamping her thighs about the complaining head, muffling the noise. The design was perfect, even allowing for suitable encouragement, and the assassin rolled onto her belly, sliding back to push the Korean's nose between her buttocks. Spread out in front of her the Asian girl's vagina invited retribution. Suitable tools hung from the coiled metal frame like bizarre wind chimes. All she had to do was select one... or perhaps several. A pair of hand crafted clamps almost begged to be used, the sharp teeth held closed by strong springs. Shalyn removed them and attached one to each of the Asian girl's labia, feeling the head jerk between her legs as the teeth bit into soft flesh. The assassin wrapped the attached chains around the girl's thighs, pulling her open, then she reached for a large dildo, far too large for the girl's tiny frame, a thing that would dwarf anything the sad bastards who had used her before would have been able to muster. Shalyn smiled as she twisted the thick shaft into the slut's cunt, pressing it when the tiny pussy refused to swallow the monster whole. The head between her legs had not gone quiet, but it was no longer complaining... pleading perhaps, pouring promises of unbelievable pleasure into Shalyn's pussy as the wriggling tongue tried to deliver. The assassin laughed, enjoying her first night in the bed as she looked along the dangling implements, carefully selecting her next toy.

The handle of the large dildo protruded from the Korean's vagina, chains from the clamps wound round the girl's thighs, and a bulbous hand inflator dangled on its tube from the butt plug buried deep in the slave's anus.

Feeling satisfied, the assassin moved on. Molly, the Greek gangster's slut, had been blended along the left side of the bed. Shalyn pulled away from the sucking, licking mouth of the Korean slave and reached down to remove Molly's gag. The assassin waited a few moments, enjoying the whimpering sobs the girl made. For some reason she knew the slut had to suffer. Even though she appeared more than willing to attend to any needs her captor may have, she'd already decided this was not going to be a pleasant night for little Molly. The crude but wonderfully crafted piercing implements glinted enticingly as Shalyn removed them from their hooks. She pushed against the top of the bed, jamming herself down onto the sobbing face between her legs, discovering with pleasure that there was a support plate behind the girl's head to facilitate just this kind of treatment, until she was satisfied that any noises the blonde would make would be muffled enough not to be irritating.

Molly had a cute pussy, and Shalyn had to use pliers to pull the slender labia out far enough to get sufficient access for the task in hand. She eased the sharp needle through the skin, then carefully inserted a polished ring, and once again an act of training was met with promises of delights, frantic pleading and damp sobbing, delivered in their slobbering glory directly to her pussy... which was, after all, the real mistress of these unfortunate girls.

Angelica waited respectfully for her employer to leave the small house that was to be the home of her creations before returning to work. The artist stripped off the black sheet, smiling at the three miserable faces. Angelica sat at the top of the bed with her bag of equipment, the thoroughness of the preparation a result of her two years in prison, but first she had to remove the results of her employer's play session. Once the girls were cleaned up she inserted a catheter into each slave's urethra, linking the three bladders so they drained into a single container. Then she inserted a tube into the slave's bowels to remove feces, the beauty of the design being the valve system, which meant that the tubes could be yanked out at a moment's notice if the bed's owner felt the urge to play.

Angelica then slid under the bed and inserted a needle into each girl's arm to provide fluid and nutrients. Finally, and most carefully thought out, were the small electric pads, adapted from home exercise kits, which she attached to all the main muscle groups, connecting them to the sequencer device that would work the girls' muscles at appropriate intervals. Angelica stood back to admire the start of her experiment; she had calculated a girl could be safely left in the furniture for several months at a time. The artist then ran her slender fingers around the external frame, feeling where the living bodies would go. It excited her so much she felt the sudden need come upon her, and climbing onto the bed she chose the Korean girl, sliding down onto the slave. She laughed at the look on the girl's face as her moist pussy lips pressed onto the slave's mouth. She winked and smiled at the angry eyes that peered up from her pubic mound, then the artist felt a surge of pleasure as the slave's tongue probed inside her.

Between Beasts and Angels

Amber leaned casually against Rebecca's office door. The older woman put down her ornate platinum pen, glanced at her wristwatch and smiled.

'If I'm not mistaken, my little Ice Angel, you have a riding session booked this afternoon.'

'It can wait. I thought we were going to check out the merchandise in the storage pens.'

'I think I can handle it, unless you think I'm not up to a basic inventory check.'

Amber smiled. 'Well, I guess you'll manage. Now I have to go tell my saddle that she's not getting the night off after all.'

'Oh, I'm sure she'll be delighted,' Rebecca smiled sarcastically. 'Why don't you meet me in the main lounge when I get back for a couple of drinks before bed?'

'Sure, see you there.'

The stable girls had lifted the slave onto the horse, laying her on her back, carefully placing her neck in the shaped groove in the adapted saddle before strapping her head in place. They then pulled her arms under the horse, connecting her wrists with a leather strap. Then they looped her legs around the beasts neck, tying them at the knees, leaving the girl's exposed vagina halfway up the powerful mount's neck, perfectly placed for the rider's crop.

Amber arrived a few moments later, wearing her crotchless riding britches. She placed her boot in the stirrup, which was attached to the slave's breast, and heaved herself up, sitting heavily on the girl's mouth and feeling the instantaneous response of a trained saddle girl as her tongue slid into her rider's anus. Amber pressed down on the stirrups, stretching the slave's breasts, then pulled the beast away from the stable and out of the gate. She soon got into her rhythm, moving the horse to a canter and bouncing pleasurably on the restrained face under her. The redhead had been riding this saddle girl for six months and her experience was beginning to show, for despite the uneven bouncing of the ass on her face she managed to slip her tongue deftly into the rider's anus each time the firm buttocks landed heavily on her mouth, giving it a swift lick and suck before the horse's momentum pulled it away from her again. The last time Amber rode the girl she had even managed to maintain an almost perfect ass-licking score while the redhead lashed at her pussy with the stinging crop, so this time out Amber had the stable girls place clamps on the saddle's labia, using thin leather strips to spread the slave's vagina so the pink inner flesh was visible. Amber tested the girl's resolve, a skilled flick of the wrist bringing the crop down to smack the inner lips of her cunt, and to her delight the slave missed her stride and Amber's ass slapped down on her mouth stifling a yelp rather than meeting a willing tongue.

Amber rode for at least an hour, training her saddle to perform under the new conditions that had been set her, and when after twenty minutes the slave had still not mastered the new distraction, her rider stood up in the stirrups, bringing her full weight to bear on the girl's breasts while delivering six lashes to the girl's exposed genitals.

Amber sat back onto the slave's face and felt her begin to sob. The wet tongue slithered into her anus and she pressed her weight down to meet it, and it was then that she noticed the strap that held the slave's pelvis to the beast's neck had come loose, causing her buttocks to slap against the horse's neck, so she turned sharply and headed back to the stable, an amusing idea forming in her mind.

The stable girls worked quickly, and had soon rigged up a large dildo that was held in place by a strap around the horse's neck. They inserted the black shaft deep into the saddle girl's ass, but on Amber's instructions did not replace the restraining strap that had come loose earlier. Amber climbed back on the girl's face and rode out of the compound once more, and now each bounce of the mighty beast drove the dildo in and out of the saddle girl's ass, in perfect time with the slave's tongue as it dipped in and out of her rider's anus, though the redhead imagined the two sensations would have been quite different.

Amber rode the beast hard, whipping the girl's spread vagina and watching the thrilling sight of the large dildo ass-fucking the hapless slave at the same time. It took another hour for Amber to break the girl completely, reducing her to a sobbing wretch, the redhead stopped the horse and masturbated herself to a powerful climax on the saddle girl's face, allowing the slave a few minutes to lick the cum from her pussy before trotting the horse back to the stable as the whimpering slave lay exhausted, slobbering into her rider's ass.

Perpetual Motion

Shalyn looked up at the slowly spinning tangle of flesh that hung above dusky gray fronds of the bed.

'This was my first one,' Angelica said as she walked over and gave the thing a gentle shove, setting it slowly spinning. Sparkling slithers of sharp metal dangled from the structure like primitive arrowheads, glittering in the sunlight streaming through the slatted blinds, the living sculpture another mark of Angelica Ramirez's art and a testimony to her twisted genius and their shared vision. The creation was strangely soothing, like a sparkling, pretty mobile gently spinning above a child's bed. The decoration had been made from two naked slaves, early morning joggers in the nearby park. Shalyn had watched them closely for weeks before making her move; the swift strike of a practiced hunter.

To produce her latest work Angelica had tied the girls' ankles to their thighs, in Japanese style, before they were laid together in a sixty-nine position and tightly bound together. A living ball of flesh, the carefully placed limbs forming a near mechanical synergy, Angelica also decorated the slaves' bodies, intricate patterns, Celtic swirls, hieroglyphs and phallic images adorning the supple young flesh in body paint. The whole bizarre sculpture had been hung on a sturdy chain above the titanium bed, and Angelica smiled in satisfaction as her employer marveled at the surrealistic object, its obvious aesthetic appeal electrifyingly enhanced by the casually arrogant cruelty of forcing two girls to dedicate themselves so completely to becoming an object of ornamentation.

'Please, *ángel oscuro*, watch,' Angelica said, pressing a button beside the bed, lowering the organic sculpture so it hung a few inches from the silk sheets, 'it is the ultimate in recycling, very fashionable, no? It was why you left me in that place.' The artist's eyes became distant as she gazed into her own memories. 'At the time I didn't understand, but now it is obvious, *ángel oscuro*, you had no choice.'

This close up Shalyn could see the intricate system the artist had designed and fabricated, each girl fitted with a rubber hose in the shape of a Y. An end of the hollow tube at the fork of the Y had been fed into each girls' anus, the other into her vagina, and near where the vaginal tube disappeared inside the slave's body a small thin feeder tube led off the main section, inserted into the girl's urethra, draining her bladder. The stalk of the Y section disappeared into the other girl's mouth and was held firmly in place by a rubber gag arrangement. It was a short journey for the interchange of bodily wastes as each unwitting participant in the work of art had her head tied between the other's thighs. The various sections of the Y-tube were only a couple of inches long, and disappeared almost immediately into an anus, a vagina or a mouth, depending which section you were looking at.

'It is like we have created a new form of life *ángel oscuro*. I call the work *Intimacy*. I imagine you can see why. There are closeable valves where nutrients and additional water can be added, but I believe they can remain undisturbed for many days.' Angelica paused, not looking directly at her employer. 'Thank you,' she said quietly. 'Thank you for my gift, and for the chance to express it. The Earth bound, they do not understand.'

'You indeed have a gift, Miss Ramirez, as do I. The only crime would be not to exercise them. Fortunately we have found considerable freedom of expression.'

Angelica smiled. '*Sí*, that we have, *ángel oscuro*...' The artist pressed the button again, raising the sculpture towards the ceiling. 'Come, I have more to show you.'

Shalyn followed the woman into her workshop, a separate extension on the side of the house. The room was a surrealistic clutter of twisted metal and heavy tools, the sullen line of chained girls kneeling in subdued silence along the far wall adding to the impression that the place was a sadistic torture chamber rather than a place of divine expression.

In the center of the room a similar hanging sculpture dangled over a comfortable chair. 'This is where I sit to paint my creations,' the artist explained, deftly sliding herself under the mobile and into the chair. The new design incorporated four girls, two arranged just like the first sculpture but two others had been added, folded carefully around the original bizarre sixty-nine wrap in the contra direction to form a kind of X. The recycling tubes had been totally reworked, skillfully adapted by the artist so that each of the four girls that made up the creation were able to *share* each other equally, achieved by the addition of a small black pump, added to overcome the drag of the longer tubes the arrangement demanded. Each girl now provided for each one of her sisters-in-art via the crisscross of tubes that resembled the idealistic vines that crept up the naked figures of ancient Greek sculptures. The design allowed each girl to share her gifts equally with the others in the composition, as well as ensuring her entwined companions reciprocated, delivering themselves directly into each other's mouths.

Angelica looked up expectantly from the chair, picked up a colored pen and began to work on her living canvas, and the artist's eyes lit up when she saw the smile of delight spreading across her employer's face, a face where such gestures were almost as unfamiliar as a tsunami in the desert. 'I wanted only to please you, *ángel oscuro*. It is for your kind that I do my work.'

'Then you have succeeded, Miss Ramirez. You have indeed succeeded.'

Whispers on the Wind

Vanessa squeezed her tanned, toned Southern Californian body into her fluorescent running kit and slipped her feet into a pair of blue and silver athletic shoes that had been constructed with as much computer simulated design work as the average fighter jet, at least, that's what the advertisement and the eight-hundred dollar price tag said. She tied her long hair back, stuck a chilled squeeze-bottle of performance enhancing sports drink into a waist holder, and set off at a steady pace. A cool breeze blew across the watered lawns of the park, the dry air picking up moisture and pleasant scents from the sprinklers and coarse grass.

After about twenty minutes Vanessa began to breathe harder, sucking air in through her mouth, her sinewy body glistening in a sheen of clean sweat. She turned left following her usual trail, heading through a sparse grove of palms and waxy leafed bushes. The bee sting came as a surprise and she yelped, slowing to a walk to inspect her thigh. She stopped, staring at the small dart in confusion. It lay in the palm of her hand, its sharp needle glinting in the early morning sunlight, the breeze ruffling its flight, a soft, purple, cotton down. There weren't usually any kids in the park at this time of day, but no doubt they found it very funny. Vanessa thought about searching the thick undergrowth for them, and then decided her schedule didn't allow for it. She threw the dart down in disgust, rubbed her leg, and jogged away.

The nearest palms began to waver, as if she were looking at them through the thick air of a desert heat haze. There was a sound like rushing water in her ears that grew painfully loud and she felt her legs buckle as she staggered forward, watching with mild surprise as the ground came rushing up to meet her.

The mood was unusually heavy; even the bright sun that stabbed its way past the swaying palm fronds in the courtyard outside the *El Sol de la Mañana* was unable to dent it. Rebecca held the piece of paper in her hand as if it were a letter from the devil herself.

'Are you sure?'

Dakota looked squarely at her boss. 'Good source, ma'am. Been with the Bureau twenty years. Been feeding us for about eight. Cruza money put his kids through college; he's in too deep to pull anything. Sends us fairly constant reports, nothing too earth shattering... well, until now.'

'So what am I supposed to read here, the FBI are actually connecting one of our authorized hits with a series of front page, TV special serial killer type disappearances? What the fuck is this? Dak? Amber?'

'I read the case file,' said Amber, sliding the document onto the table in front of Rebecca. 'Have to say, it stacks up pretty well. Trace amounts of titanium dust found at the scene where that punk dealer Slake was taken out, and at two sites where young women have recently disappeared. Not only is it unusual to find titanium dust, but forensics have been able to test the batch, same marker spikes, so same batch, little too much of a coincidence.'

'Still hard to believe. I've worked with her for years, and never seen a chink in that armor.' Rebecca sighed. 'You two go pay her a visit, and be careful. I'll handle the showcase myself.'

Angelica lay the woman on her workbench, tying down her wrists and ankles with the thick leather straps. She placed a rubber gag in the pretty mouth and set to work cutting away the modest clothing. The young woman woke halfway through the process and began to tug frantically at her restraints, but Angelica worked on unbothered by the distraction. In fact, she found the woman's muffled cries soothing. Artistic fingers had the girl naked in a few minutes, although Angelica was a little disappointed to see that her pubic region was carefully shaven, depriving her of a much loved little ritual, but then, it was the current fashion.

The well-defined body was quite beautiful, and great care had evidently gone into its upkeep. The sinews of muscle stood out as the girl fought her confinement, the sight stirring Angelica into a state of sexual arousal that pressed its way past her careful, artistic nature, demanding fulfillment. Angelica left on her baggy T-shirt, but slid out of her paint-stained sweatpants and panties, the need welling up from her groin, ripples of excitement in her chest that crept into her brain, a woozy drug. There were trained slaves in the building and she was free to use any of them, but she wanted the struggling girl on the table, wanted her badly, there was no time for training of any sort, so she improvised.

The girl's gag was removed and she began to babble instantly, pleading, demanding. Angelica swung her leg over the young woman, sitting on her upper chest, above her breasts, so that the girl's chin nestled pleasantly in her moist crotch. The girl fell into a shocked silence for a few moments, and then resumed her babble, though more frantic this time. Angelica sighed, shaking her head, then heaved herself forward, placing her wet pussy firmly over the complaining mouth. She let her legs dangle off the table, pressing her full weight down onto the girl, feeling the mouth close sharply. She smiled, looking down past the black fuzz of her own pubic mound at the pair of stunned eyes glaring back up at her, wondering what was going on inside that pretty head, then decided she didn't much care.

The artist pulled up till she was kneeling on either side of the girl's head, her vagina merely resting on the mouth now, though it remained tightly shut. Angelica began to rub herself on the girl, masturbating on those pretty features, rubbing her vagina on the routinely exfoliated, moisturized, perfumed face beneath her. After a few moments the girl's face was coated in a slick layer of vaginal juices, allowing Angelica to rub herself more frantically on her lubricated sex toy. She moaned in pleasure, leaning her palms on the girl's forehead, gyrating and grinding, feeling the lips being pushed to the side as her swollen pussy rubbed on perfect white teeth. Angelica reached down and grabbed the young woman's pert nose, squeezing the nostrils shut, and finally the mouth opened, inhaling air past the wet flesh. Angelica pressed her advantage, grinding herself onto her captive's mouth, sliding her legs off the table again so her full weight filled it with dripping pussy, and felt herself leaking into the girl's mouth as she orgasmed.

Living in Babel's Basement

No roads led to it, no maps marked it, nothing in the starkly beautiful vista even hinted at its existence. Rebecca had obtained the subterranean military complex via a Pentagon contact five years ago. What she got for her money was more than an impenetrable fortress; she inherited government level secrecy. Not even the FBI knew of the facility's existence, and in time the Cruza slowly transformed CTS93, shorthand for *Command & Testing Station 93*, into Babel's Basement. The notion that the tower of legend, intended to transport mortals directly to heaven, might have a shortcut was not lost on Rebecca's clients, and to be invited was a highly sought after honor, even if that meant traveling in the back of a comfortable but entirely sensory deprived SUV. The adapted vehicles had been nicknamed float-tanks-on-wheels by those who used them; no sound, no view and little sense of motion, all to protect the secret the desert held beneath its dusty skin.

The flat plain of sand and scrub seemed to stretch unbroken to the horizon, when suddenly a creek appeared, jumping out of the landscape a bare fifty yards ahead. Rebecca's SUV followed the steep slope, which to the untrained eye was indistinguishable from the sharp, rocky edge of the gully, down to the shallow trickle of water that ate away at the desert floor with timeless patience. The only visible marker of Babel's Basement was a crumbling, concrete outbuilding quietly decaying a few feet from the water's edge. The vehicle elevator at the rear would be invisible to anyone not actually skulking around the place on foot, which given the mass of hidden security cameras, would be a one-way exploration trip. Curiosity often killed a lot more than cats.

The SUV pulled into the featureless gray storage building, and then transmitted the security code, releasing the heavy metal doors from their hidden recess. The door slid shut, slotting together with an audible click, and the inside of the small building began to descend. For a brief moment Rebecca regretted the absence of her closest confidantes, but State Girl and the Ice Angel were busy following up on the disturbing news. Renegades were not good for business, but the Inquisitor still held hopes that the trail would lead elsewhere.

Babel's guest areas were busier than ever before as favored clients prepared for the showcase.

Rebecca bypassed the players' quarters and made her way directly to the deeper levels that held the playthings. Her heels clicking on the cool stone floor, she entered the series of rooms that held the latest influx of sex slaves. They had taken two hundred and sixteen girls from the ship, and only hours before an FBI tactical unit had descended on the Russians. The eventual elimination of the small Russian gang had been merely a consideration at that point, but the arrogant and stupid way the gang's leaders taunted federal officers with the perfectly executed switch, illuminated a macho recklessness the Cruza could not ignore. Termination orders had already gone out, though Rebecca set the date three months ahead, putting distance between the events.

Now the Inquisitor wandered amongst her new possessions like a dealer in rare art, acutely aware that each pretty face she held in her hands was hers to do with as she wished, while simultaneously marveling at the beauty of what she owned.

The girls had been divided into seven grades according

to physical beauty, and then separated out into their respective holding areas. Tradition dictated that five percent of the take be set aside for employees, to be taken equally from all grades. Rebecca rounded in their favor to give them eleven girls, one from each of the top six levels, and four from the lowest.

In a small annexed room ten naked, bound slaves lay strewn casually on the floor while half a dozen bored drivers played with the single girl taken from the seriously cute category.

A blonde, green-eyed young thing of around twenty lay struggling on a black leather couch as the drivers mauled and explored their prize. The sound of pathetic pleading in broken English and Ukrainian echoed through the underground chambers, dying away into an incoherent sobbing as one of the women decided to put the girl's pretty mouth to use.

Rebecca smiled as she continued her inspection accompanied by the delicious sound of supple leather on young flesh, and the equally tantalizing sound of a yelp stifled by a pair of ample buttocks.

Rebecca felt her own needs gently moistening between her legs. She scanned the first chamber, her eyes alighting on the cowed form of a slender girl, her tag stating she was nineteen. The Inquisitor lifted the girl's chin and gazed intently at the pretty but slightly androgynous features as the very pretty dark eyes resolutely avoided her stare.

'This one.' Rebecca stood up, smiling as the girl's head fell back into its defeated pose.

'Nice choice, ma'am.' The curator lifted the naked girl to her feet.

'Yes, I think so. She's very skilled at faking that cute defeated air, don't you think? Must be a brain in there somewhere. Take her to my office.'

Rebecca grabbed the girl as the curator led her from the room, running her fingers through the waist-length brown hair. 'When I've finished with you, you won't have to fake it anymore, sweetie.'

The Inquisitor planted a gentle kiss on the girl's cheek. 'Now, won't that be nice?'

Rebecca dutifully greeted each of the guests, and then watched the parade. The twenty or so topflight girls were led into the center of the large display room by their handlers, colorfully dressed in bright cheerleader costumes. A series of memorable party tricks followed. Each girl was fitted with a mouth-dildo, a very similar device to a strap-on, except the harness fitted around the slave's head so the shaft extended from her lips, the ball-like shape at the base filling her mouth. The handlers kept close watch on the girls making sure they were sucking on the hollow dildos. A large backdrop screen presented the audience with charming close-up shots of the slaves' faces as the dildos they were frantically sucking on were inserted in the vagina of the girl in front. The mock cheerleaders, camera in one hand, riding-crop in the other, formed the slaves into a large circle, then set about encouraging them as they knelt on all fours vacuuming the insides of the girl in front.

Crops lashed at dangling breasts, stirring the human suction pumps to greater efforts, while handheld cameras zoomed in on desperate faces. A further murmur of appreciation from the lustful crowd of female onlookers rumbled round the room as the slaves were made to remove the dildos and insert them into the poised anus of the girl in front, the close-ups exquisite. Eventually the dildos were removed and the daisy chain of slaves was forced to use their tongues directly on each other. The handlers allowed the scenario to run for about fifteen minutes, before expertly measuring the tension in the room and breaking up the show, handing out naked girls to the drooling audience like sweets at a candy fair.

Due to the size of the audience the little groups trooped off to the specially provided and equipped playrooms, three mistresses to one slave. The guests had been promised the whole night with their toys, so Rebecca considered her duty shift finished until breakfast, which gave her plenty of time to attend to some unfinished business.

Back in Rebecca's office the teenage slave hung limply in the circle of silver tubing. She moved to the rear of the wheel, admiring the red welts that covered the girl's legs, buttocks and back.

'Wake up, honey,' the Inquisitor chided, carefully lifting the girl's hair and arranging it into a tight ponytail. 'That was just a warm up. Hey, now we can play properly.' She let the long ponytail fall down the slave's striped back. 'Won't that be fun, huh?' Rebecca smiled at the girl's refusal to acknowledge her taunts.

She pulled a step over to the wheel, climbed up and attached the slave's ponytail to a rubber clamp at the top of the circular frame, forcibly lifting her playmate's head up so the girl stared directly ahead. 'Sorry honey, but I'm going to need these.' Rebecca stroked the girl's breasts. 'And you were getting in the way a little, don't you think?' The Inquisitor wasn't sure how much English the girl understood, but something must have clicked because she began to suck air past her thick rubber gag like a runner going the distance.

Rebecca walked slowly to her desk, then stripped down to her underwear, her lithe, tanned body in almost as good shape as her young plaything, despite a few decades' difference in their ages. The Inquisitor picked up the thin cane, turning it over in her hands as she made her way back to her waiting victim. Rebecca smiled up at the girl, and then caught her a stinging blow on the left breast. The girl rattled against her chains, breathing hard. Her tormentor stood back to enjoy the moment, aware that the cane was designed to be a superficial tool; the pain it could inflict was actually quite minimal and any damage would be negligible, but that's why such sessions were an art form. To break a slave properly took timing, attitude, and no small amount of theatrics.

Rebecca stroked the thin red line, cupping the breast in her hand. 'Ooh, that felt so nice, shall we do it again?' The girl's stubborn silence was broken by the swishing slap of the cane as it kissed her right breast.

An hour later Rebecca had been able to remove the gag entirely, and the slave's prideful silence evaporated as she realized she was being toyed with. There was no importance to this; nothing was wanted from her, it was a declaration… a declaration of utter supremacy. Rebecca allowed the girl to choose where on her body the cane should caress her, then she watched as the slave's mind worked, and knowing it would be foolish to select constantly easy targets she would occasionally offer up her breasts, like a form of ritual sacrifice, and Rebecca would oblige. The game was playing out well. The girl took a deep breath, and then muttered something in faltering English.

'Speak up, sweet thing,' Rebecca said, leaning closer, 'no need to be shy.'

'My poosy… please… my poosy.'

Rebecca widened her eyes in mock surprise. 'Excellent choice, little one.' The Inquisitor pulled gently on the perfectly balanced wheel, spinning it until the girl hung upside down, her smooth, hairless genitals tantalizingly vulnerable. In keeping with the unspoken rules this first blow was mild, a flick of the wrist catching the soft flesh with a sharp but very swift smack, then the girl was returned to the upright position. The trap had been laid early in the game and the girl was now held firmly in its grip, pulling like a rabbit in a snare. It would only be a matter of time before she would have to offer up her precious little pussy again, and all the while Rebecca would be watching as the girl agonized over how long she could safely wait before offering her tormentor the gift, walking the tightrope that had been so carefully laid for her.

When she grew tired of the game Rebecca called in two servants, who took the girl down and attached her to the large black leather chair behind the Inquisitor's desk. The girl was left sitting on the floor, her back to the chair, bound tightly to it with thick leather straps, her head bent sharply back and inserted through a small hole at the chair's base, so that it rested conveniently face upward on the seat.

Elena felt her will slipping gently away, the thing she had guarded so fiercely for so long. She had been an independent child, fighting back against a growing decay that not only ate at the small house she lived in, but that seemed to crawl its way into her mother with the same inexorable inevitability, the rotting wood and crumbling plaster matching its occupants' tattered, dirty clothing. Elena's mother had no weapons with which to fight this nameless menace, except vodka, but the more of the deceptive liquid she used in her little war, the worse things got. Men came, and Elena's mother had given her to them without question, her eyes empty and hollow as she watched her only child marched to a waiting car. Elena fought the men, and then she fought their killers, the ones that took her like plundered silver. And now she fought the killers' killers. She had fought in that wheel, clinging to her dignity like a life raft in a cold, expansive ocean. But the pain had been so little, really; little enough that even Elena in her naked vulnerability could sense the underlying game, see what was expected, and so she surrendered, too tired to fight. She had played the game. Now, strangely, things were more complicated than ever before. She was clean and well fed, a little sore perhaps and missing her dignity, which had been so cleverly stolen from her on that wheel, but she was so tired of fighting. Elena let her muscles relax, falling into her bonds as if they were loving arms. She stared at the ceiling, adrift in her own thoughts. It was funny, she had never even experimented with another girl, never given it much thought, but now she was about to.

The teenager watched the smooth tanned flesh as it entered her view, descending till it became her view. Elena smelled the perfume, and other very human smells, feeling the tension flow out of her as she acknowledged her own surrender, sticking out her tongue to meet the descending flesh.

Rebecca eased herself into the large, commanding chair, feeling the cool leather against her skin. A little fizz of electric pleasure danced between her legs as she felt herself settling onto the teenager's waiting face, it raced into her belly, pulsing through her breasts, making her nipples jump to attention. The girl's tongue dallied at the entrance to her anus, licking and kissing, and the slave's hesitancy had a message all its own, the simple idea of conquest sending further, harder waves pulsing through the Inquisitor's body. Then the Ukrainian took the plunge, her virginal tongue pushed past the opening to Rebecca's ass, squirming and wriggling its way inside, then it began to dance, twirling and lapping, probing deeper and deeper.

Rebecca gasped. She grasped the arms of the chair, forcing herself down onto the fleshy intruder, welcoming it into her body, demanding it tunnel deeper, and the tongue responded, squirming into the Inquisitor's expectant anus. Rebecca pulled her knees up, balancing her heels on the edge of the chair, imprisoning the slobbering, sucking, licking mouth, holding it close to her ass in a passionate embrace as an orgasm rode the nerves in her spine, crashing into her brain like a freight train and causing her whole body to spasm.

Shadows Within Shadows

The night lost its appeal, gnawing at Rebecca's impatience till she could fight the sleepless twisting and turning no longer. Conceding defeat at around four-thirty the Inquisitor threw off the sheets and climbed out of bed, literally peeling the naked, tightly bound Ukrainian teenager from between her sticky thighs. The unexpected treasure had lost none of her skill as the evening wore on, drawing orgasm after orgasm from the Inquisitor, but after hours of extremely physical multiple orgasms sleep still eluded the Inquisitor.

Rebecca left the tightly bound bundle of fun laying on the bed, her face glistening in the half-light, making her look like a wide-eyed, varnished doll. Dragging two curators from their beds, and own secret pleasures, the Inquisitor made her way to the main elevators, descending deeper into the desert to examine the lower slave pens she hadn't had time to look over earlier in the day.

The catacombs of the hidden base excited her, as they always had. The dark, cool vaults that usually held a small contingent of unfortunates, deemed unprepossessing enough for standard rental, were now alive with a throng of new inmates. Rebecca never tired of sifting through the human debris of raids and acquisitions for the diamond in the rough, and she found such treasure on many occasions, little things others had missed, like a fierce independence hidden behind a plain face, or a burning intelligence staring out from average eyes, or something as simple as pretty feet, all potentially interesting to certain clients.

The curators moved ahead of the Inquisitor, rousing the sleeping inhabitants. Her employees had wanted to turn on the main lamps, but Rebecca preferred the dull yellow light from the single night watch lamp that stared down at them all from its high vantage point like a coyote's eye, full of insatiable hunger. She reveled in the surreal edge, the pleading eyes that stared out from shadow-masked faces.

Rebecca had held the girl's face in her hands for several minutes, intrigued by the brilliant blue eyes set neatly into the slightly plump face. She reached for the zippers on the crotch of her fatigues and loosened them, and then she guided the whimpering face to her crotch, pressing the tightly closed mouth into the warm folds of her vagina. Rebecca held the girl there, she wasn't trained, and so would do nothing but quiver and whine, but the initial innocence was exciting all in itself, a fragile thing, a Chiotilla bloom, something to be enjoyed for what it was, something to be crushed. Pleasure seeped gently into Rebecca's tired mind, but there was a part of the Inquisitor's brain that never relaxed, never slept, never got distracted. Even while the rest of her toyed with the slave between her legs it was vigilant, monitoring the subtle blend of sounds in the catacombs for any unusual change, and found it.

The change was an absence, the gentle background murmur of restless slaves continued as before, and although the curators were almost silent in their work, going from girl to girl with practiced ease, the occasional footfalls and quiet whispers that marked their progress had ceased. Rebecca pushed the girl away, zipping up her pants and inwardly cursing the fact that she had felt comfortable enough in her fortress to be without a firearm. Something was moving along the far left wall, undetectable by itself, noticed only by the subtle increase in tension amongst the captives, like a flock of sheep being stalked by a wolf, except that this time it was Rebecca who was the prey.

Rebecca stroked the soft leather gauntlet strapped to her right wrist. The silver scorpion lay flat against the dark material, facing its mistress, its curved metal tail curled in a majestic arc, ready to strike at her enemies. The ruby eyes shone in the weak glow, a demon peering into the shadows, where lurked another kind of demon entirely. Rebecca pressed gently on the scorpion's bejeweled head, and heard the tiny click as the small spring in the creature's belly pushed the needle-like spike out of its tail, a slither of metal, a glinting shard… not much of an edge against whatever moved silently through the darkness, but it was all she had.

Ice Maidens Aren't Afraid of the Dark

The Ice Angel's cell phone buzzed silently in her jacket pocket and she pulled it out, flipping it open with one hand. 'Yes?'

'Someone got to the Commander-in-Chief.' McKenna's voice sounded numb, her professional detachment kicking in, as automatic as an airbag in a car wreck.

'How bad?'

'You're the leading lady, Ice. Understudy days are over.'

'Jeez, Mac, who the fuck could get to her?'

'Best guess? You're sniffing around her lair right now. Happened at Babel.'

'How long ago, amiga?'

'Maybe a couple of hours, tops. My money says she'll be at your location any time now. I sent backup, but it'll take time, so you're gonna have to handle it with what you have. Be careful, okay? You know who the next in line is, and I ain't doing this job wearing a diaper.'

The phone cut off, leaving Amber replaying the last moments in Rebecca's office in her head. Not much of a goodbye, but there was no changing that now. Amber hadn't been raised to feel loss, only the irrepressible need to get even. It rose within her like a well of liquid nitrogen, colder than death itself, inexorably wiping all other thoughts from her mind. It was her survival trick – a gift if you like. Then something sucked the light from the room. Amber's hand went instinctively for her pistol even as the smothering blackness enveloped her. The darkness was terrifyingly tangible, like a choking smoke that left her struggling for breath. Something moved where it shouldn't, behind her, off to the left.

'Dak, get the fuck out! She's got night vision!' Amber shouted into the void, feeling her instincts take control as her faltering mind struggled to keep pace. The Ice Angel was already spinning, pivoting on her toes like a ballerina, her arm snapping the pistol into the darkness like a whip. There was no hesitation, her finger squeezed the trigger loosing shards of white-hot metal into the impenetrable gloom, three sonic booms numbed her ears, and she heard the shattering thuds as the bullets missed their target and struck the walls.

There was no initial pain; a deadening blow to the midriff then a dull ache, growing in intensity with every second. When she was a child she had played a game where she wore a rope round her middle, she would run against it, her friend somewhere behind, giggling and trying to hold her back, then a big kid, unseen, had grabbed the rope, pulling it so hard and so suddenly she was lifted completely off her feet and dragged sharply backwards by her waist till she landed sobbing on her butt. It was a lot like that, the sudden force in her belly knocking her off her feet. She heard the sound of the shot a moment before she crashed into the corner of the room, a jumble of flailing limbs. Amber lay in shocked silence, feeling the warm blood soaking into her shirt, seeping onto her thighs. She raised the barrel of the gun slowly, not moving her hand, aware that her opponent could see everything in infrared clarity, then emptied the rest of the clip into the black void.

'You're empty.' The emotionless voice seemed to come at Amber from no particular direction.

'I know,' the Ice Angel said into the darkness as she let the pistol fall heavily to the floor.

'Dak's dead… shame, I liked her.'

'Me too.' Amber coughed and tasted blood in her mouth.

'You drew blood, if its any consolation. Nicked my arm.

So now I'll have a scar to remember each of you by.'

'Each of us?' Amber could feel consciousness slipping away as the blood pooled in her lap.

'Yes, my dear, Rebecca ruined a perfectly good jacket before I killed her, with that eccentric little hidden knife. To be honest with you I've had worse paper cuts.'

Amber spat blood onto the floor. She couldn't see the other woman's self-satisfied smirk, but she could feel it. 'But she drew blood?'

'A little, but I'll live.'

Amber managed a painful laugh. 'No... no you won't.'

'Sorry, child, but you're not in much of a position to make threats.'

'Why do you think she has a scorpion on the wristband, you dumb fuck...? Her sting... it was her sting. Taipan venom... most poisonous snake in the world... nothin' you can do... nothin'... guess you have to call that a draw then, huh?'

Shalyn left the dying bitch where she was. For a moment she had taken the story to be a last bit of bravado, but then she felt her legs getting cold, felt the tightness in her chest. The assassin's last moments were consumed with an irrational need to protect her creation. She hunted her artist like a ravenous wolf chasing down a wounded deer. As her dying mind collapsed into some apocalyptic Egyptian funerary right, she decided her closest servant must cross the final river with her; they must take their vision with them, forever into that sweet night. But in the end the Shadow Stalker failed, the woman had gone to ground and Shalyn's strength began to fail massively, till she collapsed onto her beloved bed, the dark, windowless house a pharaoh's tomb. In the distance she felt certain she could hear a gentle splashing as the oars of Rá's boat dipped into the river of night, ready to carry her soul safely to morning.

Epilogue

Two black SUV's growled purposefully through the entranceway to the trailer park, flanking a slate-gray Mercedes. The invasion sent the residents scuttling for cover. Like bugs when you lift a rock, thought Amber.

The entourage drove the short distance to the service road, pulling to a halt in front of the last, dingy trailer. Dusk's elongated shadows crisscrossed the park, leaving patches of golden light, pools of warm radiance amongst the clutter of human detritus, not all of which was inanimate. Amber stepped from the car and into one of the pools of light, the color of her name, bathing her in the place she was raised. Life was strange. An inheritance that had come draped in blood had left her powerful enough to crush every living thing in this miserable, forgotten slice of the world with a word… a single word. Yet now she was here she found she no longer cared. Her father was perhaps only a few dozen yards away, and it all seemed so unimportant.

Except what she came for.

Amber rapped on the flaking, dented door and waited. Jackie stared out of the gloom, looking exactly as Amber remembered her, as if time itself couldn't be bothered with the last trailer in the lot.

'I'm going to give you a choice,' the redhead, dressed in black, stared levelly into Jackie's surprised eyes, 'and I want you to think carefully, because it may be the last decision you are ever allowed to make. You can follow me to that car and I'll enslave you so thoroughly, so completely, that you'll need a permission slip just to piss…

or you can stay here. I won't bother you again.'

Jackie stared at the dark figure, her face, as always, an unreadable mask. Then she walked silently to the waiting car, and Amber stood by the trailer's open door, smiling.

Amber ran the palm of her hand over the new plaster, the smooth, flawless finish hiding the many holes she had blasted into the wall several months ago. She slid her other hand inside her T-shirt, the raised outline of the scar a permanent reminder of how close she came. The wall had fared better.

Megan had found the strange woman, Angelica, working calmly in her workshop. All she would say was that angels sometimes fought. The new Inquisitor had decided to keep the dolls' house, as Angelica quaintly referred to her life's work, despite some painful memories the house held… or perhaps because of them. Angelica continued to labor in her basement workshop, melding flesh with metal, while Amber and the higher echelons of the organization enjoyed the practical side of the woman's work, using her creations as they were intended. As McKenna had so aptly put it, 'The world's only works of abstract modern art that could lick your ass.'

The women had stripped her, then bathed and manicured her and rubbed scented oils into her skin. When they finished Jackie watched with breathless excitement as her soft leather restraints were attached and locked into place. She was then carried to a strange room, it was bright and colorful, and the sun seemed drawn to it, streaming through the delicate pink curtains, suffusing it with a rosy glow. Jackie was placed on her back in a long box filled with toys. She lay quietly while the women placed straps around her thighs, clipping them to the side of the box so she couldn't close her legs, then they piled more toys on top of her and left.

After the lid of the box was closed she lay in the cool darkness, wrists and ankles still bound, knees spread, and waited. It was a pleasant place to be. Jackie had never been claustrophobic, and the box was quite insubstantial, as the pinkish sunlight filtering in through the many gaps at the joins showed.

After a while there was an unexpected flash of light as the lid was raised and someone else climbed into the box. She was naked like Jackie, and wore wrist and ankle cuffs, but hers weren't locked. Jackie caught a quick glimpse of a pretty blonde before the lid shut again.

'Hi, new doll,' the girl said, 'welcome to *my* toy box. As I'm the senior doll and everyone likes me best, you're going to be licking *my* special places, and I like it done *all* the time, so you won't get bored.' The girl began to wriggle and squirm, and Jackie felt soft thighs sliding around her cheeks. She could smell the musky scent of the young woman's vagina as it neared her face.

'Oh, and while you get your silly tongue busy on my precious pussy and ass, I'm going to introduce you to a few of the smaller dolls.' The girl giggled, moving between Jackie's legs as her shaven sex pressed against the new doll's mouth. Jackie pushed her tongue into the succulent flesh, wondering what it was pressing against the entrance to her own vagina.